Behind My Hazel Eyes
The Fan Files

Samantha Gail

Dstar Publishing LLC

To Kelly Clarkson
All of our lives would suck without you, but especially mine.

Broken & Beautiful

I've never heard a married couple say they met during last call at their local bar, but that didn't mean I shouldn't try.

Oh, wait—

Just yesterday my boyfriend of four years decided he didn't see a future with me. And there wasn't a single man in this bar under the age of sixty to replace him.

Maybe finding a husband was too ambitious. Maybe I could set my sights on finding someone to take home for the night instead. If I was sober, I would have gasped at the prospect of a one night stand. Hook ups weren't my thing. But it turned out the more beer you chugged, the less you cared.

Except, as I looked around at the slim pickings that made up my options, a one nighter didn't seem all that likely either.

"What is wrong with me, Lou?" I moaned before downing the rest of my beer. An actual bottle of Bud Light, thanks to my last call friend at the end of the bar. Nope, we weren't drinking the cheap shit tonight.

Lou, the bartender, who would die while still wiping down

the same glasses in the same position as every other night, merely reached for the next glass. "Not sure. You need me to call you a cab?"

I scowled at him. "No. I can't afford a cab."

He shrugged as if it were no never mind to him. "I can't let you drive."

Pushing away from the bar and stretching after being hunched over for so long, I sighed. "Guess it's these boots getting me home tonight! Night, Earl!" I called to my beer patron. He raised his glass to me in solidarity. "See ya soon, Lou!"

Of course I would see him soon. I was a twenty-one year old single woman who no longer had a boyfriend, job, or an apartment. All because I had to ask the question that always sent men running for hills: where do you see this going? I had no idea that Luke Davenport, my high school sweetheart, would panic over such a simple conversation, but right about now, as I meandered down the street in the heeled boots that pinched my feet, I deeply regretted bursting the bubble by asking in the first place.

Car brakes screeched to a halt as a blue sedan pulled up to my left. My mom's voice rang out through the passenger window, "Get in, Finley!"

Busted.

A heavy sigh escaped as I dramatically threw open the door and fell into the seat beside her. "Lou is such a gossip! He just had to call you, didn't he?"

My mother flashed me a look that said she was in no mood for my snarky comments. Her graying hair was barely visible under her silk bonnet, and her threadbare robe parted to reveal a cotton nightdress. She even donned the fuzzy slippers to complete the ensemble.

The tires squealed as she pulled back out onto the road.

"Carrying on at all hours of the night like this is unacceptable, Finley!" Mom snapped. "Some of us have real jobs and need to sleep at night!"

If only her words didn't echo in my skull like they came through surround sound. How many beers did I *actually* drink?

"Geez, Mom, can you take it down an octave?" I grumbled. Leaning my head out the open window felt spectacular with the cold breeze hitting my face. It probably destroyed my makeup, but you couldn't have everything.

My mom was quiet for several minutes, allowing her disdain to fill the void. As she turned onto the main road closest to her house, it was too much to hold back.

"You smell like a distillery," Mom commented harshly.

"It's the new perfume," I quipped.

"And so what if he dumped you?" she continued, acting like she hadn't heard me. "Women get dumped all the time."

I sighed. "Always glad to be a statistic."

She eyed me sharply before turning down her street. "It's time you get your life together, Finley. You need some direction."

And here we go, folks…

"Mom, we've talked about this," I reminded her. "I want to be a singer."

I jerked forward as she harshly parked in her driveway and killed the engine. The porch light barely illuminated the walkway into the house that was overgrown with shrubs. Shrubs my now ex-boyfriend had long ago promised to trim for her. She didn't wait for me, just called over her shoulder, "You can't be a singer if you don't go out and sing!"

I was approximately three shots and four beers too deep to have this same old argument with her. We could (and would) continue it later on in the morning after I managed to get some sleep. Followed hopefully by some very strong coffee. The odds were stacked against me for it to happen in that order, knowing my mom, but I made a mental note to thank her for letting me crash on her couch. It might soften her up enough to keep the lecture under 30 minutes long.

My mom's couch was worn and lumpy, a relic passed on from my great-grandma's house when she died. Most of the furniture in her house was a hand-me-down from some relative or neighbor. As a single mom, she did the best she could, but there simply wasn't enough to go around on a preschool teacher's salary. It couldn't have been easy for her to raise me on her own.

Settling into the cushions with a throw blanket, sleep avoided me. I mulled over my circumstances and wound up drawing a blank. There were no good options. Luke's dad owned the pizza place where I worked as a server, and he promptly fired me on the spot when I showed up in tears for the shift right after our breakup. Said he couldn't have an "emotionally unstable" person on the payroll.

Asshole.

It wasn't like I *wanted* to be a waitress, and the tips sure sucked. Luke and I were so far behind on most of our bills because he decided it was better for him to go back to college to study philosophy and run everything up on credit cards. Credit cards that he conveniently forgot to mention were in both of our names until after the bill arrived.

Okay, so Luke wasn't a catch by any stretch of the imagination. In fact, many would say that I dodged a bullet when he ended things. But it was the reason he did it that stung. For him to tell me that *I* was dragging *him* down. That there was no way he could ever have a future with someone like me, someone who *only* wanted to work for his dad. Who says things like that to their girlfriend of four years?

For the time being, I needed to at least talk to my mom about staying with her until I figured something else out. I didn't need her sympathy and I wasn't going to hold out my hand for freebies. But I could admit when I was down on my luck. Mom had to respect me for that, at least.

It wasn't a pleasant thought, but it was enough of a plan that my brain finally hit the off switch and I fell into a restless sleep.

Never Again

Subtlety wasn't Mom's strong suit, as made abundantly clear when she turned the vacuum on and let it run right next to my head at six o'clock the next morning. She followed it up with lots of cabinet bangs and door slams in the kitchen as she made breakfast and packed her lunch.

"Okay, I'll get up," I moaned to no one in particular. Mom was mad enough at me without adding fuel to the fire.

Stretching my arms over my head, I let out an enormous yawn that somehow managed to offend her as she brushed past me on her way out the door.

"You have no right to be tired after what you pulled!" she barked. My mom's anger tended to blaze like an inferno, then snuff out just as quickly. It no longer bothered me since I had become so accustomed to it over the years. I tended to make her angry *a lot*.

Her arms were ladened with tote bags full of art supplies for her preschool classroom. It royally sucked that so much of her own money had to go right back into their projects, especially when she made peanuts to begin with, but she had a heart of gold and only wanted her students to feel excited about school.

"I'm sorry, Mom. I really am." I tried to give her a smile, but it made my already spinning head hurt too much. "Thank you for letting me sleep here," I added.

It was enough for some of the steam to let out. "Finley," she sighed, "I just want what's best for you. You need some direction."

I nodded in agreement. Right now she definitely had the upper hand in the logic department because the pain gathering behind my eyeballs rendered me nearly worthless. "The good news is that now I have the time to figure it out."

Mom pursed her lips tightly before setting the bags down and crossing the room to join me on the couch, my sadness softening her ire. "What if you went to see your dad?" she suggested lightly.

Witty comebacks don't kick in after a hangover, I learned. That was why I was left gaping at her like a goldfish. "You want me to do what, now?"

She rolled her eyes and got up to retrieve her bags by the door. "C'mon, Finley. What do you have left to lose?"

I didn't have a chance to answer before the door slammed shut behind her.

Her assessment of the situation might be right, but that didn't mean I had to like it. Ever since my parents' divorce when I was seven, I barely spoke to my father. He moved out to California after everything was finalized in the courts, and although child support was garnished from his checks each month, that was about the extent to which he played a role in my life. For the first couple years, he sent an obligatory birthday card and called around Christmas, but it never went much beyond that. As I got older, Mom said it was because we were both too stubborn to learn how to communicate. We could argue the whole nature vs. nurture debate all day long. The fact of the matter was, my dad and I barely knew one another.

And yet...the prospect of a change of scenery didn't sound too bad. There were no memories haunting me in California like there were here in Texas. I could start over fresh and maybe get more opportunities to sing while I was at it. Lord knew I wasn't finding them here.

The better part of the day drifted by before I gathered up the nerve to text my dad. Wanting to apologize for last night, I threw together a semblance of dinner in the crockpot and cleaned my mom's house as best I could. Hopefully that would put her in a better mood.

When there was nothing left to scrub, vacuum, or spray, I finally pulled out my cell. Normally, I would beat around the bush to get a feel for the reception of my request, but this time I figured I should just rip off the Band-Aid and ask him outright.

> Dad, can I come out to visit for a bit?

The three dots appeared instantly as he typed out a response.

> Are you in trouble?

I rolled my eyes at his assumption before remembering he was actually correct.

> Um, kind of...I'm between jobs and wanted to see if Cali suited me better.

This time around the three dots appeared and disappeared several times over the course of the next few minutes. Finally, I received:

> Just let me know when you land.

So it wasn't going to be the world's warmest welcome. But I could deal with that. After all, I was sort of springing this on him. And he easily could have said no, although I would wager my stepmother had far more to do with his agreement than any fatherly affection.

I never met my stepmom, though she sent me a wedding announcement a few years back. Thankfully, their wedding fell on the same weekend as the state choir competition, so I had a good excuse to miss the nuptials. She seemed a lot more disappointed when I couldn't make it than he did.

When my mom got home, she was in much better spirits after she saw the crockpot. "It smells good," she commented. "Thank you for not burning down my house."

I shrugged. "The firewood guy was running late. So...listen. I talked to Dad."

Mom nodded. "I know."

Blinking, I waited for the rest of her statement. "Um...how?"

Rather than answering right away, Mom began getting plates and silverware out to set the table. "Go get some napkins from the pantry, please," she instructed before returning to the cabinets for drinking glasses.

"MOM!"

"Okay, fine!" Her dramatic sigh didn't fool me for a second. "He called me to make sure you weren't pregnant or running from some kind of legal trouble."

I threw my hands up in my frustration. "Good god, is that how y'all think of me? It's a wonder you let me use the bathroom on my own!"

"We haven't ruled that out yet, dear." The twinkle in her eye let me know it was a joke, but I scowled just the same. "Once I assured him that you simply needed to get out of town for a little while, he said Deborah was looking forward to meeting you."

Of course my stepmother looked forward to it. My own father couldn't.

"So I went ahead and got you a plane ticket during my planning period this afternoon. I can drop you off at the airport first thing tomorrow morning." Mom started to spoon the contents of the crockpot into a serving bowl before suddenly dropping the spoon with a clatter. "Did you put raw ground beef AND raw chicken in here?!" She looked horrified.

I peered over her shoulder at the half-cooked meats. "I thought you just couldn't put them in the same grocery bag."

She groaned as she reached for her cell. "I'll order us a pizza."

Most of my clothes were still at my old apartment, so after dinner my mom let me borrow the car so I could go and pick up the last of my belongings. I wasn't the kind of person to nitpick over objects; at this point, all the memories of the furniture, decorations, and whatnot were tainted anyway. I just wanted enough to dress myself for my trip and then it was peace out, Luke Davenport!

I was still in the bitter, resentful space after a breakup where imagining your ex's pain and suffering makes you feel better about your life. What can I say? Texans can hold a grudge.

What I wasn't prepared for was Luke to be home. He normally had classes late in the evenings since I worked, but when I pulled into the parking lot, I saw his Mustang in its usual spot.

My stomach filled with dread. The last thing I wanted was a face off with my ex.

Not that Luke was the kind of person to confront someone. His laidback, unassuming persona was what initially attracted me to him back in high school. I tended to be the louder, more outgoing one of the two of us. When I first met him, it felt like our personalities balanced each other out. We rarely ever fought because we just fell into sync with one another right away.

As we grew up, it started to feel like more of a hassle than a sign of good luck. While I loved going out, Luke preferred to stay in. I always longed to try new things and visit new places while Luke enjoyed the comfort of all things familiar and close. I wanted to be the hostess with the most-est and have our friends over for game nights and dinner parties. He wanted quiet evenings with classical music where we played nearly silent games like chess. All of the things I once admired became the things that irritated me.

Yet the loss of the future I envisioned with him still hurt. While I could accept that we just didn't work anymore, it would probably be a long time before the pain ebbed. He was my first love. What was that line from *Eat, Pray, Love?* I had to send him some light and love or some shit.

Taking advice from Julia Roberts movies probably isn't the best life choice right now, Finley.

Steeling my resolve, I climbed up the two flights of stairs

with my mom's borrowed suitcase to our old apartment. I left in such a hurry that I hadn't given him back my key, so I let myself in and did a double take. The floor was strewn with rose petals and candles that trailed down the small hallway into the living area and then around the corner towards the bedroom, where the door was closed. As I approached, I could hear the melody to our song, the first song we danced to at a high school home-coming when we both finally admitted our feelings for one another.

Oh my god! He's apologizing! This is so romantic!

I fluffed my hair and pulled a mint from my jacket pocket to pop in my mouth before opening the door...to see my (admittedly, ex) boyfriend's bare ass thrusting into the bare ass of another woman. She had long, dark hair that cascaded down her back, parts of it wrapped up in his fist with the passion of the moment, and looked to be in her mid-thirties.

"WHAT IN THE BLOODY HELL IS GOING ON?!" I bellowed. Yes, when I get upset, I resort to British slang. It's a thing.

Luke jumped as though electrocuted, which his companion clearly wasn't ready for because she let out a howl like a wounded bison, grabbing her ass that had no doubt just stretched an extra few inches on impact. In her haste to end the pain, she shoved her bottom down, thereby forcing Luke's erection in the opposite direction. He yelped and hastily withdrew his member, clutching it in both hands to scream, "I think you broke my DICK!"

The woman rolled over, still gripping her puckered asshole for dear life while trying to cover herself with a decorative throw blanket at the end of the bed. A throw blanket *I* bought, might I add.

"Luke, we broke up TWO DAYS AGO!" I screamed. He continued to whimper about his broken penis while I advanced on him in my anger and backed him into the corner of the room. "Have you been *cheating* on me?"

The woman scrambled off the bed with the blanket over her front and dashed madly to snatch her clothing off the floor. "You have a girlfriend, you asshole?! I can't believe you!" she shrieked at him.

This man had brass balls the size of Texas! I shoved him backwards, screeching like an owl with incoherent gibberish in my rage. Words failed me.

Luke started to cry, crumpling in on himself, hands still firmly clasped around his penis. "I really think my dick is broken, Fin!"

"Sometimes karma arrives on time, now, doesn't it?!" I yelled.

By now, the front door slammed as the woman left, taking my throw blanket with her as she tried to wrestle into her clothes while leaving as fast as possible. I dropped my suitcase to the floor and made a mad dash through the dresser drawers, yanking everything out and tossing it in without any regard for folding, sorting, or even whether it was mine or not. I pushed Luke out of the way to get to the closet behind him. Everything, including the hangers, was tossed into the suitcase, too. Thankfully I only owned a few pairs of shoes, so even though I had to lay myself across the top to get it closed, I pulled that suitcase zipper with a vengeance.

"Wait!" Luke called after me when I headed towards the door. "You have to take me to the hospital! I can't drive myself like this!"

"Then it sounds like you have a real problem!" I snapped. While I had never considered myself a petty person, I snatched his phone from the kitchen counter and then left it on the hood of his car when I reached the parking lot. He wasn't gonna call anyone for help getting out of the bed he made on this one!

Tears started to flow freely as I drove off like a bat out of hell. I drove around the outskirts of Fort Worth for a while, wanting to regain my composure before facing my mom again. It wasn't like I didn't think she would take my side, but my "dramatics" wouldn't exactly be welcomed in this situation.

It was definitely time for a fresh start. California was my last chance to turn my life around so that I was actually, well...*living*.

Piece by Piece

Landing in LAX made me realize two things: one, drinking like a sailor on leave to fill my time on the plane was decidedly not a good choice. Two, holy hell, was California *bright*. It was like the sun had a vendetta against all the plastic faces everywhere. My clothes were sticking to my back the moment I stepped outside.

My dad and a woman who could only be my stepmom waited for me in front of an idling SUV outside of baggage claim. Although I had never met her before, Deborah was exactly the way I envisioned her—hair like gold, matching Lululemon workout outfit, and enough perfume to alert others to her presence from five feet away. She beamed at me before enveloping me in a bone crushing hug.

"Oh, you're just darling! Isn't she just darling, John?! You really are!" she squealed in one breath.

The tequila lacing my veins didn't like it. "That's exactly what I was going for," I replied.

My dad leaned forward to give me an awkward, one-arm hug. "You smell like a distillery," he commented.

I blinked at him. "Did Mom send you the script or was that improv?"

Our lack of relationship meant he didn't know how to take my sarcasm. He merely arched an eyebrow at me before taking my suitcase to load in the back end.

"C'mon, dear, let's get going! We're gonna take you to lunch!" Deborah sang. She waved me into the back seat like I was a flight risk, then jumped into the front seat. "You're just gonna love it here!"

Instead of responding, I merely offered her two thumbs up and a cheesy grin. To my surprise, she repeated the gesture back to me from the front seat, though her smile was definitely more sincere. If I didn't have a migraine from the seventh circle of Hell, I would probably feel bad.

Maybe.

It took forever to pull out of LAX and get on the highway. Although I grew up outside of Dallas/Fort Worth and was no stranger to big cities, even I thought the number of cars was excessive. We were gridlocked on a ten lane highway, barely making any headway. Deborah continued to yammer incessantly about their house, their dog, and how excited she was to have a "daughter" to show off to her friends. She never seemed to notice my lack of response, so I got away with monosyllabic replies that barely sounded like words.

My father did notice, however. "So, you gonna tell us about the kind of trouble you're in, or do we need to piece it together ourselves?"

Thank God for oversized sunglasses because right now they were hiding how hard my eyes rolled.

"Like Mom said, I'm not in any trouble. Just trying to figure things out." I gritted my teeth at his insinuation that made me simultaneously feel like a toddler and a failure all in one.

"Of course you are, honey! John, don't grill the girl! She just got here!" Deborah swatted at her husband, looking deeply offended on my behalf.

At least I had one person on my side in all this.

Dad finally moved enough to take the exit and take us on the main roads through central Los Angeles. They lived in Glendale, which Deborah assured me was a "friendly" part of L.A., and after driving for a half hour in awkward silence, we pulled into a small Mexican restaurant called Amigo Buenito.

Deborah insisted that we sit outside (because clearly the Universe realized the sun as punishment worked). My father glared at me when I ordered a Bloody Mary and the world's tallest glass of ice water. We weren't off on the best foot, but as Deborah tried out conversation topics that I had no interest participating in, the three of us simply stared at one another in more awkward silence. My stepmom kept giving Dad furtive looks with her eyebrows raised as if they had discussed all of this previously and my dad wasn't living up to his end of the bargain.

He glared at her and finally asked, "What are your plans while here, Finley?"

I shrugged. Right now my only plan was to sleep off the hangover that awaited me. "Find a job, I guess. Get enough money to get a place? I don't know."

Dad frowned, with deep creases contracting between his eyebrows. "You kind of *need* to know, don't you think?"

"John!" my stepmother scolded sharply. They both sat across from me and it looked like she might have tried to kick him under the table. He didn't react, so she must have somehow missed or not put enough force behind it to matter.

"What, Deborah? I can't just sit by and let my twenty three year old daughter be a loser!"

I could blame it on the alcohol, or whatever it was Jamie Foxx said. Or I could blame it on a lifetime's worth of resentment for the father who essentially abandoned me after my parents' divorce. Hell, I could even blame it on my loud, impulsive nature.

Ultimately, the blame didn't matter because the damage was done when I stood up and growled, "Twenty *one* year old daughter. TWENTY ONE. Which, had you ever actually been a father to me, you might even remember! And no worries, Dad, we don't have to let a loser darken your doorstep!"

More than one customer turned to stare at my outburst. Even the waiter hovered near the door with our drinks. I snatched the Bloody Mary off his tray and downed it in one gulp before loudly dropping it back on the tray. A few of the onlookers gasped and clutched their chests as I clambered up on the small metal fence separating the dining area from the sidewalk and hopped over, gangly falling onto my feet with my arms waving like a windmill.

Great, now I even looked like a cartoon version of my drunk self.

"FINLEY, GET BACK HERE!" my dad roared.

"Yeah, I'm not really interested in earning your love and approval!" I called back over my shoulder. "Ask Deborah—she can help with that!"

I inwardly cringed at the low blow because thus far my stepmom had been nothing but nice to me. Still, I powerwalked down the street as fast as my legs would carry me, without a sense of direction or destination in mind.

Dᴵᴅ I mention that Los Angeles is huge? Because holy fuck, this city never *ends*. I aimlessly walked for hours, not really paying attention to my surroundings. My feet were starting to hurt by the time I walked past a restaurant with open doors and windows where a caterwauling wail brought me up short. The neon flickered in the sign labeling it the Songbird Lounge.

A visibly drunk group of women stood on a stage with two microphones, a small screen in front of them. They all tried (and failed) to read the words, and more than one tried (and failed) to keep pitch, but it was all a jumbled mess. No one could even recognize the song.

And this was why I hated karaoke.

Still, it seemed as good a place as any to rest. I pushed through the group of patrons gathered near the door, many of them wearing Navy uniforms and cheering for the girls in skimpy dresses on stage, and found a seat at the bar where I could easily watch the train wreck onstage as it unfolded. All of them were teetering in sky high stilettos and tight Bodycon dresses that left little room for movement. At least they were having fun, which was a lot more than I could say.

The bartender, a cute Latino male, came over and winked at me. "You look like you need to cheer up," he greeted.

I groaned, making him laugh.

"What'll it be?"

My hand instinctively itched towards the purse in my lap. I had approximately $78 left in my account, so now wasn't the time to drink, as much as I wanted to.

Look at what a responsible twenty one year old I am now, Dad!

"What do you have that's free?" I asked.

The bartender grinned even wider. "I have some moonshine back here that some sketchy lookin' dudes dropped off and we can't sell. You're welcome to try it."

What did I have to lose? If I was gonna contemplate all my life choices, wouldn't all my options sound better with something from the cast of *Deliverance*?

"Sure, why not?" I shrugged and settled as much of my torso on the bar as I could, chin in hand. "Do all your karaoke-goers sound this bad?"

My new friend walked further up the bar and pulled out a mason jar of clear liquid that he poured over a small glass of ice. He set it back down in front of me, then with a glance full of pity, grabbed a bottle of cherry grenadine and poured a couple ounces in the glass.

"Every once in a while we get someone who knows the words," he offered. "I'm Max."

"Finley." I took his hand in mine for a quick handshake. "This is hard to watch."

Max chuckled. "Yeah, but you can't beat the free entertainment."

Another woman, much older but no less drunk, hobbled onto the stage. She wore a business suit and kitten heels, and I had the distinct impression this was the first time she'd let her hair down in years. The first few chords played of Katy Perry's "I Kissed a Girl" started playing and the woman's hips gyrated offbeat to the music. When the very first note out of her mouth was sharper than a razor blade, I grimaced and shot my hands over my ears.

Max looked equally pained. "And then there's that!" he yelled.

Once the woman left the stage to the applause of her friends, also in business suits, a guy who looked like he belonged at a biker bar walked up to the stage. I took the opportunity to sneak a drink of the moonshine and came up sputtering. That didn't just burn on the way down—it blazed! Some of it dribbled down my chin as Max grabbed a napkin for me to wipe up my face.

"What the hell is the alcohol content in there?!" I cried. "That tasted like feet mixed with cherries!"

Brown eyes twinkling, Max shrugged. "Free is free, baby."

We continued to watch the shit show on stage as progressively more drunken people sang their hearts out in the form of incoherent words, off key screeches, and dorky dance moves. Before long, a man slid onto the barstool on my right, the corner stool, with a cocky smirk on his face. He was older than me by at least ten years, with thick, caramel-colored hair and tan skin.

"You look like you're having fun," he commented. He had an aura of confidence and charm, like he already knew I was a sure thing. "The name's Billy Anderson." A large hand crossed his body, waiting for mine.

I stared at him with my eyebrows raised, letting his hand continue to wait. "Did I miss the part where I asked?"

That earned a chuckle. "Sorry, I just couldn't resist sitting down and enjoying the fun you seem to be having. What's that your drinking?"

I crinkled my nose. "Moonshine that'll put hair on your ass," I replied.

Max, who was restocking the empty glasses next to me, gave me a look that told me he was unamused.

"Well, I'm sorry, but it will!" I argued.

The new guy laughed even harder. "Why do I get the feeling that it's always like this with you? How about I buy us a real drink?"

What was it people used to say back in the day, YOLO? "Eh, sure, why not? What are we drinking?"

Billy's smile grew wider. "We'll take two pomegranate mojitos," he said. "Reyka, or whatever's close." He turned back to me and I caught a scent of his cologne, a rich, woodsy smell.

Vodka wasn't my usual choice, but then again, beggars couldn't be choosy. Or whatever the stupid idiom was. Right now, I was partially drunk on moonshine and happy to let Billy Anderson flirt with me. It was a distraction from pondering the dumpster fire before me while ridiculing the people singing karaoke.

"What are we drinking to?" I asked as Max set our glasses down. He placed mine on the far side of my left elbow, well beyond Billy's reach, for which I was grateful. Good looking out and all.

Billy picked up his glass and held it in front of his face as he contemplated his answer. "Let's drink to royal fuck ups because my royal fuck up might have just cost me my job!"

"Cheers." Billy and I were riding the same wavelength right now.

Pomegranate mojitos with top shelf vodka might also be my new drink of choice. It went down a hell of a lot smoother than the feet moonshine. I smacked my lips with a contented sigh.

"So how did you fuck up?" I asked. Max leaned against the back counter, seemingly joining our conversation.

Billy winced. "We had someone back out of a pretty big project, and I've only got tonight to find a replacement. I haven't found a single person who can fill in." He laughed as if it was the funniest thing in the world. "I guess I'll be jobless tomorrow!"

Max and I both joined in, although I knew better than

anyone that losing your job was more disaster than funny. Top shelf vodka tends to turn everything into a comedy, however.

Yet another drunken disaster scrambled offstage after a rather heartless rendition of "Dancing Queen" by ABBA. I mean, honestly—who screws up *that* song?! I groaned loudly.

The crowd had grown bigger, the streetlights now on outside. A warm breeze blew through the door, reminding me that I was in Los Angeles, California, where the only people I knew were my dad and stepmom, and my two new bar friends. My dad barely even counted. Anyone who saw me as a loser while simultaneously forgetting my age wasn't really someone who knew me. Not the real me.

Could I name one person who did? Me included?

Gulping down the remainder of my third pomegranate mojito, I noisily wiped my mouth on the back of my arm and shakily stood up from the barstool. "I'm gonna show these clowns how it's done," I announced to Max and Billy, who both wore bemused expressions.

Walking towards the stage, I hastily scrawled my song choice to the karaoke DJ and handed him the slip of paper. He nodded enthusiastically and gestured for me to get on stage.

I didn't need the words for this song, though. Singing had been a part of me long before I could talk right. All I had ever dreamt of was performing on stage for thousands of people screaming my lyrics right back at me. My mom paid for vocal lessons as soon as I turned ten, and despite how much money and time it cost us, I enrolled in every singing competition I could find until I graduated high school. Adulthood might have halted my plans for super stardom, but that all ended right now in this karaoke bar.

Pomegranate mojitos and feet moonshine were the secret to confidence. I made a mental note to jot that down somewhere.

No matter how much alcohol flooded my system, stepping on stage and placing a microphone in my hand brought everything into crystal clear focus. Their lighting setup might have been weak and there wasn't a single person in the crowd who knew my name, but I felt the serendipitous draw of the universe. I needed to show everyone just what Finley Smalls could really do.

The opening melody of Madonna's "Express Yourself" played and I was transported. Music had a way of doing that for me. Nerves never really impacted my performances because I simply *felt* the music. Like it became such an integral part of me in the moment that the only way to let it free was to sing out the words.

I wanted to perform all the time as a child, which was why all our free time and money went towards music lessons. Although my mom pursed her lips and remained silent about my decision, my announcement to forego college and simply pursue a life of music wasn't exactly supported.

And then Luke Davenport happened, and everything changed.

Singing karaoke right now brought back the floodgate of reminders. This was what I was meant to do. God put me on this Earth to entertain people, simple as that. As I leaned more into the performance, letting my intuition guide my voice into their own runs and harmonies that weren't part of the original song, more and more people in the audience became captivated. The room grew silent as everyone stared at me in awe, some of them with their mouths literally hanging open.

As I belted out the final note, the karaoke music fading away, the room broke out into uproarious applause. We're talking, walls-thundering-glasses-falling kind of applause. Their cheers were so loud and positive that I started to giggle and waved at everyone from the small stage.

I momentarily wished my father was here so that he could see what a *loser* I could be.

My new friends in the corner were beaming at me. Max whooped louder than the rest, starting the crowd on a chant of "GO FIN-LEY! GO FIN-LEY!" But Billy? He looked downright delighted, standing up and clapping above his head.

I made my way back to them, accepting praise from everyone as I moved through the crowd back to my seat, and when I reached Billy, he had stars in his eyes.

"What did you say your name was?!" he shouted above the din.

Laughing, I stuck out my hand. "Finley Smalls, nice to meet you!"

"Finley Smalls, you just solved my problem!" Billy yelled, vigorously shaking my hand.

Miss Independent

"Mom, I'm telling you, this is legit!" No matter how many times I repeated that phrase over the phone, her Spanish Inquisition continued.

"If it sounds like it's too good to be true, then it *is*!"

Dr. Phil was in the house, y'all.

"I told you, Billy is a producer for a singing competition! They had a contestant drop out for medical reasons at the very last second and they needed somebody to fill in. It's like Fate wanted me to find him."

"Finley Brianne Smalls, that is *not* how life works! How am I supposed to be happy that you're now living in some random house that I've never seen with eleven strangers?! Have you even met them yet?" My mom's anxiety made my heart rate spike.

I held my cell phone to my chest and counted to ten in my head on an exhale so I could tone it down a notch before answering. "I briefly saw my roommates this morning, but we have a bunch of promo stuff to film soon, so I'm sure I'll meet them all then. We have security and everything here, so you don't need to worry about me."

Last night was a dream come true. When I triumphantly left the karaoke stage to thunderous applause from the crowd, Billy stood there with a smile that stretched to the farthest corners of his cheeks. He told me that I was the answer to his prayers, then dragged my drunken ass out to his car to bring me to this house.

On the car ride, he explained that he was a television producer for a brand new reality singing competition called *America's Music Star*, and that their most promising contestant overdosed during sound checks earlier that afternoon. She was in critical condition, but as Billy assured me, even if the girl made a full recovery, the network wasn't willing to take on the risk of a drug addict.

Since filming was slated to start the next morning, he was desperate to find someone and I more than fit the bill. When he offered me the spot, I slurred out a word vaguely resembling "Sure!" before passing out in the front seat beside him. I barely grasped what was going on by the time I called my mom from the bedroom I woke up in.

Clearly my attempt at lowering the volume on our current phone call didn't work because my mom's voice continued to go up an octave. "And what about your father?! This was a chance to make things right between the two of you!"

As much as his words hurt me, ratting my dad out to my mom wasn't going to help the situation. This was one of those rare moments where I was self-aware enough to know that telling her what he said would only infuriate her on my behalf. She didn't need to be angry in addition to panicked—I couldn't be cruel.

"Except it was also about making something of myself...and look, on my very first night, opportunity knocked with the dream of a lifetime. So I'm taking it!" I waited with bated breath for her defeated sigh, thereby eradicating my guilt. "This is going to be great, Mom!"

"Lord knows you deserve it," she grumbled. "There was no way you could be so talented for nothing!"

I laughed to cover my relief. My mom's support was the most important factor in this show. There was no way I could get through it without having her as a sounding board.

An abrupt knock came from the door where a male voice called out, "Smalls, you're up next!"

"Mom, I have to go!" I whispered. "I'll call you later tonight, I promise!"

"Break a leg, kiddo!" Mom cheered. "Love you!"

Another harsh knock rang through the room as I darted to open it. A harried looking man, well below average in height, stood there with a headset and a clipboard. "Come on, you're on the last shuttle over to the studio and we're already running behind since we had to change everything over to your name." He darted away at a brisk pace down the hall so that I had to jog to catch up to him.

"Wait!" I called out. "What's your name? Are you in charge?"

He snorted in derision, giving me a side eye that said he didn't find me amusing. "The name's Kyle, not that you'll ever need to use it because I'm at the bottom of the food chain and therefore not worth remembering. You already charmed the big guy, remember? Billy Anderson himself."

By this point, Kyle had to be in on some sort of practical joke because I was all but sprinting to keep up with him. I barely had time to notice the layout of the house, which included more bedrooms for contestants, music rooms, a lounge area, and a massive kitchen that my mom would have loved to cook in. Everyone lived in the house together, along with a few of the production assistants, and although I briefly saw her outline when she got up hours earlier, I had a roommate I needed to officially meet. Hopefully she was a talker like me.

"I've been ordered to have you sign all this paperwork, and we don't have time for you to send any questions over to Legal," Kyle said. We stepped out the front door, where a car waited. "It's a standard contract. We'll provide the house, your stage wardrobe, hair and makeup, along with vocal coaching and any appropriate music instruction. You'll also receive $1,500 per month while you're here that you can use for toiletries, your cell phone bill, etc. No drinking, no drugs, no sex tapes—nothing that will get you bad press. You are officially a representative of the U.S. Broadcasting Network, so don't do anything stupid that will make Billy get involved, and you'll be just fine."

He was talking a mile a minute and it was enough to make my head spin. Kyle's irritated monotone made me wonder how many people had toed the line with rules previously to make him hate his life this much. "And what's so wrong with that? Billy was really nice to me."

Kyle snorted again. "Yeah, go figure, the tv executive was 'nice' to the pretty singer who saved his ass at the last second. You're gonna be under an even brighter spotlight because of the way he went to bat for you. Every other contestant had to go through rounds of auditions and interviews to be on this show. Watch out for the knife in your back."

God, who pissed in his Wheaties?!

Pulling a pen out of his shirt pocket, he handed me a clipboard with a stack of paperwork. There were teal tabs to mark where I needed to sign, initial, and date everything. "So I'm only signing away my firstborn, right? Or did you need the blood of a unicorn, too?" I joked.

My joke was met with crickets. Kyle just stared at me like he wanted me to disappear.

"So what even happens on this show? All I know is that it's a singing competition." If Kyle was anything like the men back at the pizza place, he simply needed an opportunity to mansplain something to me and his mood would improve.

Bingo.

"Oh, it's gonna completely revitalize reality singing shows. On *America's Music Star*, nobody gets voted off. We really give the audience a chance to get to know the contestants, so that the person who wins is someone who truly deserves to win. And the grand prize is way bigger than any of the other shows," Kyle added, a hint of pride in his voice.

I was instantly intrigued. Maybe Billy explained all of this to me last night, but I couldn't remember all of these details. "Oh, yeah?" I prompted him.

"The grand prize winner will receive $2.5 million, a five album contract with Zone Records, and a headlining world tour. We've already been selling tickets. You're really gonna have to win over the hearts of America because ads have been streaming for the show and the other contestants for weeks. After each show, viewers can vote, so the leader board will constantly change. It's anyone's game."

My heart sank as I considered his words. But then again, I hadn't backed down from a challenge yet. And hell, even if I didn't make it, $1,500 a month for four months was enough to help me start over without my father's help. There had to be some place cheap where I could find some roommates in L.A. and live on that money for a while after the show wrapped up. And I could continue looking for a singing job afterwards.

It was enough of a plan that some of my nerves settled. Now I just had to figure out a way to win over the hearts of America.

So, you know, no pressure or anything.

A Moment Like This

The contract was far too long and detailed for me to read in a single car ride, but Kyle said I couldn't step foot on set without signing it. When someone dangles your dream in front of you, especially when you're on the edge of rock bottom, you have to take a leap of faith. Praying the scene didn't look like Ariel's fated first meeting with Ursula the Sea Witch, I signed where all the tabs indicated and hoped I was making the right decision.

All I could think of was my mother telling ten year old me that sometimes you make the right decision and other times, you make a decision, then make it right.

Entering the studio completely blew my mind. I couldn't exactly articulate what it was that I assumed a set would be like for a reality show, but this wasn't it. There were people *everywhere*, many of whom were wearing headsets with built in microphones like Kyle's. We rushed so quickly down the hallway that I didn't have time to take any of it in, but he said I was already too late for wardrobe, and then I had to join all the contestants for group shots that they would air as trailers for that night's live shows.

"I hope you already have a song picked out," added a snarky Kyle. "You'll only get fifteen minutes to practice with the band before the show tonight."

Um, WHAT?

I instantly went into panic mode, my brain flipping through my usual set list. Nobody gave me any kind of parameters as far as music choices. The deck was already stacked against me since nobody in the audience would have any real clue as to who I was. I could vaguely recall Billy saying every night would have a theme, but Kyle hadn't mentioned it so far.

"What kind of song am I supposed to pick?" I asked. "Will the producers normally pick my songs?"

"They have to approve all song choices," Kyle explained. "You'll meet them after the promo shoot. Here's where I leave you." We stopped in front of a red door with a plaque that read WARDROBE. Kyle didn't spare me a second glance before he paced down the hallway at an outright run again.

Inside resembled the most chaotic walk-in closet I had ever seen. Racks upon racks of clothes in every conceivable color created a maze. Sparkles, feathers, patterns—there was something for every style. Elton John would have loved some of the platform shoes underneath the clothes. Most of them were just as trippy as the fabrics hanging above.

"Hello?" I called out as I walked down an aisle without encountering anyone.

"Over here!" came a faint voice.

I followed the aisle down to a crossroad, then turned right, then another left. Bright lights that reminded me of a fashion runway formed a spotlight at the end of another aisle to my left, so I went that direction. A tall, black man with a closely shaved head and a nose ring kneeled with a row of pins poking out of his mouth. He measured the hem of a shimmery halter dress on the most statuesque woman I'd ever seen. Her warm, golden eyes found mine in the mirror and she greeted me with a smile.

"Hey, sleepyhead!" she gushed. "It's nice to meet you while you're conscious."

I grinned. "Yeah, top shelf mojitos will put me into a coma."

"Girl, they'd put *anybody* into a coma!" the woman replied. "I'm Zephyr, your roommate."

Wow, cool name. "What's your last name?" I asked.

"Just Zephyr. I figure if a sister like Zendaya can do it, I'm gonna follow suit." She popped out a hip, making us both laugh, while the man on the floor cast her stern look.

"Unless you'd like me to pierce your ankles, I suggest you stand still!" he ordered in a British accent. "Name, please?" He turned in my direction, appraising me over the rims of the glasses perched on the edge of his nose.

"I'm Finley Smalls," I replied. "The new girl."

"Ah, yes." The man nodded to himself, returning his attention back to Zephyr's hemline. "The replacement."

Kind of a weird way of putting it, but a lot of people would probably look at me that way.

"I take it you're in charge of the clothes?"

He stood up and pulled the glasses off his face. "You're done, love," he said to Zephyr while keeping his eyes on me. "Turn." Using his finger, he gestured for me to twirl.

Slowly, I spun in a circle as his eyes raked me from head to toe. "You look like you have a bit of an edgy side to you," he said.

"I can work with that. I'm Ashford. My friends call me Ash. We are not friends, so do not call me that."

I chuckled. "Aw, that's not how we do it around here, Ashy! It's great to meet ya!" I pulled him in for a fierce hug, pinning both of his arms to his sides.

"Oh my god! Not another American hugger!" Ash fixed his rumpled shirt and fixed me with a glare. "Why can't Americans ever give someone personal space?"

"Because that's how the West was won," I replied solemnly. Zephyr chortled on the stand behind him.

Ash's scowl turned down even further. "And a comedian, too. How fortunate we are to have found you. If we're going to make you look like a rock star, you should wear black. Go find a dress you like down there." He pointed over my shoulder towards an aisle of clothing racks behind me. "All of those are your size."

I glanced backwards before turning back to him. "How do you know my size?"

He rolled his eyes and walked over to a worktable with a sewing machine and scraps of fabrics, mumbling something under his breath that resembled "Americans!"

Zephyr joined me, still chuckling. "Come on, I'll help you find something," she offered.

We walked towards the two racks with black dresses. Some of them were plain and simple while others looked like they would barely cover the important parts. Those were NOT my kind of dresses. She started browsing through each dress, zipping through the hangers faster than I could have.

"Do we have to wear dresses for every show?" My reluctance must have shown on my face because she laughed again.

"No, but they wanted tonight to be more formal since it's the first one. Sort of a 'dress to impress' thing." Zephyr held up a slinky silk dress that I wouldn't be caught dead in. Thankfully, she put it back right away and continued onto the next hanger.

"Is everyone as nice as you?" I asked. We were competing for the same grand prize, after all. I certainly didn't expect her to be so helpful.

Zephyr snorted. "Hardly. I haven't met everyone yet, but I can tell you the one you need to watch out for is Jessica Harris. She thinks her shit don't stink and then some. Girl's already walking around here acting like she won the damn thing. Don't trust a word out of her mouth. And don't eat or drink anything she gives you. Rumor has it she brought laxatives with her and ain't afraid to use 'em!"

My eyebrows rose to my hairline. Yeah, I wanted to win, but not at the expense of someone shitting themselves on national television. What a monster!

"I'll definitely steer clear of her," I agreed. "Thanks for the head's up. I figured everyone here would be out for blood."

She shrugged. "The only competition I see is when I look in the mirror. I'm here to win, but if I have to tear somebody down to do it, that's not really winning, is it? People go their entire lives for a chance like this. I'm not wasting it."

Her take on it made me smile. Look at me making friends on my first day.

Who's the loser now, Dad?

Glancing at a dress that caught my eye at the end of the other rack of black dresses, I darted forward to snatch one of the hangers. "Oh, this is it!" I cried. My stomach flipped with excitement.

"Really?!" Zephyr looked at the dress dubiously. "I don't think Ashford will go for that."

"Why not? All it needs is a pair of combat boots and we're in business! This is so rad!"

"You are not wearing combat boots and an evening gown on this stage!" Ashford's heavy British accent rang out over the racks of clothes.

Zephyr and I both laughed.

"Watch me," I whispered.

Stronger

Ash was going to love me by the end of the show, I just knew it. The way he groused during my fitting was a clear sign. We would be besties for life. Obviously, that was the reason I donned what I called the Evil Bride dress and paired it with black combat boots that hit just below the knee. Who wouldn't want to wear a solid black dress with a puffy, tulle skirt and silk corset that made my girls perk up and sing, too? With a heavy sigh, Ashford agreed to pin up the front of the skirt into more of a hi-lo design to show off the boots. They had a bunch of silver buckles on the side that I loved.

Fully committed to the ensemble, I added a loose belt with purple spikes. The purple seamlessly matched the chunky purple streaks throughout my hair. The dark wedding gown felt like the perfect way to signify my move from the old life in Texas to this new one in Cali. I made sure to text Luke so that he knew to tune in that night and watch me live out my dreams in front of millions of people. Playing the Evil Bride could be my personal "fuck you" to him. He might have broken up with me, but I would come back stronger and better than ever.

Once my wardrobe was nailed down for the show that night, I headed off to have my hair and makeup done for the promo shots. The stylists assured me that wearing jeans with a solid color tank top, AKA my go-to outfit, was perfectly acceptable for that. All the contestants would simply be thrown together in front of a white back drop to interact while photographers and videographers captured the moment.

Although the makeup artist was a little heavier on the eye liner than I was used to, overall I liked the new look. The hair stylist gave me a light trim to even out the layers in my hair. We discussed my preference for the purple streaks, a look that she wanted to maintain to help set me apart from the other contestants. I could be the "alt girl," as she put it.

If it led to a record contract and $2.5 million, she could label it whatever she wanted.

After setting my hair in soft, beach waves, another production assistant with a clipboard led me to the soundstage where the promo shots were being filmed. We would have individual photographs taken, too. The rest of the contestants were already there, milling about the snack table set up in the corner while the camera crew finished up the lighting and sound checks. The atmosphere crackled with excitement and adrenaline.

"All right, gather round!" a woman called. She also wore a headset with a microphone and carried a clipboard, but her outfit looked far more expensive and carefully put together. Big shot energy swirled around her. I saw Kyle off to the side immediately stand up straighter when she stepped to center stage, confirming my suspicions.

Billy Anderson sat in a chair against the wall behind all the photographers, along with a few other people in perfectly tailored suits. I was willing to bet money that they were the producers from the corporate network. When he saw me, Billy smiled and waved. I nodded, but turned away before he could wave me over or try to introduce me. Since Kyle already had the impression that I was Billy's pet, I didn't want to give the rest of the contestants a reason to agree with him.

I spotted Zephyr right away and went to stand beside her. She handed me a water bottle in greeting before turning back towards the woman on stage.

"Now that the replacement has joined us," the woman said without looking at me, though the rest of the contestants certainly turned to glance my way, "I'm going to go over everything a final time. For those of you who don't remember, I'm Veronica Crewe and I am your lead contact for your time here with us on *America's Music Star.*"

She continued, repeating the same rules that Kyle provided in the car on the way to set, adding that there was no rule against contestants dating or having sex, but that the entire network encouraged us to make "safe choices." The only rooms in the house that did not have cameras were the bathrooms, though no one would have access to any of the video feed from the cameras because it was all loaded to a hard drive kept off site.

"And yes, that does mean that we reserve the right to share your sex tapes with the American public if we think it will boost ratings," Veronica stated flatly, "so be sure the sex is worth it!"

I glanced around to see if anyone else was as wide-eyed at her candor as me, but most of them merely nodded in agreement.

Each week there would be candid interviews and each

contestant would get to film a confessional-style reaction to all of the "drama" in the house. If there wasn't any drama, the producers had the right to stir some up.

"This is a television show, folks," Veronica reminded us. "Entertain them at all costs. Never forget that."

We would work with a guest mentor each week along with vocal coaches, instrument instructors, songwriters, and choreographers. All the contestants had creative freedom "within reason," which Veronica summarized as being tastefully appropriate for the average American family to watch together. I interpreted that as keeping our song choices clean and our genitals covered, but maybe I was a prude.

By the time Veronica started going over the daily schedule, I was too bored to pay attention. My eyes began to wander, assessing each of the contestants standing in the group. None of the women stood out to me as the kind of person who would slip you a laxative while you weren't looking, but then again, spray tans and mini-skirts made great camouflage.

A guy I estimated to be a few years older than me caught me staring and gave me a roguish wink. His dark hair was nearly jet black, and he wore it long and wild. Several piercings lined his ear. There were tattoos covering every inch of skin that I could see, starting from the neck down, a motley assortment of skulls, flowers, and symbols. His clothes were all black, which matched the leather cuffs around both wrists. Easily the sexiest man in the room.

The bloom of embarrassment hitting my cheeks made his lips twitch before he turned his attention back to Veronica.

"Zephyr," I whispered, leaning towards her ear. "Who is that guy? The one with all the tattoos?"

"Bowie Baird," she muttered back. "He seems like a bit of a bad boy."

"Yeah..." My voice trailed off as my fantasies went into hyperdrive. Bowie looked like every other millennial and Gen Z rock star, but something told me it wasn't just a vibe for him. He genuinely had a middle finger locked and loaded for everyone around him.

I needed to take a pregnancy test just from looking at him.

Luke...who...? a voice in the back of my mind asked.

Suddenly, I was aware Billy was on stage and all eyes were now directed towards me.

"I'm sorry. What was that?" I asked.

Billy rolled his eyes. "I invited you up here to introduce yourself first since you haven't had a chance to meet anyone. Ladies and gentlemen, I give you Finley Smalls."

It was like the worst first day of junior high school all over again. All eyes were boring into the back of my head as the group parted so I could cross over to the center of the room. Billy vigorously shook my hand as I joined him, stepping back so that I could take over. A girl who looked to be my age in a baby pink mini-dress and perfect curls glowered at me from the front row. She crossed her arms across her chest in challenge, jutting a hip out to one side as soon as we made eye contact.

Why, hello, Jessica Harris.

"Hey, y'all. I'm Finley Smalls," I introduced myself. "I'm twenty-one, and originally from Fort Worth, Texas. And, uh... yeah. I'm just really happy to be here." Shrugging, I cast a quick glance over to Billy, who nodded in return. That was my exit cue.

The girl I assumed to be Jessica immediately stepped forward to go next, intentionally pushing her shoulder into mine as she passed me. Her hips swayed as she walked. This was a person used to being the center of attention and getting her way. I doubted she struggled with anything a day in her life.

"I'm Jessica, and I'm here to win," she said, her hands in fists on her hips.

Billy's eyes widened as we all waited for her to say something else. After an awkward pause, he asked, "Anything else you'd like to tell us about yourself?"

Jessica rolled her eyes. "There's no need. I'm not here to make friends." She stomped off stage. Everyone gave her wide berth this time around.

I returned to my spot next to Zephyr, who had her eyebrows raised and her nose crinkled. "Damn, what kinda dog shit did she step in?" she whispered to me.

Water went down the wrong pipe as I snorted while taking a sip from my water bottle. The rock god, Bowie, came over and thumped me harshly between the shoulder blades.

"Easy there, cowgirl," he said in a thick Irish accent. "Do we need to have a doctor on hand for ye?"

Zephyr and I exchanged an incredulous look.

"You're not American?" I asked in surprise.

Bowie grinned. "Nothing gets by ye."

Billy called his name, causing Bowie to flash us another smirk. "Later, cowgirl." He casually strutted over to the stage, commanding everyone's attention. More than one woman did a double take as he walked up.

"He's barely come out of his room since we got here," Zephyr whispered to me in a hushed tone. "I've never heard him speak before, let alone come up to someone on his own!"

"Good afternoon, everyone," Bowie said, giving a half-hearted wave. "I'm Bowie Baird—"

"You're Irish!" Jessica yelled.

"So glad ye told me, dearie. I've been wondering." Bowie rolled his eyes at her and tried to finish his introduction when she interrupted again.

"But it's *America's Music Star*! Being an American should be a requirement!" she argued. Crossing her arms over her chest again, Jessica rounded on Billy and Veronica. "Why isn't there a restriction for contestants from other countries?"

"I think it's rad!" I offered, making the rest of the group chuckle. Bowie shot me an appreciative smirk.

Jessica sneered at me. "Of course *you* do!"

Before I could ask her what that meant, Bowie held up both hands in a placating gesture. "Easy, dames. There's plenty of me to go around." Everyone tittered. "And not that I need to go over my tragic back story, but I'm a dual citizen. American dad, Irish mum. We're done here, yeah, Billy?"

Without waiting for Billy to answer, he stepped back onto the ground, pushing past everyone to come grab a water bottle from the table behind me. He stood close enough to me that I couldn't move an inch to the left or I would bump into him. My arms broke out in goosebumps as I realized he was gazing at me with that irreverent smirk again.

"How'd I do, cowgirl?"

"Sir, the closest I've come to a cow is a steak at Texas Road-house, so you might wanna cool your jets with the nickname." Lord, if my mom heard me talking to somebody like that, she would probably smack me on the back of the head. Why was I suddenly feeling so sassy and ready to spar?

My comment didn't seem to bother Bowie in the least. On the contrary, he gave me a devil-may-care grin that had to routinely make women's panties disappear because Lord have mercy. "Ye and I are gonna be the best of friends by the time this is all over, yeah?"

Zephyr gave me a wide eyed look that clearly asked what to make of Bowie's sudden interest in me. And as I took in his tattooed, lithe frame, I kinda wanted to find out, too.

I gulped. I was in so far over my head.

The rest of the contestants all had a chance to introduce themselves since everyone had been trickling in over the past few days to start the season. This was the first time we had all been assembled together. Thankfully, Jessica seemed to be the only one with an attitude problem, although every teacher I'd ever had told me I could have made friends with a wall. Cattiness just wasn't in my nature.

Cooper Davies was the stereotypical Southern gentleman. He worked on his family's farm back in Mississippi and loved country music. With his baby blue eyes, carefully tousled curls, and trim beard, he looked like the perfect guy to grace the halls of the Grand Ol' Opry. And yet, his manners and laidback personality seemed natural, not something that he faked for the cameras.

Gretchen Osenbaugh was the oldest contestant of the group at thirty-five. She already had a husband and three kids at home who would be cheering her on every night. Her introduction mostly included references to musical theater; getting a part on Broadway was her greatest life's ambition. I liked her.

Kameron Potts had to be selected as the season's heart throb. There was no way God made someone that handsome and talented all in one. His cheek bones were sharp enough to cut glass, and he had the most brilliant green eyes I ever saw in a human head. Once his introduction was done, Kameron joined us next to the water bottle table and adjusted the colored contact lenses. The illusion burst for me, but I knew he would have the female viewers at home eating out of the palm of his hand.

Tessa Seeley reminded me of a college cheerleader. She had the perfect tan skin, blonde hair, and athletic body that most women would kill for. If Tessa didn't win the grand prize on the show, I had every confidence she could get a modeling contract the moment she stepped off stage. Her introduction was perky and bubbly, thereby completing my cheerleader assessment. I hoped her positivity stayed up for the duration of the show because sometimes I needed an attitude like that in my corner.

Miles Henshaw was an older black man who grew up singing gospel. Even his speaking voice was deep and rich, and I couldn't wait to hear him sing. He was the youth choir director at his church back home in Atlanta. All of the kids in his choir wanted him to audition for the show, so he submitted a tape to encourage them to follow their dreams. "I never actually thought I'd get picked," Miles explained.

Isabela Caravelli, or Issy, as she asked us to call her, studied classical music in Italy during college. After graduating last year, she went on a spiritual retreat at an ashram in India, where she had a vision that told her she should return to the United States and pursue a career in music. Issy firmly believed it was her destiny to share more classical music with younger generations so that it wasn't lost or forgotten. It was a weird flex in my opinion, but I admired her spirit.

Riley Varnowitz was the youngest contestant on the show at only sixteen. Due to his age, Riley would be permitted to stay at a hotel each night with his mother, but had to remain at the contestant house during the day. My first impression was that Riley would feel more at home in a computer lab; large square glasses kept sliding down his nose and the button up shirt he wore looked like it had been starched from the way it crinkled when he moved. A woman I assumed to be his mother stood off to the side, nodding her head and prompting him to smile as he talked.

Joey Perez wore a football jersey that only served to make his indomitable frame even larger. At close to 6'5, the man had to be 230 pounds of solid muscle. He said that his coaches wanted him to pursue a career in the NFL, but he was going to give *America's Music Star* one shot to prove whether or not he was actually cut out to be a singer. Joey and Kameron immediately bonded with bro hugs and back slaps.

Zephyr winked at me when she went last, her brown curls flying every which way around her face like a halo. She grew up in New York City, but spent every summer with her grandparents in Pennsylvania who "beat the accent" out of her. Music had always been her greatest passion and her entire family planned to host viewing parties down the Eastern seaboard to vote for her.

It was an eclectic mix of tales and talent. Exactly the kind of thing that would make for great tv. I already wanted everybody to win...though I probably wouldn't mind if Jessica came in second place. Her scowl remained firmly in place during all of the introductions.

Once introductions were over, the photographer gathered us around and took various group shots. Some were more posed than others, and it was obvious who had taken professional photos before. Jessica simpered in front of the camera. The smile changed her face entirely, morphing her into a girl who looked like America's Sweetheart.

"That girl is gonna be a thorn in my side the whole time," Zephyr muttered. I tried not to laugh since I was the one getting the dirtiest looks from the photographer already. Modeling was not in my skillset. We were currently posed on the floor as the photographer stood on a stepladder to look down at us.

"Don't worry about her," I offered. "We're gonna have a blast and that's all that matters. What are you gonna sing tonight?"

"Un-Break My Heart by the queen, Toni Braxton," Zephyr replied with a smile. "What about you? How are you going to perform if you haven't had any chance to practice?" She shifted so that her chin lifted up, exposing more of her long neck and angular features.

"I'll probably do something a cappella and make it easy on myself," I joked.

Zephyr nodded, though. "Go for a classic like 'Thinking Out Loud.' That always slays."

"Wait—can we play our own instruments here?"

"Yeah, girl. You can do anything that will set yourself apart. Go for it."

That was all the encouragement I needed. I had enough of this picture nonsense and scrambled back to my feet in search of Billy. He and the bigwig execs had moved closer to the food table, animatedly discussing something.

Sliding up to Billy's shoulder, I whispered, "I need a practice room."

"Finley," he greeted me, a tight smile plastered on his face. "I'm just talking to the board members of the U.S. Broadcasting Network. They're very interested to hear you sing tonight."

I waved my hand over my head in an exaggerated hello. "Great! That's why I need a practice room."

Billy sighed. "There will be time for you on the schedule later."

"Yeah, a whopping fifteen minutes! I need more than that, Billy! How am I gonna win over America if I don't prepare?"

Glancing around at the wide-eyed expressions of the board members, Billy ground out, "Fine. Go find Veronica and tell her I approved it."

He didn't need to tell me twice. I zipped around the back of the photographer, holding two thumbs up and calling out, "Looking rad, y'all!" before I found Veronica near the seating area on the other side of the room. She barked out orders about lighting to two production assistants who looked as though they wanted to shit themselves.

"Hi, there! I just spoke with Billy—you know, the producer Billy—and he said it's okay if I get some extra time in a practice room. Since I haven't had rehearsal time and all." I flashed her my biggest smile to layer the charm on thick.

Judging by her frown, the charm didn't work. "I don't have time for the band to give you extra rehearsals. Billy said you're a natural and wouldn't need the extra help."

"Oh yeah, totally. I *totally* am a natural. That's why I'm not asking for the band. I just need the space for me. Me, myself, and I." As if she couldn't understand who I meant, both index fingers pointed at my face.

The frown stayed firmly in place. "Follow me."

She led me down the hallway to a small music room,

complete with piano, acoustic guitar, and a wall of mirrors. Without any further instruction, Veronica swept from the room.

I had no idea why but being left alone so abruptly triggered a lot of feelings. In only twenty-four hours, I experienced every facet of the human emotion, and yet now loneliness crashed over me like a tidal wave. No matter which way you sliced it, I was completely on my own.

Sitting down at the piano and running my hands across the ivory keys woke up the feelings I had been suppressing since the moment Luke told me our relationship was over. Music always had a way of doing that for me; emotions became crystal clear when I paired them to a melody. All of my favorite break up ballads swam through my head as the loneliness and sorrow took over.

Even though I knew our breakup was a blessing in disguise, it was painful to look back on the memories. Luke was the staple in my life for four years. I lost my virginity to him. I graduated high school with him. So many milestones now lost to a man who had no place in my future.

Although I didn't dedicate as much of my time to playing piano as I did to singing, I could still play well enough to accompany myself. Going through some scales, I warmed up my voice and prepared to test some songs. The acoustics in the room were incredible. Every note rang out clear as a bell.

I was so lost in my feelings while trying to nail down a song that without thinking about it, my fingers started to play the opening notes to one of my favorite Whitney Houston songs, a Finley Smalls' idol if there ever was one. Dolly Parton might have coined "I Will Always Love You," but nobody sang it like Whitney did. I wanted to convey the hurt that came with letting go of someone you cared about, just like she did.

My fingers moved on their own accord as I moved through the harmony of the song. Even I could hear the pain and emotion lacing through the words as I sang the ultimate goodbye to Luke. Only it wasn't to Luke, I realized. It was the version of my life that I had to grieve. Cathartic tears streamed down my face as I belted out note after note, letting the words bury themselves in my skin.

By the time the last chord faded, a slow clap of applause came from the door behind me. I hastily wiped the tears from my face as I turned to find Bowie, Zephyr, and all the other contestants crowding around the door. It was Bowie who leaned against the door frame, gazing at me in a way that was equal parts awestruck and equal parts expectant. He clapped loudly, which prompted Zephyr and the rest to join him. Jessica, as I expected, narrowed her eyes in scorn.

"Well, well, ladies and gents," drawled Bowie. "We have ourselves a true talent here."

A slow smile spread across my face. Luke never once paid me a compliment on my singing, just told me how he couldn't wait for me to be famous so we would have lots of money. Somehow, hearing the flattery come from Bowie's lips made it true.

It was like I could breathe again. Dreams I had long since forgotten came surging back as I realized the possibilities open to me now that Luke wasn't in the picture. Now I could go after what I wanted.

And for the first time since Billy offered me a spot on the show, I realized winning *America's Music Star* was it.

Breakaway

Despite Ashford's grumblings, I was pretty damn pleased with my appearance for the show. The hair and makeup people gave me an elaborate faux hawk along with a smoky eye of silver, black, and a hint of purple that extended towards my ears. I opted for a simple black choker necklace because I knew having anything dangling would just give me something to fidget. And I *loved* to fidget.

If anyone ever tells you that they aren't nervous to perform, they're lying. Having any kind of audience is the biggest thrill you could experience. Their emotions feed into your emotions, and if you're a good artist, you'll help them navigate the full gamut through your entire set. Music helps people connect to the human experience. I just happened to the be the lucky bitch who could share it with them. Thankfully, my "nerves" weren't really nerves, but more of a pumped up excitement.

Tickets for the show sold out as soon as *America's Music Star* announced Enid Wexler as the host. She was an up and coming TikTok sensation with over three million followers and the interview savvy of a young Barbara Walters. It was the perfect fit to get a younger audience to tune in along with fans who had already devoted years to other reality singing competitions. Enid was kind during our brief introduction, assuring me that she wouldn't put me on the spot or make comments about sensitive subjects, which I appreciated.

However, a sold out show meant a room packed full of people. To date, the largest gig I ever had was during my senior year of high school when the honors choir competed at a state tournament and there were 150 parents in the room. Tonight's show doubled down on that and then some. Excitement was tangible as everyone rushed around to prepare for the big opening number.

Since I was a last minute addition, I didn't have the chance to learn the choreography to the opening song that all the contestants had prepared. Billy said the plan was to have me stand next to Enid so that when the contestants moved out of the shot as the camera zoomed in to her, it would look like I naturally belonged there. We only had time enough for one rehearsal that afternoon, so I hoped everything went according to plan.

That alone proved my giddy optimism for tonight. Nothing ever went according to plan.

Nerves tap-danced through my system. I wanted to cry, vomit, and scream all at once knowing that I was about to be on national television. Fans were out in the audience already cheering for their favorite contestants from all the pre-show promos that had been run for the last month, and several of them had signs to hold up in support of one person or another. Zephyr told me earlier that Jessica, Tessa, Kameron, Joey, and oddly enough, Bowie, already had substantial social media followings.

We were all encouraged to post things on our socials to get more viewers and votes.

Social media management was one of those things I always assumed I could hire out once I made it big. I couldn't even tell you any of my handles. Luke set them up for me when we were still in high school and the dreams of super stardom seemed far more realistic.

"Okay, everyone, get into position!" Kyle screamed.

Zephyr and I turned to each other for what we decided was our Friend Check. Hair, teeth, makeup, jewelry, shoes—nobody deserved to go out on stage with food in their teeth or a stray wisp of hair sticking up. We both nodded when we were satisfied with each other's appearances. Zephyr, being tall and thin in a way that I could never achieve, wore a floor length halter dress that had flecks of gold woven into the multi-colored fabric. A long chain of tiny gold rings traced down her spine with the completely open back. She had large gold hoops in her ears and metallic makeup that made her eyes pop.

"Go!" Kyle waved forward the rest of the contestants. The lights turned off on stage, signifying the start of the show, and the crowd went crazy. I just barely caught a glimpse of Bowie in a low rise pair of black leather pants and a tattered gray henley that gripped his torso so tightly that I could see every line of muscle on his arms and stomach. Even the guyliner did something to me.

I bit back a moan, picturing the stern face of my gran, as Enid joined me.

"Ready?" she whispered.

Suddenly, I was too nervous to do anything but nod.

The rest of the group burst on stage, fanning out to sing "Walking on Sunshine," complete with dance routine. The cheering reached new decibels as fans screamed for their favorites. Kameron winked at a group of teenage girls waving signs with his photo on it and I thought we might have to call the paramedics. Literal swooning like a Bugs Bunny cartoon.

Enid and I waited in the wings. She seemed completely unfazed by the whole thing, adjusting her earpiece. Without looking in a mirror, I'd be willing to bet money that I looked like I was trying to keep the contents of my bowels inside.

Which I was, if we're being honest.

In a slow motion montage worthy of John Hughes, we scurried across the stage to our mark, with me on Enid's right. The lights were getting brighter, the contestants were twirling out of the way, sparklers were shooting up from the edges of the stage, and there was the camera, right in my face. I smiled and gave a little wave. Hopefully my mom knew it was for her.

This time around it was Bowie on my right. During our run through earlier, I was next to Joey. My confusion must have been written on my face because his lips turned up for the briefest of moments when my eyes caught his.

Leaning in, Bowie barely breathed the words, "I had to be close to ye."

The cameras no longer mattered because my heart stopped. Either he was the world's biggest flirt or *he* felt the same kind of magnetism towards me that I felt towards him. Both options were dangerous in the worst kind of way. Not that I had time to consider them when we were filming a frickin' tv show!

The production team cued for a commercial and everyone was ushered into what we were affectionately calling The Pen. It was really just a slightly elevated seating area surrounded by a glass partition for all the contestants to use while we watched everyone else perform. It also had a small space in the back, away from the prying eyes of the audience, where we could freshen up. A makeup artist, hair stylist, and Ashford all waited there and watched the live feed on a monitor in case one of them needed to swoop in for a style emergency.

Sadly, the space didn't offer a bucket for vomiting, which was still a very real possibility for me. Between Bowie's whispered comment that made my thighs clench and my anticipation to sing in front of millions of people, I was ready to spew my guts out on the drop of a dime. Trying to push away thoughts of sexy guyliner and taut muscles might be my biggest challenge of the night.

Enid Wexler returned to the side of the stage under an enormous spotlight. Rather than having the same judges each week like other singing competitions, *America's Music Star* wanted to keep a steady rotation of musicians, actors, and comedians who all had their own new releases to plug. This week's judges included legendary music producer Johnny Cho, the frontman of a boy band, Nate Hall, and a Victoria's Secret model who just dropped her first single, Eliana Rivera. Rumors swirled that Nate and Eliana were dating and neither would attend an event without the other, which was what caused the unusual line up.

We were not allowed to meet the judges beforehand so that they couldn't form a "preconceived bias" for one of us over another. As if all the interviews and propaganda hadn't done that already.

I truly was the odd man out since nobody knew who I was. The song tonight was my only shot to make a good first impression. All my fingers and toes were crossed that I nailed it.

The producers decided that we would start off tonight in alphabetical order based on first name. After we performed, Enid would ask a few questions about our song choice, families, or whatever she thought up before we received feedback from the judges. By the end of the last commercial break, the viewers had to vote on their favorite performances of the night, and we would be ranked. Our rankings would determine our performance order for next week. No one got voted off, so at the end of twelve weeks, it could be any one of us winning the grand prize.

Based on first names, Bowie was the season opener, with Cooper on deck. I was third, just after the second commercial break. I hadn't seen or heard any of the others practicing other than the vocal exercises we did with a voice coach before filming started tonight. They all sounded like professionals to me.

Squealing girls caught my attention as Bowie took to the stage with a chrome plated Les Paul guitar in hand. A string of women wearing tight Spanx dresses lined the front row and looked ready to throw their panties at him. They were probably already huge fans if what Zephyr said about his social media following was true.

With a rallying cry, Enid screamed, "And our first performer of the night, BOWIE BAIRD!" The rest of the audience went nuts.

Bowie ripped out a guitar solo with all the style and musicality of Slash before segueing into the opening chords of "Second Chance" by Shinedown. The song choice surprised me since some of the runs in that song required a more experienced singer, but Bowie blew me away. The high notes were as pure and clear as the original, and he never needed to go into a falsetto to get there.

Even more distracting was the way he moved with the guitar. Bowie had a hypnotic way of rolling his hips along to the music that made me imagine what it would be like to have him use the same move while naked. He stayed on beat the entire time while playing lead guitar and singing. Pure talent wrapped up in all the required casing of the stereotypical bad boy your mom warned you to stay away from.

Now I understood the fan section in the front row. They could count me amongst their ranks because I was a Bowie girl for life!

When the final note ended, the entire room erupted in a standing ovation. Between the tattoos, the sexy way he played the guitar, and the smolder, Bowie Baird was definitely a rock star. The television show was just a way to prove it.

Everyone in The Pen whooped and hollered for him, though Jessica's looked to be against her better judgement. Whenever a camera zoomed in for shots of our reactions, she made it a point to appear interested and excited. But the moment the cameras dropped so did the act. A bit counterproductive, in my opinion, since we had a live audience who could see the difference for themselves. But I wasn't a social media personality, so what did I know?

Cooper Davies made all the women in the audience collectively sigh. Wranglers tight enough to make his butt pop out along with an open flannel and rolled up sleeves made him the quintessential country singer. His cream-colored Stetson and worn leather boots completed the ensemble, but it was his bright smile that won the crowd over. He walked on stage with an acoustic guitar on his back. Greeting everyone with a simple, "Howdy, y'all!" received thunderous applause and wolf whistles.

The band started playing behind him and I recognized the opening chords to "Somebody Like You" by Keith Urban. Cooper joined in on his guitar as more pyrotechnics went off. Fans were dancing in their seats and singing along. He successfully brought smiles to everyone's faces. It was infectious; I found myself humming and dancing along with the rest of them.

In short, after just two contestants I could already tell the stakes were a lot higher than I originally thought. If I wasn't already battling a case of the jitters, I sure would be now.

Half-way through Cooper's song, Bowie returned from backstage where he had freshened up with a new white V-neck. His long hair was now up in a bun at the nape of his neck. Man buns had never been an aphrodisiac before, but then again, when had I ever met someone with the raw sex appeal of Bowie Baird? Even his name could make your lady parts wet.

Bowie immediately came next to me, a bemused smirk on his face as he watched me dance along from the corner of his eye. Once Cooper's song ended, he whooped and hollered along with the rest of us, but his body faced mine as he did so.

"Ye're gonna blow them all away, cowgirl," Bowie said quietly.

My eyebrows scrunched together as I considered him for a moment. "Why do you care so much?"

He bit down on his lower lip, a move that made him look even sexier, as he pondered his answer. "Don't know," Bowie admitted. "But they're waitin' on ye."

Oh, shit! It's my turn!

A tech crew member waved me forward so I could grab the sound piece for my ear. After practicing on my own for the better part of the afternoon, I opted out of using the band and decided to just accompany myself on the piano. The other producers were reluctant at first, but Billy vouched for me, saying that I had earned the right to make an executive decision like that since I was doing them all a favor by joining the show at the last minute.

The stage was now black while the interior lights brightened. Audience members were rushing to and from the bathroom or taking selfies, so no one really paid attention as the production crew wheeled out a magnificent, white grand piano to center stage. Bowie and Zephyr each gave my hand a gentle squeeze as I left The Pen to take my place on the piano stool.

Adrenaline coursed through my veins as I felt myself shedding the girl I used to be. It was time to break away from the Finley who kept her dreams at bay because her worthless boyfriend couldn't be bothered to earn his keep. All I ever wanted was to sing to a crowd of my fans—people who actually paid money to see me. Even if I didn't win, taking a chance by being on this show was the closest I had ever come to making that a reality. I was damn proud of myself.

Lights started flashing to signal that recording was about to start, and the people in the audience scrambled to their seats. Enid Wexler went to her cue next to the judges' seats so that she could welcome back the viewers at home before introducing me.

Deep breath in.

Deep breath out.

The lights died out so that a single spotlight shined on me at the piano. It was just me and the music, a melody weaving my heartstrings as every emotion came out. Luke's face hovered in my mind's eye as I made a musical vow of eternal love. Raw, tortured pieces of my soul said goodbye to the boy I used to love along with the girl I used to be. Like a phoenix, I, too, would grow from this fire.

Tears ran freely down my face as I let my feelings guide the runs my voice took. Each time I sang this song always felt unique; I was never quite sure where the heart would take me. This rendition was powerful. Hopefully my old vocal coach was watching and recognized the breath control I gave from my diaphragm because it sounded mighty to my ears.

As the last chord faded, awareness returned. The muffled sounds of the audience slowly amplified until I realized that I was receiving a standing ovation. All three of the judges had tears streaming down their faces. Glancing over at Zephyr, she beamed at me, both hands in fists above her head.

Bowie simply stood with his arms crossed, a small smile barely tipping at the corners of his mouth. Pride shown through his eyes. Which was crazy.

We barely knew one another.

Stepping over to stage right, I joined Enid for my interview.

"Wow!" she gushed. "You moved everyone here tonight, Finley. I'm sure you did the same thing for everyone watching at home. What do you have to say about your song choice tonight?"

I half shrugged. "Whitney is one of my biggest idols, so I hope she's proud up there in Heaven."

Enid laughed. "You were a last minute addition to the show. How did you have time to prepare a song like that?"

"It's one of my favorite songs, and it just really fits where my life is at right now, ya know? I recently went through a bad breakup, so this was my swan song from the old me. Time to embrace the new!" We both shared another laugh and the audience joined in.

The camera man came a step closer as if he was zooming in for a close up. I tried not to think about how awkward it would feel later to see my face plastered all over tv and social media. It was a weird juxtaposition to want to be the center of attention while simultaneously hiding away from the world.

"Well, I just have to mention, before we get the feedback from the judges, your hair slays!" Enid smiled so wide that her cheeks must have burned. "This whole alternative pop princess vibe really works for you! Do you think you'll see a bunch of fans with chunky purple streaks now?"

"Um...maybe?" I would hardly call myself a trendsetter.

Sensing my nervous laughter, Enid placed a gentle hand on my elbow before turning to the camera to announce that the judges were ready with my critiques.

Since no one was voted off on *America's Music Star*, the judges didn't have to assign scores. They would simply give feedback to help contestants improve for next time. Billy said judges were supposed to nitpick to stir up controversy and not to worry about the things they critiqued. It was all for ratings.

Eliana went first, waving at the fans who cheered for her. "Finley Smalls," she said, her accent thick, "you really have a set of pipes on you, lady!" Roars of approval from the audience followed. "I think your song choice was perfect. I'm so sorry you went through a breakup, but he's the one feeling stupid now!" More applause.

I didn't want to look over and check, but I would have sworn I felt Bowie's eyes burning into the side of my head. It was a ridiculous idea because why would he do that? We hadn't even had a full conversation yet.

Enid introduced Nate and asked what words of wisdom he had for me.

The crowds didn't scream as loud for Nate as they did for Eliana, but his boy band fell out of favor over the past few years when one of their members left the group to make a solo album. People knew him now more so because of his rumored relationship with Eliana the supermodel.

"Yo, yo, what up, Finley, baby?!" Bright stage lights reflected off the sunglasses he wore and nearly blinded me. "That was fresh! You just keep yo' head up and keep doin' your thing, and you'll be a'ight!"

I smiled as wide as I could, thanking him and blowing kisses.

We moved onto Johnny Cho, who was the only opinion out of the group I actually cared about. Johnny worked with some of the best names in the industry, and albums with his signature style always topped the Billboard 100 charts. He was one of the most sought after music producers in the world right now.

"Yeah, so you did what not many people can do," Johnny said, "and that's wow me. You've got *it*, Finley. And I don't say that lightly."

You could've knocked me over with a feather. His comments validated everything I worked for leading up to this performance. Spending every spare minute practicing, joining all the school and church choirs, begging my mom for more voice lessons...it all had a purpose.

I cried in earnest now as all the adrenaline, pride, and happiness filled my chest. It swelled like a peacock spreading its plumes.

I frickin' did it!

In a daze, the next transition allowed for me to exit backstage where Ashford and the team of stylists waited to fix my hair and makeup. As much as I loved the Evil Bride look, it was starting to hurt having my boobs squashed as high as my clavicle bone. And I was not pencil thin by any stretch of the imagination—my stomach would undoubtedly have marks from where the bones of the corset pressed into flesh.

I vaguely heard their praises as they fixed the eye shadow and added more hairspray to the faux hawk. My fingers burned to check my phone. Mom would have left me a message about my performance, and right then I longed to hear the comfort of her voice. Shock started to take effect as my adrenaline crashed, leaving me shaking and gasping for breath. Ashford called out for the paramedic the studio kept on standby. I tried to decline but my teeth clattered too hard to be understood.

"The lass doesn't need a medic," Bowie said. He appeared almost out of nowhere, coming to squat down in front of me. His rich brown eyes caught mine and he clasped my hands in his own, squeezing tight. "Go on and fetch her some water." They all scattered.

Maintaining eye contact, Bowie started to slowly inhale and exhale. I mimicked his actions. "That's a good girl," he whispered to me. Within minutes, my heart rate started to go back down and I no longer shook in my seat. When I completely settled, he grinned at me, the most wickedly seductive smile to grace this Earth.

"Why are you being so nice to me?" I asked.

Bowie leaned back so that his weight rested more on his heels. A thumb gently rubbed soothing circles on the back of my hand as he considered my question.

"Maybe I find ye interesting," Bowie finally admitted.

I rolled my eyes. "You find me interesting? When you walk in a room there's a line of women fainting behind you."

"Does that include ye, cowgirl?"

I flushed beet red all the way down to my toes. Flirting was never my thing. It's too hard to flirt when your mouth is always twelve seconds ahead of your brain. Even I'm surprised with what comes out half the time.

"I'm not really the swooning kind of gal," I settled on. It sounded cringeworthy out loud, but I didn't want to take it back. I just got out of a serious relationship, and I was now living in a goldfish bowl the entire world got to see. This was not the time to start something with a new man, no matter how sexy he looked playing his guitar.

Bowie didn't look offended, however. He stood up, offering me his hand to help me out of the makeup chair. "That's because ye've only been with a wee boy who didn't know what he had, cowgirl. Not all of us are that foolish."

Okay, so maybe now I *was* going to swoon. The suggestive edge to his voice sent Morse Code straight between my thighs. Luke never talked to me like that. In the beginning there were the sweet sort of things you say when you're in high school and think puppy love is real. But Bowie? He spoke like a lover who knew his way around a woman's body. I had a gut feeling that he could make me sing in more ways than one.

Rather than encouraging his flirtation, I laughed it off. "Well, you can't win 'em all! And since I'd rather win this competition, I'm willing to let my dating life stay a dumpster fire. C'mon, before Kyle comes after us with a shotgun!"

I didn't wait to see if he followed as I took off towards the concealed door for The Pen.

The rest of the night passed in a blur of music, lights, and sparkly wardrobes. For all of Kameron's posturing as a heart throb, his voice wasn't as impressive as I thought it would be. He was a hell of a dancer, however, leading a group of back up dancers to NSYNC's "It's Gonna Be Me." Gretchen's performance was impressive, but she definitely had more of a theater sound. She deserved to be on Broadway. I admired the way she tackled "How Far I'll Go" by Alessia Cara.

Jessica's performance confirmed her status as a pop princess. Her rendition of "Toxic" by Britney Spears was actually quite impressive. I would never tell her, though, because her ego didn't need any more inflation.

Riley, being the youngest one of the group, was...different. The producers allowed him to use an all-in-one setup that a DJ at a night club would use, so his song was infused with synthesized sounds that played off the topics highlighted in the Fall Out Boy version of "We Didn't Start the Fire." It wasn't a song choice or mix I would have initially pegged him for, but apparently teenage Riley was a bit of an activist. He certainly had more of an opinion on current events than I ever did in high school.

All of the contestants were talented; there wasn't a single one who didn't deserve to be here. Once I returned to The Pen, I stayed glued to Zephyr's side, unsure of how to act around Bowie. His words kept ringing in my head.

Maybe I find ye interesting.

Was it even really a compliment? Perhaps it was one of those loosely veiled insults that I was just too gullible to understand. Freak circus side shows were interesting. People who shared plates of food with their dogs. Bedazzling body hair. All things that were *interesting*.

Bowie Baird had all the inherent sex appeal of a rock star. Given how many girls were already filling the audience for him, I strongly suspected he had the sex part down in the "sex, drugs, and rock n' roll" lifestyle. And if my dating history hadn't already indicated it, I would happily spell it out for him: I didn't do hook ups. I wasn't a one night stand kinda girl.

Unless he took me to a bar first. But we weren't gonna tell him that.

Zephyr moved me to tears as she belted out the notes to Toni Braxton. She had to be as destined for greatness as Toni herself. Zephyr was a natural on stage already, walking out to touch the hands of fans who stood captivated. And while it couldn't be called dancing per se, Zephyr had a natural body rhythm that allowed her to move to the music in such a way that you wanted to see and hear more. Her voice had a natural breathiness to it that allowed her to create spectacular runs.

I made some talented new friends, y'all.

Thankfully, the judges had wonderful things to say about

everybody, even Riley. By the time we all had to return on stage for the final votes, it was really anybody's game. We all deserved to be in the top spot...although Jessica's attitude might be worthy of second or third.

My heartbeat was so loud in my ears that I could barely hear the roar of the crowd. Zephyr and I had clasped hands for balance as we walked up on stage in a fever dream, and we shared the same wide-eyed look of terror over what was to come. Even though none of us could be voted off, the possibility of ranking low amongst so many fantastic singers would bring out my downward spiral of self-destruction again.

Although, if that came with more pomegranate mojitos, I could stomach the suffering.

Enid had to go through an entire spiel to remind the audience of the importance of their votes, how all of us would be joining them next week, and to follow the show on socials for more info. The lights dropped so that a jumbotron screen behind us illuminated most of the venue. A drumroll rippled through as Enid threw out an arm and the leader board appeared...

And I was in second place! Bowie took the top spot, earning a raucous round of applause from the crowd. Miles, who sang a gospel infused rendition of "A House is Not a Home" by Luther Vandross, was in last place. Zephyr managed to secure fifth, which made her squeal in delight. We both hugged one another as tears threatened to spill over again.

Enid was gesticulating wildly towards me, which I realized after Zephyr pushed me forward meant that I needed to join her at the front of the stage. Bowie smirked down at me on my right, wrapping one arm around my waist to pull me into his hip as the other arm waved to his screaming legion of fans. I didn't want the action to mean anything to him, so I pulled Jessica, who rounded out the top three, in on my other side. Surprisingly, she didn't fight me on it, merely copied Bowie by waving to the crowd.

I stood in the middle as the beaming center of our Top Three Sandwich. The lights were so bright that they blocked out all the faces in the crowd. As the top three, we would give an exclusive interview with the hosts of *Rise and Shine, America* the next morning, which was the national news program on the U.S. Broadcasting Network.

Triumphant. That's what it felt like to bask in that kind of attention. I bet Mom was back home losing her mind over the results. Part of me wondered if Luke had tuned in and what he thought, but I shook the idea out of my mind. His opinion no longer mattered.

Veronica stepped forward from the recesses of the back to signal that the show was no longer filming. Enid immediately relaxed, massaging her jaw that was sore from all the smiling. "Thanks, guys, that was great!" she said to us.

Jessica also dropped the happy demeanor, stepping away from me as if I burned her. "I can't believe I got third place," she sneered. "You better watch your back. That top spot is mine!" She stomped off stage, hastily signing a few autographs for waiting fans on her way.

The rest of the contestants surrounded us, giving me the perfect reason to put some distance between Bowie and me, who tried to catch my eye through the crowd of people. I steadfastly ignored him. Zephyr gave me a fierce hug, a blessed distraction.

"Oh my god, that was stellar!" she yelled. "Imagine what you can do next week with all that time to practice!"

"Should be enough time for my cirque du soleil routine," I agreed with a laugh.

"Hey, we should celebrate!" Kameron cried. "We did it, guys! We made it through the first week!"

Everyone nodded in agreement.

Tessa was the one with the words of wisdom. "But first, let's shower!" We all laughed.

HOT SHOWERS ARE the best location to do some deep contemplation. It definitely wasn't the healthiest of rituals, but I tended to overanalyze my performance for hours after it ended. What if I would have worked the crowd more? Should I have spent more time looking at the camera so that people at home felt included? Did my outfit make sense with the song choice? Would it have been worthy of the top spot if I projected more at the end?

It was an anxious loop that I wouldn't get out of until the dust settled. Since I let Zephyr use the shower first for our shared bathroom, the cold water made the dust settle a bit earlier than I hoped.

Reality singing competitions were nothing new. But what they never shared on television were the crashes after a performance. How fatigue settles into your very bones when you're finally able to switch yourself to "off" mode because you no longer have to keep up an image in front of other people.

That's not to say entertainers aren't being true to themselves while on stage. Art imitates life and all that jazz.

But it's a façade. The Finley I am on stage can't be the Finley I am in real life because I could never experience the same kind of emotions I feel when I'm singing. I would explode.

Zephyr was already wearing fuzzy slippers and a battered

school t-shirt with her hair in a silk bonnet. Pillows were piled high around her so that she reclined on clouds. I knew without having to ask that she wasn't going to join everyone for the celebratory fire and drinks in the backyard.

"Don't look at me like I kicked a puppy," she said, holding up her hands in placation. "I am too tired and comfortable in this bed to go deal with all the negative chi out there."

Longingly, I shot a look at my own bed. My side of the room wasn't decorated like Zephyr's, but the bed looked to be queen size with a thick, blue duvet and fluffy pillows. We each had a gray curtain that hung from the ceiling that we could pull around our beds for privacy. The nightstand next to my bed only had my cell phone and a water bottle on it while Zephyr's had an array of crystals and a Himalayan salt lamp.

"I'm only going out there for one drink," I assured her.

The look she gave me in response called my bluff, but Zephyr didn't argue. "I'm putting in my Airpods so I can still hear the thunderstorms that help me sleep at night. Remember to set your alarm for three A.M.—you have to get up to film for *Rise and Shine!*" With a last warning gaze, Zephyr pulled an eye mask down and popped her Airpods in.

Stifling a laugh, I slathered on some of the green apple lotion my mom gave me as a parting gift and ran a brush through my hair. My choice of pajamas had always been yoga pants and tank tops, which is what I had on. It didn't occur to me to change, but as soon as I stepped out into the living room, a camera greeted me and I immediately regretted that choice. Every move would be filmed from here on out.

Some of the group was already outside, visible through the open sliding glass door that led out to the backyard. A fire roared in the pit, surrounded by Adirondack chairs. Lights from the city of Los Angeles twinkled beyond. The studio house was nestled into the hills of the Valley, creating a beautiful panoramic view of the L.A. skyline.

I grabbed a bottle of beer from the counter before heading outside. My arrival was met with a cheer of welcome from Miles, Joey, Tessa, Kameron, and Issy. Jessica sat in silence, scowling into the flames as if they personally offended her. Bowie sat on the ground close to the edge of the property. He had his elbows wrapped around his knees as he gazed out in the Valley; he wasn't even facing the revelry.

"What's up, y'all?!" I plopped down into the only vacant chair left around the fire. "Sure is nice out here!"

"Your accent is so funny!" Joey commented playfully.

"Yeah, it's hard to take you seriously!" chimed in Issy.

I shrugged. "They made me take lessons before I left Texas. So that was some show, huh? Everyone was on fire tonight!"

Jessica sneered at me. She seemed to do that a lot. "Of course you can say that. You were in the top two!"

Glancing around at the rest of the contestants, I hesitated to respond to her. Almost automatically, my gaze shifted back to Bowie, wondering if he heard—or cared—about Jessica's accusation. "I mean, you were third. It's not like we're that far apart. A lot can change by the end."

"Ugh, I can't stand another second of Mother Theresa over here!" Throwing the blanket off her lap, Jessica stormed back into the house. A cameraman followed her.

Miles shook his head as he stared after her. "We should pray for her. I sense the Devil at work with that one."

"Amen," I muttered as I watched Jessica's retreating form. "So what happens next? There's an interview in the morning, but then what?"

Several of them looked askance at one another before answering me.

"Is this another one of your jokes?" Tessa asked skeptically.

"You know, I've heard a fairy dies every time I try to be funny and miss the mark," I quipped. Just like before, some inner-autopilot stole a glance at Bowie. He still hadn't moved from his spot on the ground.

Crickets...Tessa actually looked mildly alarmed.

"Sorry, that joke normally kills." I grinned at my own humor. "Anyways, no, I have no clue what's going on."

"Where's your itinerary?" Joey inquired.

"My what?"

"Your itinerary," replied Tessa. "The producers should have given you an itinerary by now because we have a very strict schedule to follow. Like, down to the minute. Veronica said heads will roll if we don't follow it precisely." She swallowed thickly as if she genuinely believed Veronica had the means to cut off her head as punishment.

"Don't worry, I'll make a copy of mine," Kameron offered. "I basically have it memorized anyway."

"Really?" Issy asked. Now she was the skeptical one.

Kameron smiled, displaying his even, white teeth. I might have been the only one who noticed the way Issy fidgeted in her seat upon receipt of it. "Yeah, I actually have an eidetic memory."

"Shut up! Do you really?!" I asked in excitement.

He nodded. "It's helpful when it comes to learning new music. But other than that, it's more of a hindrance than anything. Imagine always remembering what someone said in an argument."

"Yeah, but at least you'll always know she's lying when a

groupie accuses you of something stupid!" Joey laughed so hard he fell over from his own joke. Issy frowned.

"Why is Bowie over there by himself?" I asked quietly, nodding towards his back. Not that I cared.

Much.

Miles, Joey, and Kameron looked over their shoulders at him. Bowie was still sitting in the same contemplative stance.

"He said he needs to decompress after a performance," Miles said, his voice low. He leaned over so that he was only a few inches away from me. "He told us he was out here waiting for you." He wiggled his eyebrows suggestively, making everyone else laugh.

I frowned outwardly, but inside my stomach flipped like an Olympic gymnast. Bowie would make everyone in the house believe there was something going on between us if he kept carrying on like this. I couldn't afford the distraction when my dreams were on the line.

Maybe I needed to outright tell him. Sometimes guys couldn't take a hint.

Resigning myself to the difficult conversation, I sighed and went to join him. Flopping down on the ground next to him, Bowie didn't even glance at me. We sat in companionable silence for a few minutes. The view was spectacular, I'd give him that. I wondered how many other people were down there just trying to hustle their way to the top like us.

"So..." I finally said. Awkward silences made me uncomfortable. All of my teachers always marked me down for talking too much in class, but I just couldn't help it. Silence felt unnatural.

"The town in Ireland where I grew up is barely a blight on the map," Bowie replied suddenly. "Ain't nothing to do but raise sheep and twiddle yer thumbs. My grandda left me an old guitar when he died, so I spent all my free time practicing with it. All hours of the day. Drove me ma bonkers."

I chuckled softly. He still wasn't looking at me, but based on the glaze in his eyes, he wasn't looking out on Los Angeles either.

"After a while, we found an old radio in the trash. It could only tune to one station that played classic rock. I started listenin' to the music and realized I could recognize most of the chords. Started playin' along.

"Once my ma married my stepfather, things started changing. He's a mean drunk, and he ain't never seen a bottle he couldn't stomach. The more I stood up to him, the worse the beatin's got. At sixteen, I lit out of there because I knew it was either him or me, and I wasn't ready to die yet."

"I'm so sorry, Bowie," I murmured. I scooted closer to him and gently rested my hand on his elbow for comfort.

He nodded his thanks. "I never really knew my da. He sent a check every month, but we never talked much."

"I can definitely relate to that!" I muttered bitterly.

Bowie continued. "When I came out here to America, I found out why. Got himself a whole new family, and the new missus didn't know anything about me."

Gasping, my hands went to my mouth. "What did you do?"

Bowie's shoulders looked stiff, the tension rippling off him so that I lived the pain with him. His long hair hung around his face like a curtain. Maybe he liked it that way. His hair served to block out the rest of the world.

"My da got me a small apartment nearby. Let me live on my own. Didn't pay much attention so long as I left his 'real' family alone. I started pickin' up gigs to bring in more money. Some girls at a bar one time started filming me for Instagram and the following blew up from there. Basically been playing to earn my way ever since.

"A couple years ago, one of the singers in the band I was playing with was too drunk to go on stage. They pushed me behind the microphone, and I realized I could sing the songs, too." Bowie shrugged as if the whole story was no big deal. "Heard of the auditions for this new show and figured, 'Whadya have to lose, mate?' And here I am."

I paused for a moment to consider his story and how vulnerable he must feel from sharing it. "Why are you telling me all this?" From what I gathered, Bowie wasn't much of a talker and kept himself isolated from the others. Since Riley couldn't sleep at the house as a minor, Bowie was the only contestant who had a room to himself.

Bowie turned his head towards me, assessing my face like it held the clues to the Universe. I felt my cheeks flame under his scrutiny. "Because I recognize the same drivin' force in you."

My eyebrows rose in question.

This time Bowie gave me a sad smile. "Desperation."

While the conclusion hurt, I couldn't actually disagree with him. I *was* desperate. I just wasn't exactly sure what for at the moment.

I swallowed thickly. My harsh truth was hard to admit out loud. "My dad didn't even remember how old I was. Dads are kind of overrated."

Bowie snorted derisively. "The piss poor da's are." His brown eyes softened as he turned to look at me. An unspoken bond forged between us as we shared a universal experience of shitty fathers.

To lighten the mood as the tension mounted, I shrugged again. "I'm still not hooking up with you."

Mr. Know It All

Fun fact: three A.M. is not the best time to wake up in the morning. Zephyr cemented herself as my best friend forever when she set her own alarm so that she could force me to get up; I hit the snooze button when left to my own devices. I was never much of a morning person to begin with, but there was something about getting up before the sun that was super depressing. A bed as soft as a cloud with sheets that smelled like lavender certainly didn't help.

Zephyr told me not to bother doing anything other than washing my face. We would always have a makeup and hair person when we did anything associated with the show. That was fine by me because until I had at least a gallon of coffee in my system, I wasn't going to be good with a makeup brush anyway. One of the production assistants knocked and handed me the clothes I was supposed to wear. A high necked blouse and dark washed jeans riddled with holes. Thankfully they were paired with glittery black Converse, otherwise I would have had to riot.

There was already a small breakfast spread on the counter when I joined Bowie and Jessica. I went straight to the Keurig, filling a mug to the brim and inhaling its rich scent. Heaven smelled like freshly brewed coffee and you couldn't tell me otherwise.

Jessica sat in a chair as a makeup artist applied products to her face. Bowie simply sat at the end of the kitchen table with an acoustic guitar in his lap. He strummed a few chords mindlessly, smirking at me as I guzzled the nectar of life. We didn't talk at all after his confession to me last night, and I wasn't sure how to act around him now. My lady bits still wanted to get up close and personal with him, but I knew my heart wasn't ready for the devastation Bowie would bring. If he could already intuitively peek into my soul like that, something told me recovering from him would be ten times worse than it was with Luke.

I plopped down beside him with my coffee and grabbed an oversized muffin from the table.

"Morning, cowgirl," Bowie offered.

"Are you seriously going to eat that muffin?" Jessica queried from her chair.

There were at least a dozen muffins in the basket. She couldn't possibly have an issue with me eating one.

"Uh, yeah," I replied slowly. "There's plenty to go around."

She cringed. "I would never eat carbs like that. You really shouldn't either."

"I mean, corpses don't eat carbs either, and look at how it turned out for them," I deadpanned. Rather than respond, Jessica's eyes narrowed. "I think I'll be alright."

"You would just think you'd want to watch your figure," she continued, despite the fact that nobody asked her opinion.

I rolled my eyes. "Watch my figure do what? My voice doesn't change with my weight, so who cares?"

Bowie outright laughed at that. "Trust me, Finley has nothing to worry about with that figure."

Faint red blotches mottled Jessica's skin at Bowie's praise. She pursed her lips, returning to her usual angry silence. One of the cameramen stepped closer to get a different angle of her reaction.

As much as I wanted to compete on the show, having cameras follow us around was already proving to be a thorn in my side. I couldn't imagine how the Kardashians lived like this every day. I valued my privacy way too much.

"Are ye ready for the interview?" Bowie inquired as he continued to strum random chords on the guitar. His long hair looked tamed straight. There was a small section with a braided leather strip in it that pulled back just enough of his hair to reveal Bowie's strong jawline and an ear full of earrings. It had to be some kind of felony for him to look *that* good at three in the morning.

Since I'd never had a reason to do an interview, I didn't have a frame of reference. Why would people feel nervous to answer questions? Public speaking might not be high on my list of fun, but there were worse things out there. Besides, my mom always watched *Rise and Shine, America,* so there was something kind of cool about picturing her turn on the small television set in her kitchen and seeing me on the screen.

"They're not gonna ask me much. I'll be fine." Leaning forward, I helped myself to a cheese danish. "Oh, no! Somebody better tell the carbs in this to run away before I eat them!" I took an obnoxiously large bite to drive my point home.

By now, the makeup artist was done with Jessica. She looked

ready to walk the runway at Fashion Week. "Nobody thinks you're funny," she scoffed.

I caught her eyeing a small stack of pancakes, but managed to hold my tongue. There wasn't enough caffeine in my system yet.

The stylist team moved over to me, frowning at the hair piled in a messy bun on top of my head. One of them snatched the muffin out of my hand. "You have to be camera ready in a few minutes!"

Bowie snickered at my scowl. "Why can't they just see me like this?" I whined.

Both of the stylists exchanged looks of horror.

"I don't look *that* bad!" I mumbled under my breath.

Hair came tumbling around my face as she (rather aggressively) yanked out the ponytail holder and immediately went crazy with the flat iron. Judging by the amount of foundation the other one used, covering up the bags under my eyes was the makeup artist's top priority. Maybe they shouldn't get us up in the middle of the night if they didn't want the evidence to show?

"It's go time, people, look alive!" Kyle shouted from the doorway. His usual headset and microphone were already in place, clipboard in hand. He was just as harried now as he was yesterday when he took me to the set.

"Come along now, cowgirl," Bowie drawled. "Let's see how long it takes for us to make Jessica crack." We exchanged a matching set of wicked grins, then followed Kyle down the hallway.

Since *Rise and Shine, America* filmed in New York City, our interview would be conducted via video. One of the music rooms now had a full camera and lighting set up. Jessica already sat in the farthest chair, taking selfies. I internally cringed.

"Have you guys checked your socials yet?" she inquired. "We're blowing up right now!"

Bowie and I slid into the seats beside her. I wound up in the middle again. The circular formation was tight enough that our knees were close to touching. I was spared answering her when they started the countdown to indicate we were filming. A small flat screen on the right side of the camera played the video as the news played it. Another flat screen on the left played back our live footage, causing me to sit up a little straighter in my seat.

"Good morning!" Kathy Whitehouse, the *Rise and Shine* anchor, cooed through the video. "Bowie, Finley, Jessica, thank you so much for being here today!"

Jessica simpered in front of the camera. "Thank you so much for having us!"

Kathy continued, "Now, I know it's early morning still out there in California, but we just couldn't wait to celebrate your top three placement after last night's premiere! What more can you tell us about the show?"

Jessica immediately answered. "It's unlike any other singing competition! Nobody gets voted off, so you can root for your favorites all season long. You can see more of our day to day lives on America's Music Star dot com, too!" She beamed at the camera, ever the picture perfect girl next door.

"Well, I'm just happy to be here!" I interjected.

Bowie snorted, which he quickly covered with a cough. If Kathy noticed, she didn't say anything but instead focused on me.

"Yes, Finley, you're the new girl! All the viewers are dying to get to know you! Tell us about yourself!"

"Let's hope they don't die because I need them to keep voting for me," I quipped. Jessica shot me a look of annoyance.

"Um, yeah...there's not much to tell, really. Fate stepped in at the last minute and gave me a shot on the show, so I'm just trying to earn my place here."

Kathy laughed. "I'd say you've done more than earn it! Second place! And with hardly any time to practice, I heard! That's quite impressive!"

Holy shit, that was a lot of exclamation points. How could anyone be so perky in the morning?

"I guess everyone gets lucky once in a while. I'm gonna have to work hard to keep up with these guys if I want to stay in the top three." I hiked my thumbs over both shoulders to point out Bowie and Jessica. Anything to get the attention off me.

Kathy took the bait. "So true! Bowie, what's it like holding the top spot?"

Bowie angled himself so that his body faced me, allowing his left arm to rest on the back of my chair. His fingers casually played with my hair as he smirked at Kathy through the screen. "Ask me that when the show's done, and I'll tell you."

Jessica had to be boiling over with that comment, but there was no way she would correct him on national tv. I was damn proud of myself for not turning to gauge her reaction, which only would have fueled the drama. And quite frankly, the offhand way his fingertips caressed my back as he ran them through my hair was kind of soothing.

The news anchor let out a peal of laughter at Bowie's response. "Oh, I hope we can! Fans were especially taken with the way you play guitar, Bowie! Where did you get all those moves?"

For once, Bowie looked sheepish, and it was so out of character for him that I pressed my lips together to keep my mouth in check. "I just do what feels natural while I'm up there," he admitted. "My hips move on their own accord."

Oh, please.

It was a click bait answer that would make all his female fans go into overdrive. Nor did I think it was a genuine response to Kathy's interest. I sucked in a shaky breath to stop my face from cringing like I wanted to. It was a welcome reminder that Bowie was the kind of bad news I didn't need right now. His backstory last night almost made me forget.

Ever so subtly, I sat forward in my chair, distancing myself from his touch.

"Well, we are so looking forward to seeing what you and the rest of the cast has in store for us this season on *America's Music Star!*" gushed Kathy. "Thank you so much for joining us!" She encouraged everyone to download the app associated with the show for more information on all their favorite singers and then plugged the next episode before it cut to commercial and we were done.

Snarky as ever, Jessica stood up with a huff of irritation. "Clearly neither of you have ever done an interview before!" she snapped before stomping out of the room.

"That girl needs to find Jesus," I commented.

"Or get laid," added Bowie.

I rolled my eyes, but smiled just the same. "Reach for the stars. Let her do both."

"At the same time."

"No sex is that good."

With a tip of his head, Bowie considered my statement for a moment. "Guess ye'll just have to find out, won't ye, cowgirl?"

"You're making me want a cheeseburger," I whined. There was no way I trusted myself to respond to the invitation laced in that question. Turning to Kyle, who was typing rapidly on a cell phone, I asked if we were free to go back to bed.

"Yes, but only for a couple hours. Dance rehearsal for next week starts at six thirty sharp." His warning glare made me think of those horrible Easter bunny costumes people wore at the mall.

Sighing, I thanked the camera guy and left the room. Bowie followed close behind, grabbing my wrist as I reached my bedroom door.

"Let's go get breakfast somewhere. Just the two of us." His voice was barely above a whisper so that he didn't wake anyone up. Or maybe it was just that he stood too close, his face only inches away from mine. I was like a fun sized candy bar at only 5'2, but Bowie wasn't actually that much taller than me. It was his persona that made him seem larger than life.

"I need more sleep," I argued.

"Ye just need more coffee," he countered.

For some reason, the entire exchange reminded me of Luke. My ex always used to give me unsolicited advice, sometimes even outright demanding that I do things or act in a certain way, and I hated it. Nobody had the right to tell me what to do or where to go. Bowie had no idea what I needed any more than Luke did.

"Nope. But thanks for playing." Pulling my wrist from his grasp, I opened the door to slip inside.

Love So Soft

Sleep evaded me as I considered Bowie's actions. Everything around my breakup with Luke still hurt. It was pure luck that I had the show to distract me or I would probably still close down the bar with Lou every night back home. I was way too young for an engagement or anything with Luke; that wasn't even why I had asked him where we were headed. But I wanted the assurance that something more committed was at least on the table as I watched life pass me by while I paid off *his* debt.

If I was being honest with myself, I needed this opportunity. I needed to have a purpose again. Singing was all I ever wanted to do with my life and Billy wouldn't have picked me if he didn't see something in me. Something that Luke couldn't.

But maybe Bowie did?

My feelings were all a jumbled mess at this point. In a typical Finley move, I planned to ignore them. Feelings would only get in the way if you let them. It was far easier to focus on the show and building a fan base than to consider the train wreck that waited me outside these walls. *America's Music Star* could be my safety bubble for the next 16 weeks since we would have another four weeks of press and touring afterwards.

I was more than ready.

When Zephyr's alarm went off, I promised myself that I would do everything possible to avoid Bowie Baird along with any residual feelings for Luke. Winning the grand prize was the only thing that mattered.

Darting out of bed, I checked Zephyr's schedule, which she conveniently left on top of her dresser and saw that we had dance and music rehearsals all day. I was free to wear leggings and a tank top—score! My hair went up in another messy knot on top of my head before I slipped on a pair of Chuck's and called it a day.

Zephyr had a beauty regimen that included rolling a quartz crystal over her face, moisturizing, and teeth whitening. I watched in fascination as she performed the ritual in the bathroom mirror. She was already gorgeous enough to model, with long legs, a lean torso, and smooth brown skin.

"How did the interview go?" she asked.

I sat on the tub while she went through her morning routine. It was either this or risk going out into the common area and running into Bowie. Zephyr was better.

"It was fine, I guess," I admitted. "I've never done an interview like that before."

She nodded in understanding. "I haven't either. I'm kind of surprised they didn't have producers coaching everyone on what to say."

"We muddled our way through it." I shrugged, not worried at all about how the interview went. Who even watched the morning news anymore anyhow? Other than my mother and all her teacher friends. I frowned at the thought.

Zephyr started applying her own makeup. When she caught sight of my questioning brow in the mirror, she sighed. "Their makeup artist isn't good with people of color. I'd rather just do my own."

"Why do you need makeup for dance rehearsals?" I asked, dumbfounded.

It was her turn to look at me like I was crazy. "Because we'll be filming." Zephyr spoke slowly so that I could understand. "Every move we make is now on camera."

"Why would they want to film us in rehearsals?"

"People like seeing things behind the scenes." She shrugged as if it didn't really matter. "I don't mind having more time on camera. This is our chance to make a name for ourselves." Nodding towards the cell phone that poked out of my pocket, she added, "You might wanna start making more of a social media presence for yourself. That's what everyone expects nowadays."

I crinkled my nose in disgust, but pulled out my phone to log into my socials anyway. When I saw my follower count, I gasped and dropped my phone. Without posting any recent videos in the past six months, my followers now approached thirty thousand. There were over 10,000 notifications of others tagging me in videos and comments. They all featured footage from *America's Music Star* or my interview on the news that morning. Eagle-eyed viewers zeroed in on Bowie's hand placement; thousands of them wrote things like, "Shipping these two-OMG!" and other equally cringeworthy statements.

"What's wrong?" Zephyr asked while brushing out her artfully sculpted eyebrows.

"I have like thirty thousand new followers, and they all think there's something going on between me and Bowie!" I shouted. "My mom is gonna strangle me!"

My friend turned and leaned a hip against the counter, crossing her arms at me quizzically. "Aren't you single?"

"Well, yeah, but—"

"But what? If you're single and he's single, what does it matter?" she pressed.

It was hard to put my relationship with Luke into words. "My mom never really liked Luke. Or at least, she didn't like that we were so committed so fast. He's really the only boyfriend I've ever had. And it put a huge rift between us when I moved in with him right after I graduated high school. If she thinks I'm immediately dating somebody else right after breaking up with Luke, she won't be supportive."

Zephyr nodded. "I bet Billy and the other producers will want to push the love story narrative," she admitted. "It's a good angle to get more viewers."

I snorted in exasperation. "Then let it play out between Kameron and Issy, damn it!"

She tilted her head back and laughed like I was a comedian. "That'll be the day!"

"I'm serious! I think there's something between them!" Her continued laughter made me frown.

Returning to her makeup routine, Zephyr commented playfully, "But they aren't the ones in the top two this week," causing a shiver to run down my spine.

If what she said was true, I not only needed to avoid Bowie like a debt collector, I needed to act as if he didn't exist.

As soon as we got into dance rehearsals, I realized how impossible my plan would be. Billy and Veronica hovered near the door, waiting to pounce on me, and dragged me back into the hall where Bowie already waited. He didn't say anything, just casually leaned against the wall to hear them out.

Billy clapped gleefully. "Our socials are blowing up after your interview on *Rise and Shine* this morning! Viewers want to see more of your relationship!"

Glancing at Bowie, he remained silent and uncharacteristically stoic. Not even an acknowledgement of my presence.

"I'm sorry—what relationship?" I finally asked.

Veronica's head shot up from where she was poring over her precious clipboard. "You mean there's nothing going on between you?" The skepticism was thick in her clipped tone.

I hated liars above all else. I was terrible at it, too. My face would instantly give me away along with clammy hands and a nervous foot tap. Teachers always knew when I hadn't done my homework. My mom knew the ticks well enough that before I even opened my mouth, she'd tell me to hold off with the lie on my tongue.

But I had no clue what this was between Bowie and me. Did I find him attractive? Sure. Any straight woman with a pulse would. That didn't mean there was anything more than a lust-filled attraction swirling around us. Something that probably would've been satisfied if I could break my hook up rule. We'd only known each other for all of forty-eight hours, after all. We could slow our roles using words like "relationship."

"Can we get to the point of all this?" Bowie inquired.

Billy gave us what I'm sure he thought was a dazzling smile. It actually looked rather menacing. "We're going to make next week's show a 'couple's night' and pair everyone off to sing duets. If America wants to see you fall in love on screen, that's what needs to happen."

I shook my head in horror. "That most certainly is NOT! I just broke up with someone! I'm not ready to fall in love with someone else!"

Billy rolled his eyes as if those points were worthless. "Just pretend for TV! Higher ratings mean more votes, which means more top placements! Don't you want to win?"

My shoulders slumped. Yeah, I wanted to win, but I wanted to win on my own merit. Because people fell in love with my voice and wanted to hear it on the radio. This felt like a cheap tactic to get there.

Now I felt Bowie's eyes on me, and when I lifted mine to his, an unreadable expression crossed his face. Our gaze held for a long moment before he shifted off the wall. He crossed his arms over his chest and inquired, "So what do ye want us to sing?"

Bold of him to assume I would be able to sing with how tightly my jaw clenched. But if he wasn't going to say anything about their crazy plan, neither was I.

"You don't have to sing this song, but one of the producers thought 'No Air' by Jordin Sparks and Chris Brown would be a good choice." Veronica waited with her pen poised above her clipboard.

What a stereotypical choice. The producers had no flair. If it would help me win the grand prize, though, I would sing whatever they wanted.

"Fine," I muttered, turning on my heel to go back into the dance studio.

I could feel rather than see Bowie moving behind me into

the room just to stand with his chest abnormally close to my back. The rest of the contestants were also standing in a semi-circle, some of them stretching as they watched who I assumed to be the dance instructor go over the sheet music.

"This is all *your* fault," I hissed at him. "Why did you have to play with my hair like that?!"

Since I refused to look at him, I felt rather than saw Bowie lean in right next to my ear. "I think I might've rattled ye, cowgirl." His tone was so seductive, like a slow caress against my jaw, that an involuntary shiver trailed down my spine. I didn't want him to rattle me, damn it!

"Good morning, everyone," the dance instructor said, preventing me from snapping any further. "I've just been told that next week's show is themed around couples. You'll all be performing a duet and our dance routine is now centered around couples dancing together. I envision something along the lines of *Bridgerton*. We're gonna take a creative spin on a classic for the opening number. I'm going to pair you up. No, you can't change it."

"Lord have mercy on Jessica's partner," Zephyr whispered to me as she came up beside me holding the water bottle I forgot in our room.

I snorted. Loudly. Everyone turned to stare at me, so I shook my head and mumbled something that passed for an apology.

"Ah. The new girl," greeted the dance instructor. "I'm Nicola. Finley, right? You'll be paired with..." Nicola consulted the stapled papers the producers provided.

"Bowie," I supplied. It was hard to keep the bitterness out of my voice.

"Yes. Bowie," she finally agreed after finding our names. "So then Zephyr, you are with Cooper..."

Cooper tipped his head to her from the other side of the semi-circle.

"Good luck!" I whispered to her.

Zephyr winked at me. "He better hope he can keep up."

Nicola went through and paired everyone else. Zephyr and I had to look away from one another when poor Riley got paired with Jessica and actually burst into tears. Stammering, Riley admitted he was too scared to dance with her. Miles gallantly offered to partner with Jessica instead, pairing Riley with Issy. Only I noticed the longing look Issy shot Kameron's way when he partnered with Tessa. That left Joey and Gretchen together.

The song was an orchestral rendition of "Still Into You" by Paramore. Edgy guitar riffs were replaced by romantic violins, and if I weren't so pissed off about being paired off with Bowie in order to propagate a love story that didn't exist, I would have loved the arrangement.

For his part, Bowie still hadn't said a word. Then again, he really didn't have to. I could feel his presence everywhere. Nicola wasn't kidding when she compared the dance to something you'd see on Netflix. The choreography was the love child of a modernized Regency period. While I wasn't a bad dancer, I would never call myself a good one either. Tessa and Zephyr were the only ones who really moved with the grace and agility of a dancer. Kameron wasn't too bad either, which made me wonder if he was self-taught whereas the girls had formal training.

Bowie moved like someone who was used to moving his body without thought. As soon as you forced him to move a certain way, all the dexterity went out the window. Nicola was far more patient with him than I could have been. She stood next to us counting out the beat with gentle reminders. "One, two, three, left foot, two, three, right foot, two, three..."

When she finally moved on to help Riley, who was close to tears again, Bowie grimaced as he stepped on my foot once more. "Sorry," he muttered. "I'm really bad at this."

I wasn't a total monster. "You're not bad at dancing. I've already seen you move on stage."

He shook his head. "That's different. I don't even realize I'm doing it. Music just flows through me."

Abruptly, I stopped, causing him to step on my foot again. I didn't even notice. I had never met someone who articulated the same feeling I had whenever I sang. "That's how it is for me, too."

"Well, duh." Bowie rolled his eyes and gave me a small smile to let me know he meant it softly. "Nobody has a voice like yers without having music live inside."

You know those silly emojis with hearts for eyes? I'm 99% certain that's what I looked like in that moment. As much as I loved my mom, she never understood the way I felt about music or performing. She supported me in every way possible; she was there in the front row for every choir concert and she drove me all over Fort Worth for practices, lessons, and auditions. But trying to connect with her? We might as well have been speaking Mandarin because my mother couldn't fathom music at a deeper level than a hobby.

Wait—didn't I make a pact earlier about ignoring Bowie completely?

Heart, you traitorous bitch.

My throat felt thick as I breathed out a thank you. Glancing up at him through my lashes, I saw him take a shaky inhale before rewarding me with the same small smile. It was almost incongruous with the harshness of his tattoos and long, dark hair. But Bowie might be softer than his image let on. He noticed so many things about me already, and I was still confused as to whether or not I liked it.

Bad Reputation

The rest of the week passed by in a blur. Sadly, I did start to forget that there were cameras everywhere. It was easy to get caught up in our own little bubble because living in the house with everyone was so unlike anything I'd ever experienced before. All of the contestants became my new brothers and sisters—with Jessica being the possible exception—and we clung to one another as tightly as any other family unit that was isolated onto themselves.

Veronica and the production assistants encouraged us to post things on social media all the time. The network was working out endorsement deals so that every contestant would leave the house to spend a few hours at a photo shoot for whatever brand signed with us. I hadn't signed on with anyone yet because none of them felt authentic to me. A hair dye company wanted to film a commercial with me to promote their own line of bright colored hair products, but I couldn't bring myself to close the deal. My mom's nagging to get a contract attorney didn't help. To no one's surprise, Bowie signed a deal with

Calvin Klein for a six month exclusive underwear modeling gig.

Believe me, I was *very* well acquainted with Bowie shirtless now that we were in rehearsals together for seven hours a day. The man never bothered wearing a shirt, and the millions of hits on social media had Billy seeing dollar signs rather than Bowie's sculpted abs. It was on the tip of my tongue to ask Billy if he stole all of Bowie's shirts to boost ratings, but Billy seemed to constantly be in a state of panic from the network's board and I didn't want to push my luck. Besides, I couldn't exactly say the view sucked. Bowie's tattoos extended down past the waistline of his jeans, so I let my imagination run wild with the way they looked underneath. Despite being a lankier build, Bowie had the seductively sculpted abs of an Olympic swimmer, and if I let my mind wander too much, I could imagine myself tracing the tattoos with my tongue.

Lord help me, but that man was fine.

It rankled me, but our duet was actually incredible. At first, I tried to throw him off by changing a run or adding a crescendo where we had previously arranged for the music to be softer. But Bowie stayed toe to toe with me every time. Then it turned into a thrill because I had never performed with someone as vocally accomplished as him. I either had to step up my game or get out of the fight.

Whenever we weren't practicing our duet, we were practicing the choreography. Nicola was as patient with Bowie as she could be, but he continued to struggle his way through the dance. The footwork wasn't particularly simple, yet even practicing as often as we did, Bowie's skills hadn't improved. I started whispering small reminders under my breath just to prevent him from crushing my feet. It worked in the dance studio with only a small speaker to play the music, but we both knew that once the noise from the audience and the stage audio system played, he would never be able to hear my commands.

One of the production assistants, Tiana, had been tasked with managing the show's social media accounts, but all of her focus remained primarily on the top three from last week's show. It kept Jessica's guard up because she didn't want to look bad on camera. And trust me, Tiana used that to her advantage. The house was far happier when Jessica remained on her best behavior.

My favorite time of day, though? Every night when we all gathered outside around the fire pit just to talk. It was the best way to unwind as a group. The producers started becoming more respectful of that time so that by the end of the week, there was only one cameraman hanging out with us, and he only filmed if he felt there was something really important happening. We talked about everything under the sun, opening up more about our lives, goals, and past struggles as we became more comfortable with one another.

Gretchen, for example, wanted to leave her husband. She had never been permitted to work during their marriage because he wanted her to rely solely on his income, but he became greedy at the prospect of the $2.5 million dollar prize and "allowed" her to compete on the show. If she won, she planned to use the money to leave him. We all rallied around her and promised that even if she didn't win, we would help. I wished I could be as strong as her. None of my struggles meant much in comparison.

Miles battled to take a break from his church back home. Clearly, he was a vital part of their institution; they called him constantly throughout the day to ask quick questions about administrative things that he had always done. He admitted at the fire pit one night that the guilt of leaving was crushing him. Poor Miles just wanted to make his own dreams come true as well as his church's.

Kameron was actually entertaining the idea of forming a boy band after the show ended. Jokingly, he said winning *America's Music Star* was his first choice, but he wouldn't feel bad if he didn't. And that made him wonder if it was fair to compete in the first place since so many of us *needed* to win. I assured him that hearing his plans only made me realize the importance of figuring out Plan B for myself. Jessica rolled her eyes, of course, but several of the housemates nodded in agreement.

Tessa had a boyfriend back home in Connecticut and she became more homesick as time went on. He planned to visit next week when he was out in Los Angeles for work, but Tessa said this was the first time they'd been apart in the six years they had been together. From what I read between the lines, Tessa came from a rather well off family and her boyfriend almost sounded like a family-arranged relationship, yet they were very happy and planned to get married anyway. Singing on the show was the first time she had ever done something for herself.

Jessica didn't share as much about herself as the others. That girl had figurative spikes coming out, keeping everyone more than an arm's length away at all times. I couldn't understand why she remained so hostile. Especially when she continued to join us every night and participated in our discussions. She was the first one to assure Gretchen that we would all try to find a way to help her if one of us won, so I knew there was a heart somewhere under her gruff exterior. Jessica was just a cactus personality. That was all I could figure out.

When it was my turn to share more about myself, I found

myself tongue-tied. I never considered myself a private person before, but there was something about the possibility of examining my life that seemed too overwhelming. Somehow, I managed to dodge the conversation, for the most part, only sharing superficial information about my life back in Texas. All anyone asked about was the breakup anyway. Producers were trying to cash in on my "romance," so it was only natural for my new family to be curious about Luke. When I revealed the state I found him in our apartment with his new lady friend, Joey and Kameron both flexed their hands into fists and offered to take care of him "the right way." We all agreed that the best revenge would be Luke seeing my success on the show.

My conversations seemed to be the only ones where Bowie paid attention. For the most part, he continued to sit on the outer edge, keeping to the shadows. But he positioned himself where he could see my face, and I felt his eyes on me every time. The different desires in my head were always at war with one another. On the one hand, I was insanely attracted to him. Fans shipping us made sense because there was definitely *something* there. But on the other hand, I refused to explore anything. My feelings were still too much of a knotted yarn ball since my life fell apart, and if this show was doing anything, it was making me hyper-aware of how much I needed to get it together.

Every night, as everyone started departing for their rooms, Bowie would come lace his hand in mine and walk me back to my room. There wasn't a signal or anything, it was just an uncanny sense he had that alerted him when I hit my breaking point for the day. His gesture would serve as my sign off for the night so I could leave the fire pit without feeling guilty or having FOMO from their continued conversation.

It was always on the tip of my tongue to say something

during those walks. Why hadn't he said anything when Billy and Veronica pressured us about our "love story"? How did he feel about it? Yet it never felt like the right moment. I would never admit it out loud, but I secretly loved having him walk me to my door every night. His broody presence at my side became oddly comforting.

We would reach my door, his dark eyes would seek mine, and some unknown understanding would pass between us. I swear, I'm not crazy, but I could literally feel it in the air around us. Bowie's lips would turn up in the tiniest of smirks, I would flush and thank him, and he would end it with, "Til the morning, yeah?" in his cheeky Irish accent.

I usually called my mom before bed, even if it was just for a five minute conversation. She was worried about me, I could tell, but didn't want to rain on my parade.

"There's a whole lot of photos of my daughter on the internet next to a half-naked criminal," Mom said on our call the night before the next show.

Groaning, I scolded her. "Mom! You know tattoos are no longer a sign of criminal activities!"

"I know more about the tattoos on his body than I know about his personality and that's a problem! Especially when he's supposedly in love with my daughter!" she shot back.

"In love?! Who said Bowie is in love with me?!"

Mom sighed. "The TV. It's all everyone's talking about, including the commercials they keep showing. Everyone has to tune in tomorrow to see what happens next with 'America's favorite couple.' Did you know you were America's favorite couple? I didn't know that. I thought it was still John Krasinski and Emily Blunt. Or do they not count since she's British?"

"MOM!" I interrupted.

She continued like I hadn't said anything. "No, that can't be it since your new boyfriend is Irish. That's a much nicer accent, in my opinion."

"I know what you're doing and this isn't something I want you to distract me with," I informed her. "If that's really what's being said about me, I need to know it."

"Look, Finley, I don't want you to think I'm not proud of you, because I am. But if you have to pretend to be in a relationship to win, it's probably not the kind of thing you should be winning."

Practical Mom. What would I do without her?

"It's doing me a favor," I insisted. "Nobody knew who I was since they added me to the roster so late. Now I have more fans to vote for me."

"And more fans out for blood. That hot rod of yours has a lot of women who hate your guts."

I frowned. It hadn't occurred to me until now. Bowie *did* have built in female following. Would they try to vote against me out of spite?

Even though she couldn't see me, I shook my head. "No. That's not gonna happen. Besides, Bowie and I haven't said anything. It's all just a smoke and mirror show."

"If you say so, kiddo," Mom placated me. "Bad reputations have a way of lingering, though. I'm heading off to bed. Knock 'em dead tomorrow!"

We said our goodbyes and ended the call, but her voice echoed in my head long into the night. What kind of lingering reputation had Bowie and I created?

I Hate Love

Zephyr had to shake me awake the next morning. I didn't fall asleep until almost three, giving me all the grace of a zombie on *The Walking Dead.* Anxiety was thick in the air already. I found Riley practicing the dance steps as he moved through the kitchen getting breakfast. Issy was writing out notes on sheet music when I joined her at the table with a pastry and the largest cup of coffee we had. She gave me something that was half-grimace, half-smile by way of greeting.

"Does anyone else feel like they're being run over by a train?" I grumbled.

"YES!" came the collective cry of everyone in the kitchen.

Bowie walked in and slid into the seat beside me. "Predicting how I'm gonna muck up the dance, are ye?"

Issy's pencil dropped from her hand. "That's the most I've ever heard you speak, Bowie," she gasped.

I snorted into my coffee as the laughter bubbled out from the rest of our housemates.

Bowie glared at both of us. "Only Americans have a word limit to reach every day," he jabbed at us.

We both continued to chuckle.

"It's gonna be a great show," I vowed. If I said it out loud, that had to make it true, right?

By the time we were all in our opening costumes with our hair and makeup done, I very much doubted that statement. In keeping with the romantic theme, all of the women wore slinky silk dresses with open backs and high slits. I had never felt so naked on stage before. They also wanted us to wear a much higher, thinner heel than I was typically comfortable with and had never practiced in. Bowie was given permission to wear only a vest, leaving his rippling abs visible for his legion of female fans. After a lengthy protest from Joey and Kameron, who both had equally impressive physiques, they were permitted to wear vests only, too.

America loved sex.

Hairstylists created an elaborate up-do, complete with silk flowers woven into my hair. The makeup was softer this time, giving me more of an angelic face. Once the opening number was done, Bowie and I would have to run to the changing area off stage and slip on new clothes for our duet.

This week's guest judges included R&B legend, Eddie Taylor, Broadway icon, Melanie Willems, and the actor on the new teen drama *K-Popular*, Ye-jun Park. I didn't know much about any of them, but Miles was freaking out over meeting Eddie, and Gretchen almost started hyperventilating over Melanie. For both their sakes, I hoped their performances shined.

It seemed like there were even more people out in the audience than last time. Billy had gleefully reported in our group huddle earlier that the next three shows were already sold out. Hits to social media were skyrocketing, and the network needed tonight to be even bigger than last week's. He looked pointedly at Bowie and me as he said it.

I felt like a tea kettle ready to explode from the pressure.

My nerves were on overdrive, especially when my mom's words rattled in the back of my mind. I was likely to start singing them rather than the words to the song. Bowie looking like a forbidden snack didn't help. Guyliner shouldn't look that good.

We were all lined up in the wings, waiting for our cue to go on stage. Enid Wexler looked regal in an off-white ball gown that highlighted her tan skin. Fans loved her as the host. She had job security with the network for the rest of the season with how high her approval ratings ran.

Zephyr and I executed our friend ritual and she assured me that the dress was very flattering on me. Friends had to lie to one another when they're about to go on stage; it was a rule. She would always be too kind to tell me that I actually resembled a busted can of biscuits anyway. That was just Zephyr, I learned. She might talk shit all the time, but she never backed it up.

"Good luck!" she whispered before taking her place beside Cooper for the opening number.

I found myself fidgeting far more than usual as I waited. Bowie and I were in the middle, placing us directly next to Enid when the cameras focused on her for the opening announcements. We were who they were tuning in to see, after all. Billy wanted us front and center as much as possible.

Suddenly, a large hand gripped my hip, a hip that had been shaking with my mounting anxiety. Bowie leaned close to my ear, the tip of his nose just barely grazing my earlobe in a way that made goosebumps break out along my forearms. This position was becoming a habit for us, but that didn't make my heart race any less.

"Take a deep breath, cowgirl," he murmured. "It's just ye and me."

I glanced down at the possessive hand on my hip before looking up at him through my lashes. His eyes were clouded like an onyx storm. It grounded me in a way nothing else had before a performance. I wanted to get lost in eyes like that.

Bowie licked his lips, his eyes flicking down to my mouth. Leaning closer, I found myself pushing up on tiptoe. We were only an inch away, close enough that I could feel his breath mingling with mine...

"And we're on in five, four...!" the production assistant called, pointing towards the stage entrance. The music started, resulting in more thunderous applause from the audience, and I barely had time to get my stammering heart under control before the bright lights were on us.

What happened next would make the blooper reels on all the major news networks for years to come. As I moved through the motions of choreography that had been permanently stamped into my brain, the dreadful high heels I was forced to wear landed on the tiny train of my silk dress. My hips kept moving through the routine, however, resulting in the skirt tearing at the waistline in the back. Only Bowie got the bird's eye view of the shapewear I wore underneath, but the skirt fluttering across the stage was a dead giveaway that my backside was entirely exposed.

I froze at the same time that I felt Bowie stiffen behind me.

An audible gasp broke through the audience, and even though I could barely make out anyone's faces, I could see several people standing up to point at the fabric that should have been covering my butt. Bowie yanked me backward by the waist so that his chest was flushed with my back, twirling us backwards off stage before I had time to scream. Ashford met us with the skirt and cropped sweater combo I was going to wear for our set.

It wasn't until I had the remnants of the dress off and started tugging down the shapewear that I realized Bowie and Ashford were both watching me undress. "Excuse me!" I barked out. "A little privacy here!"

Ashford rolled his eyes. "Honey, I've seen more naked women than a straight man at a Vegas strip club. Trust me, nothing you have is gonna do it for me. Change!"

I shot Bowie a meaningful plea not to look. Mortification was already making me turn a particularly hideous shade of puce. His eyes held mine for a long moment, and I saw something flash in them before he turned around to give me his back. With Ashford's help, the tattered silk was quickly replaced with the white cropped sweater and A-line black skirt. He unfastened the flowers pinned in my hair so that it fell in a gentle cascade down my back.

Tapping on Bowie's shoulder, he turned around and looked at my new ensemble appreciatively. Keeping eye contact, he unfastened the buttons on his pants and let them drop to the floor, exposing his hunter green boxer briefs. And they were...*full*. My eyes widened in shock. How could Bowie be so bold with me?

"It's just ye and me, remember?" he asked.

A smile tugged at my lips. This was Bowie's way of

distracting me so I no longer felt humiliated. It wasn't going to work, but damn, I'd like to memorize the view. Why did Kameron get to have an eidetic memory?

"C'mon," prompted Bowie, tugging on my hand as he ran on stage still in the middle of yanking his jeans up. The whole country got to see him getting dressed next to Enid Wexler. While she looked astonished, Enid masked her initial reaction well enough to give us an introduction. Bowie was just tugging a black V-neck shirt over his head when the lights cued the music.

Would anybody care about my wardrobe mishap now that Bowie dressed himself on national TV? Had he just made a fool of himself to make me feel better?

There wasn't enough time to consider everything before the opening notes started and I gave my all to the performance. Bowie's soft tones melded into my powerful vocals as the angst rose between us like a phantom. It truly was just me and him. I no longer had a sense of the audience or the cameras.

When we got to the final chorus, where our vocal ranges were truly tested, Bowie spun me around so that once again my back was pressed to his chest. A hand splayed firmly across my stomach, binding me to him. He leaned his head over my shoulder, singing into my microphone rather than his own. I gazed up at him in wonder. We were so in sync in that moment that I couldn't tell where one voice ended and the other began. A song that started as a ballad turned into a love anthem.

This was pure bliss.

Lights slowly came back into focus as I panted my way back to reality. Cheers roared around us, but Bowie and I couldn't take our eyes off one another. Something changed in me at that moment. An invisible tether connected us.

A tether that could NOT happen.

My vow to remain distant from him returned and I jumped forward like I found a spider on my shoulder. Bowie was also panting like he had just run laps. He gazed at me with a look that said he felt the connection, too, and was equally as stunned. We could not let this happen. Thankfully, Enid wrapped an arm around my shoulders and brought me back to the present moment.

"WOWZA!" she screamed. Fans in the audience were going nuts— shouting, stomping, and clapping so loudly that it almost hurt my ears. Several cameras zoomed in on our faces, and a quick glance over my shoulder confirmed that the jumbotron had a close up of my slightly bewildered expression.

Bowie recovered enough to step next to me, slipping a loose arm around my waist as he waved out to the crowd. They roared even louder, prompting me to return the gesture. That led to outright pandemonium. It was hard to tell if they were chanting "Bowie" or "Finley," but one of us was definitely getting the all star treatment. Enid had to start waving to signal to people that she needed to speak.

"You guys, THAT. WAS. ELECTRIC!" She enunciated every word as its own separate sentence. "How do you feel?"

The power of speech left my body. I was so flustered with the adrenaline from the performance, the confusion over Bowie's antics, and the mental war of disassociating with my attraction to him that I was all but mute. Turning to him, I waited for him to answer.

"It was an honor to partner with an entertainer like Finley Smalls," Bowie gushed. "Everyone in America better vote for her tonight, d'ye hear me?"

The crowd roared in approval. Now it was a definitive "FIN-

LEY" chant that met my ears. They were all freaking out over *me.*

"Finley, what do you have to say for yourself after a performance like that?" Enid cried.

"Well, I couldn't have done it without Bowie," I managed to get out. The audience cheered again.

Enid winked at the camera as if she was sharing a secret. "There's been a lot of talk about you two! Would you like to say a few words on that?"

Again, my head swiveled automatically to Bowie, my heart beating erratically in my chest. Did I really want to have this conversation on national television? Was I ready for the answer?

Bowie smirked at me before smiling back at the crowd. It was so fast that I almost doubted I saw it, but he pulled my waist closer as he replied coolly, "Finley is unlike any other woman I've met before. They don't make 'em like her back in Ireland!"

A few teenage girls in the front row were simpering with hearts in their eyes. They had our fairytale wedding planned out in their heads, for sure.

Meanwhile, my face felt so hot that I half expected it to burst into flame. Enid didn't ask another question, but automatically moved the microphone in front of me as if awaiting my answer.

"I think my poor mom would thank God for that one," I quipped lightly. Enid laughed and I saw the judges join in. "When you're working with a guy as talented as Bowie, you just have to step up your game."

Enid leaned in conspiratorially. "But is it really all work and no play? We saw the way you both came on stage!"

OH. MY. GOD. My *mother* heard that! I could already picture the 25,000 texts she was undoubtedly sending at that very moment. This was so much worse than a wardrobe malfunction on stage!

Bowie was either far more used to the attention or more comfortable speaking in double entendres because he flashed a lazy smile that had every woman in the room clenching her thighs. "Do I look like a man who kisses and tells?"

And there went my hearing. The cries from the fans reached new decibels, rendering Enid incapable of asking another question. She cued for a commercial break rather than get our feedback from the judges because the crowd wouldn't take the hint to calm down. My mouth could have landed a plane from how far my jaw hung in horror.

Screw the commentary. I needed to get as far away from Bowie and Enid as I could. No, I didn't handle that as smoothly as I should have. Even I could admit that. But neither one of them should have set it up to where those questions were asked. This was a singing competition, not a matchmaking service.

I stormed off stage to where Zephyr waited with a water bottle and a look of concern. I could sense Bowie's presence following. She enveloped me in a hug and whispered, "Everyone is still watching!"

By everyone Zephyr must have meant Billy because his booming voice let out a gleeful shout. "You're both going viral!"

I broke away from Zephyr's embrace in time to see Billy clap Bowie on the shoulder, holding up a tablet for him to see. Bowie only had eyes for me, though.

"I didn't mean to upset ye, cowgirl," he insisted. His dark brown eyes shone with sincerity, but I was too aggravated to care.

Taking a step forward, my tiny 5'2 frame pushed into his.

"My MOTHER was watching!" I pointed a finger in his face to emphasize how livid I felt.

Bowie bit his bottom lip, clearly trying not to laugh. High heels only made me so intimidating when the top of my head still barely came to his chest. "She'd've found out about us at some point, I reckon, cowgirl."

That egotistical, Irish bastard! I stomped my foot in frustration. "I don't want to yell because it would ruin my voice!" I snapped. "But if I could, I'd scream so loud that your ancestors would hear me!"

Stomping back towards The Pen, I heard the boom of Bowie's laughter. He called out after me, "Someday I'll make ye scream, and ye'll like it!"

Zephyr trailed after me with wide eyes. "What the hell is going on with you two?" she asked.

I glanced around, ensuring we weren't overheard. "The ratings went up after our interview on *Rise and Shine* when viewers saw Bowie playing with my hair and started 'shipping' us. What a stupid term anyway! Why would you 'ship' people?!"

Being the object of the shippage is where the offense lay. I'd shipped characters on shows every time I watched one.

My friend rolled her eyes at my dramatics. "Finley, it's an angle! If it gets you a boost in publicity, use it! No one has to know what goes on behind closed doors!"

"Except they do," I reminded her, "because the cameras are on us twenty-four frickin' seven."

"Yeah." She nodded slowly, waiting for me to catch up. "And Bowie is always with you. The dude only comes out of his room if you're there."

"What?! No, he doesn't!" I shot back.

"Girl, I didn't even hear him speak until you joined us!"

countered Zephyr. "Who knows what he's thinking or feeling, but unless you feel something for him, just play it out!"

I shook my head, "I don't know how he feels. About me or any of it."

"And you?" Zephyr prompted. "How do *you* feel?"

The lights started flashing to signal the end of the commercial break, saving me from having to answer her loaded question. I still needed to get feedback from the judges, so I hightailed it back to stage left where Enid and Bowie waited on their mark. I noticed Jessica glaring at me with her arms crossed from the recesses of The Pen, just out of view from the cameras. She could take a number because no one was angrier at me than me.

If I wanted to go on a dating show, I would've applied for one. My love life shouldn't even be part of the conversation. I was here to sing songs. To make people escape for just a little bit because of my music. Why couldn't that be enough?

And Bowie...he needed to stop flirting. Having the raw sex appeal of a rock star in training meant he had a moral obligation to put a leash on himself. There was only so much a girl could do to cool off around a man like that!

Stupid feelings! *Just focus for once in your life, Finley!*

Squaring my shoulders, I held my head high as I joined Enid and Bowie on stage right as the opening credits ended and the live feed began. In one of my rare Petty Betty moments, I moved to stand on Enid's other side so that she separated Bowie from me. I refused to look at him, instead waving to the crowd with both hands and a huge smile. Their excitement felt like a drug. That was a feeling I could focus on!

"Alright, welcome back, everyone!" Enid called. "We didn't have a chance to get the judge's feedback on this one, so let's start with you, Eddie!"

Eddie spun in his chair so he could wave to all the cheering fans before turning back to us and holding up both thumbs. "Bowie, my man! Finley, my girl! That was FIRE!" A roar of approval followed his words. It took several seconds for him to continue. "Seriously, I wish I could sing a duet with someone and have that kind of passion between us. You made every single person in this room feel things. Wonderful job—great way to start the night!"

Enid grinned before prompting, "Then let's hear from our Broadway superstar judge, Melanie Willems!"

Like Eddie, Melanie did a brief rotation in her chair to smile and wave at the audience. When she turned back to us, her smile dropped and she sighed heavily into her microphone as she dabbed at her eyes. "I'm sorry, but I'm still so emotional over that performance, you guys!"

The audience cheered.

Melanie stood up and bowed to Bowie and me, making the audience go wild. "I don't even have the right words to tell you how much I loved it. Simply magical!"

"Thank you so much, Melanie!" Enid called. "Ye-jun, what do you have to say to our two lovebirds?"

Rather than turn in his chair, Ye-jun focused on the camera, pointing towards it and giving a nod like he wanted to greet America. "So I thought it was pretty solid," he said. "I'm gonna keep it real with you, though. The way you interacted together was so distracting, I barely paid attention to the song. Like, we get it, you're feeling each other. But the music's gotta count, too. I'm just saying." Ye-jun held up both hands in surrender as the crowd booed. Several fans screamed out names like "Asshole!" and "Sellout!"

It took extra effort to remember that I was still on camera

where my reactions could and would be broadcasted for the world to see. They might have already gotten to see my fanny sticking out, so the best thing I could do was keep the smile plastered on my face despite my disappointment in Ye-jun's feedback. Billy warned me the judges were meant to stir up controversy. Maybe that was why Ye-jun had to be so negative.

"Well now," Enid said, her eyebrows raised in surprise. "That's some unexpected feedback from judge Ye-jun Park! Bowie, do you have anything you'd like to say in response?"

Against my better judgment, I chanced a look in Bowie's direction. His eyes caught mine as he smirked, leaning into Enid's microphone to reply, "I think the world just discovered Ye-jun's sexuality because no straight man could look at Finley Smalls and blame me for wanting to get closer. What a buck eejit!"

Hold it in, Finley! Hold it in!

The smile felt tight across my cheeks as members of the audience stood and clapped for Bowie's comeback. Ye-jun looked murderous while Enid appeared stunned. I didn't know what to do or how to react, so I stood there as still as a statue. Only my eyes darted around seeking a safe place to land. The crowd morphed into an absolute madhouse.

Enid quickly recovered, blinking twice before giving her head a small shake and beaming into the camera, "We'll be back with the next couple right after this!" Stage lights flashed to indicate another commercial break.

I made a mental note to ask Billy if they named the show episodes because I was pretty certain this one needed to be titled "Mortification." Between the wardrobe issues, Bowie's flirtatious words needling me, and now this, I would be lucky if I didn't find my mom waiting for me at the house to take me back to

Texas. It was humiliating to have so much speculation on my looks and dating history. I didn't want any part of it.

Spinning on my heel, I stomped towards The Pen, where Zephyr waited with her mouth open.

"Finley..." she said in a low voice. I snatched the water bottle out of her hand. Drinking meant my mouth had a filter from everything my brain wanted to say.

"Cowgirl, I didn't mean for it to come out like that!" Bowie followed me to the back of The Pen, where Ash and a hairstylist, Rowan, waited. "C'mon, ye can eat me head off all ye want! I acted like a tosspot!"

"I CAN'T EVEN BLOODY UNDERSTAND YOU!" I growled.

British slang when angry, remember?

Ashford moved to come in between us, an uncharacteristic display of chivalry I would never expect from him. "Why don't you leave her alone, mate? Give her some space."

Equally surprising as it was for Ashford to intervene, Bowie actually listened. He cast a furtive look my way before returning to the front of The Pen.

I sank down into the styling chair, letting my head sink into my hands. "This show has been a disaster!"

Something cold and hard nudged against my elbow. I peaked through my fingers to see a glass with a thumb full of amber liquid. Ashford slid it in front of me as he shoved a flask back inside an interior jacket pocket. "Nobody likes a hero," he prompted.

"What even is this?"

"Best you don't know, love," Ashford replied with a wince.

Drinking blind *was* a talent of mine. "Bottoms up," I sighed before tipping back the glass. It burned its way down my throat and I gagged.

"Now get back out there," ordered Ashford. "The show must go on, after all!"

I hated that he was right. Votes still mattered and I couldn't afford to lose any because the media started speculating that I was too emotional. By the time filming was over tonight, I should add 'actress' to my resume.

Zephyr raised a brow when I joined her at the front of The Pen, but accepted my nod. Yes, I was okay, but no, I didn't want to talk about it yet. Maybe I would forego the firepit tonight.

None of the other songs stuck out to me as I tried to regulate my feelings for the rest of the show. I moved on autopilot, cheering and clapping when the others did around me, moving to the music when it looked like the cameras were facing our direction, but my mind wasn't in it. Bowie stayed on the other side of The Pen, seeming to take Ashford's advice and give me space. I cringed at what tomorrow's headlines would say about that.

By the time the rankings came out, I no longer cared where I placed. I just longed for a moment alone, where the cameras couldn't follow, away from the prying eyes of the world.

All of that evaporated when Bowie and I placed first for our duet. The shock kept my feet rooted to the spot. Zephyr had to shove me forward so that I could join everyone on stage. Bowie dutifully came to my side and wrapped an arm around my waist. Even if it made my jaw clench, I knew we needed to maintain our united front for all the fans watching. And besides, the top spot *was* something worth celebrating. I just wish it didn't feel so tainted by our bogus love story.

Bowie hugged me tightly, much to the crowd's delight, and murmured in my ear, "This is all ye, Finley!"

The ending music played as the rest of the contestants joined us on stage. Zephyr and Tessa pulling me in for a hug prevented me from responding to Bowie, and somehow as everyone celebrated the end of the show, we became more and more separated. The judges joined us on stage, too, which played during the final credits.

As soon as the house lights came on to signal the end of filming, I bolted.

Me

"Why am I not surprised to find you here?" Billy said as he slid onto the barstool next to me.

I was back at the Songbird Lounge, where Max had greeted me warmly and fixed a strong pomegranate mojito right away. Since I still wore all my stage makeup and fancy clothes, I tried to shrink down as much as I could without outright laying on the bar. The Uber driver who brought me definitely recognized me, asking for an autograph rather than a tip. It was the first time someone ever wanted my signature before and now I was even more of an emotional mess.

"When words fail, mojitos speak," I quipped, taking a long pull from the straw. My bank account couldn't afford as many of the top shelf drinks as Billy's had on my first visit, so I was trying to drink slowly. It hadn't worked out well so far.

Billy sighed. "Let's get you back to the house." He withdrew a credit card from his wallet, handing it to Max with a nod. "I'd appreciate your discretion, too."

My friend shook his head. "Nah, for Finley, it's on the house.

I wouldn't say no to a couple tickets for one of the shows, though. Maybe impress my girlfriend." Max winked at me before looking expectantly at Billy.

"I'll leave two tickets for you at Will Call for next week's show," Billy agreed. "They'll be under 'The Bartender Savior.'" He wrapped an arm around my shoulders and steered me towards the exit.

Forlornly, I waved back to Max as each step towards Billy's waiting car filled me with dread. Rationally I knew I couldn't close down the bar like I used to back home, but going back to the house didn't hold any appeal for me either. Facing Bowie was the last thing I wanted to do. Zephyr, too, since my new best friend had superpowers that allowed her to read me like a book.

We drove in silence for a while as Billy wound us through the never ending traffic congestion around L.A. It wasn't until we were back on the freeway that he finally spoke up.

"So are you gonna tell me what this is about?" he asked.

"That depends. How good are you at interpretive dance?" I mused.

He shot me a look that said he didn't find my sarcasm funny at the moment. "Finley, you placed in the top spot. That should make you happy."

I picked at one of my fingernails as I mulled over how to answer. It wasn't that I wanted to look a gift horse in the mouth, because I truly was grateful to be on the show. But it no longer felt like Billy wanted me on the show because he saw talent. And that's ultimately what I wanted.

"I would be happy if it wasn't based on you manipulating viewers into thinking there's something between Bowie and me," I finally admitted.

"But there *is* something between you two!" Billy countered. "The chemistry is there and it's undeniable!"

I grimaced, hating that everyone could so clearly see the effect Bowie and I had on each other. They always said that celebrities have no privacy, and while I was far from a celebrity, this seemed like the first dose of reality where my personal life was up for grabs. Did I really want to live under a microscope like that for the rest of my life?

After a long pause, Billy sighed. "At the end of the day, Finley, people will come and go in this industry. One day you're on top of the world, the next day you're a 'has been.' My advice? Don't let go of the people who make it all bearable."

We drove in silence for a few minutes more as I considered his words. Being in the house felt like living in an alternative universe. It was its own little bubble, only everyone in the world had the right to peek in and pass judgement. Competing against eleven other amazing singers was hard enough without having strong feelings for one of my housemates. Adding in everyone's commentary made it distinctly *un*bearable.

"I just want to focus on the show," I decided out loud. "I really want to win this, Billy."

He nodded. "I'm pretty sure Bowie wants you to win, too."

Rolling my eyes, I snorted. "Over himself?"

"Why do you think I personally drove around L.A. looking for you? Bowie erupted at the house, said he was going to walk out and get on the first plane back to Ireland if we didn't find you! I can't lose both my headliners in one night—they'd have my head on the chopping block!" Billy gulped as if he actually believed someone from the network would resort to capital punishment.

My comeback died in my throat. Bowie was that upset over me leaving? Did that mean something?

Would I care if it did?

"I would just rather we focus more on me as a singer and contestant than as a love interest." I frowned at how odd that statement sounded. But that was my life now, after all.

Billy nodded. "We can do that," he agreed. "I didn't mean to pressure you, Finley. But you know it only helps people vote for you. And at the end of the day, that's what matters, right?"

Why did everyone keep saying that to me? "No, that's not all that matters! If I'm going to win, I want to earn it. Allow me to have a little integrity here, Billy."

"I had to carry you over my shoulder to even get you in the house in the first place," he pointed out.

I scowled. "All the more reason to allow me to keep what little bit of dignity I have left!"

By now, the house came into view at the end of the drive. Billy pulled the car around the circular driveway, stopping right at the door for me to get out.

"Finley?" he called through the open window as I reached the front door. I turned back to look at him. "You deserve to win either way. Remember that." The window went up and Billy sped away to return to his own home. Wherever that was.

Twisting his words around in my head, I tried to creep in as quietly as possible, bypassing the kitchen altogether to head directly to my room. Zephyr already had her Airpods in and her eye mask on with the curtain drawn around the bed. The only light in the room came from the faint glow of her Himalayan salt lamp that danced on the ceiling. Although I knew I would regret it in the morning, I ignored all the makeup and hair spray on my face and in my hair, stripping down to my panties and pulling an old t-shirt over my head.

When I settled down under the covers, snuggling onto my stomach, a heavy limb swung around my middle. I yelped right as I recognized Bowie's voice in my ear.

"Finley?" he murmured.

"BOWIE!" I whisper-shouted. "What are you doing in my bed?!" I rolled over onto my other side so that I could face him. Our noses brushed against one another as we shared a pillow.

"I wanted to make sure ye came back," he replied, his voice low. "Cowgirl, I'm so sorry. I never meant to hurt ye!"

Sincerity rang through his words, making my heart soften. That, and all the vodka from my mojitos. "I believe you! But that doesn't mean you belong in my bed!"

"I was a right miserable little pox without ye. It was the only way to get me t'shut me mouth. Poor Zephyr there needed a break."

That meant she and I needed to have a serious heart to heart in the morning.

"Well now you know I'm back, so get out!" I tried to shove him off, but it only served to tighten his hold around me.

Bowie gave me a lopsided grin as he nestled in closer to the rest of my body. His legs wound around mine and he tucked his head under my chin. "It's better if I stay here for the night," he countered. "Someone's gotta keep an eye on ye."

I rolled my eyes, but made no move to force him out. Maybe I was too tired. Maybe the mojitos spoke for me. Or maybe having Bowie Baird in my bed was just too damn comfortable.

So many years of my young life were dedicated to a worthless prick like Luke Davenport. Luke never deserved me, let alone the time I wasted on him. Turning Billy's advice around in my mind, I realized that competing on *America's Music Star* would have been horrible if I was still with Luke. He would have made the entire thing about him, dimming my light rather than stoking the flames. Bowie was the exact opposite. He made me better. I wanted to try harder because of him.

It was time I started living my life for me again, which also meant opening up my heart. While I wasn't certain if I was ready yet, I liked the fact that I felt comfortable with it being my choice, not Luke's. His insecurities didn't rule me anymore. In short—I was free.

And at that moment, freedom meant letting myself drift to sleep in the comfort of Bowie Baird's embrace.

Favorite Kind of High

"Finley Smalls!" Zephyr shook me awake with the shrill cry of a pterodactyl.

I jerked up, pummeling my elbow into Bowie's diaphragm. The gasp he emitted as he tried to suck in air would have been worthy of a Bugs Bunny cartoon. Guilt laced through me, so I tried to pull him upright and make it easier. I pulled a little too hard, though, and ended up yanking him right into my forehead so that our skulls clashed with a loud crack.

"Jesus bloomin' Joseph, what the devil is goin' on with ye?" Bowie yelled, cradling his head. His voice sounded raspy as he continued to struggle breathing through his chest.

"Sorry!" I cried. Turning back towards Zephyr, I cried out again, "So sorry!"

Her warm brown eyes widened in a way that told me Zephyr could give my mother a run for her money on a round of Twenty Questions. "Bathroom. Now!" she hissed.

"Uh...be right back," I mumbled to Bowie, scrambling out of bed to follow her into our joint bathroom.

Zephyr's pink silk robe billowed around her like a cape worthy of Harry Potter. She paced in front of the mirror like a caged animal. "Finley, what were you thinking?!"

"Shh!" I hushed. "He can *hear* you!"

"And all of America can SEE you!" countered Zephyr, stopping me in my tracks.

Oh God. *Oh my God!* Why hadn't I thought of that?!

Vodka, that's why.

"Shit, I need to call my mom!" I sprinted out to my bed where Bowie laid forlornly, still clutching his chest. The dark tinge of a bruise was just starting to form around the knot on his head. It looked like he was retraining himself how to breathe.

Snatching my cell from the nightstand, I saw I had over thirty texts waiting from my mom. There were even a few from my stepmother. I also had eight missed calls.

I quickly dialed Mom's number, torn between wanting her to answer so I could calm her down and wanting to leave her a voicemail so that I didn't have to face off against her version of Cruella de Ville.

"FINLEY BRIANNE SMALLS!" my mom screamed. "Where have you been?!" I held the phone away from my ear to protect my ear drum.

"I'm sorry, Mom, I just—"

"You just didn't think is what you did!" she finished for me. "Typical Finley, flying by the seat of her pants without any regard for everyone around you!"

"Mom, that's not exactly fair—"

"FAIR?!" Mom repeated with a screech. "Do you wanna talk FAIR, Finley Smalls?! How is it FAIR that I'm getting calls from producers in the middle of the night because they're out combing the streets of L.A. looking for you?! Would you say it's FAIR that I watched my only daughter lose her skirt on TV only to have some half naked man follow her back on stage a moment later?!"

"If you'll just let me explain—"

"No, Finley, you're done talking!"

"How can I be done talking when you haven't let me finish a sentence?!" I barked.

"Don't you sass me! I'll fly out there and whoop your behind!" She sounded like a bull in the ring, panting heavily in her anger.

Bowie still laid beside me, trying so hard not to laugh. His brown eyes gleamed with mirth as he stuffed a fist in his mouth to stifle his reaction. I threw a pillow at him that he promptly blocked.

"I'm not sassing you, Mom. I just wanted to call and let you know that I'm okay, I'm not dead in a ditch somewhere, or whatever other awful thing you conjured up in your head. I'm really sorry I didn't call you back last night."

Bowie shook his head, mouthing "no, you're not" at my words before shaking with repressed laughter again. I glared at him, but it only made things worse.

"What's that sound, Finley?" my mom asked. "Is somebody with you?"

"Um, yeah, the production guy's here. I gotta go, love you, mean it, bye!" Hitting the end call button had never been so satisfying before.

My Irish companion finally lost the battle with his laughter, clutching his side as his body rocked with chuckles. "May the sun always shine on yer poor ma!" Bowie crowed.

This time I grabbed the pillow and flung both arms over my

head to smash it down on his face. A loud cackle was barely muffled underneath.

"Finley. Bowie." Zephyr emerged from the bathroom with her hair in a braid over one shoulder, wearing a sports bra and bright colored leggings. "We're supposed to report to the dance studio for practice in about fifteen minutes..." Zephyr's voice trailed off as she took in the scene we created.

It dawned on me how bad it must look. Bowie was shirtless, with the duvet covering his lower half, leaving everything to the imagination. My shirt gathered around my hips, leaving my lacy black panties on display. Last night's makeup was still caked on my face.

"Yeah-I'll-take-a-shower-real-quick-be-there-in-a-minute!" I squeaked out in a single breath. Scampering into the bathroom, the only place where there were no cameras, I didn't dare risk a glance back at Bowie. I was scared shitless at what emotion I'd see in his eyes.

A shower hot enough to melt plastic did little to soothe my nerves, even if it did jolt me awake as well as a cup of coffee. Why did I always find myself in these situations? My impulsivity would literally be the death of me one day! I always used to scoff when a family member told me that I operated fifteen minutes in the future after fifteen seconds of reflection, but it's true. Jumping without a parachute was the only way I knew how to live.

What if you start treating this as the business opportunity it is? a voice in the back of my mind inquired.

Bowie made my knees weak, that much was obvious. But that could be true a year from now. *America's Music Star*, and all the chances that came with it, could only happen *right now*.

After my conversation with Billy last night, I could take a break from the star crossed lovers guise and really give this competition my all. I just needed to talk to Billy first and do some damage control over the whole sleeping arrangement thing.

Oh, yeah—and let Bowie know it could never and would never be repeated.

By the time I got done with the shower and brushing my teeth, I barely had three minutes to spare to get down to the dance studio. To my surprise, I found Bowie waiting outside in the hall. This was his version of fully dressed in a ripped up pair of black jeans and nothing else, bearing a travel mug of coffee. He smirked at my squeal when he placed the sacred cup in my hands.

"So, I reckon yer about to read me my rights," commented Bowie. We fell into step beside one another, neither in a hurry to face the music from our housemates and the producers.

Why could Bowie read my mind better than I could?

I winced, afraid of the way my filter-less mouth would make the words come out. "We both need to focus on the competition," I explained. "Whatever this is...it's too distracting. Fans will find some other couple to ship."

Although he didn't look my way, I could feel Bowie's walls going up, like my statement caused him to withdraw into himself. We paused just outside the door to the dance studio, Nicola's voice filtering through the cracked door as she started to mark out places for next week's performance.

"What about what I want?" Bowie asked, his voice low. Leaning against the doorframe, his body language appeared casual, but there was a coldness between us that I hadn't experienced before.

I rolled my eyes. "Oh, and what is it you want?" Sarcasm laced my words, making it sound like a joke more than a genuine question.

Bowie shrugged. "Ye never stopped to ask, now, did'ye?" With that, his dark brown eyes found mine, giving me the briefest flash of the pain he felt, before he strolled inside. I stood in the hall, dumbfounded, before slipping in after him.

HAVE you ever experienced something that made you so happy that you thought you were high? Like, you almost couldn't trust the joy because it felt too good to be real? That was what the next few weeks felt like for me. Performing in any way set my soul on fire. Spending all day in dance rehearsals, then music rehearsals, only to wake up and do it all over again turned out to be the exact way I wanted to live my life.

I finally gave in and booked the endorsement deal with Avalon Hair Care. Their new ad campaign would start the day after the show ended, which would only help me stay relevant if I didn't win. I took my mom's advice and consulted a contract attorney beforehand. It was the best decision I had made yet; the attorney negotiated a far higher payout than any of my house-mates received on their deals. Seeing that many zeroes in my bank account made my head spin. Living large and in charge wasn't so bad.

Zephyr helped me with building my social media following, too. It became habit to take photos and videos all the time. Honestly, it wasn't as scary as I thought it would be, but it felt kind of weird to have so many strangers interested in my daily life. I couldn't understand why anyone found me that interesting. Each week my fans in the crowd seemed to multiply, though, so I must've been doing something right. That became my favorite kind of high—building a fan base who genuinely loved to hear my music.

I worked my ass off to keep myself in the top five each week. Our themes ranged from genre specific to personal storytelling. A rumor began to float through the halls that we would get to work with a songwriter to write and produce a song of our own to sing at the finale. All of the songs would be professionally recorded for an album that the network could promote along with the tour at the end of the season. Billy and Veronica would not confirm or deny this rumor, which made me think it might be true. I started jotting down lyrics or randomly playing melodies on the piano as emotions swirled around in my head. What would I really want to say if I actually had the chance to write the music?

The only downside was my situation with Bowie. Fans still clamored for more between us. While he remained committed to feeding their addiction with loosely veiled innuendos and flattery aimed at me, when the cameras were off, Bowie acted like I didn't exist.

It royally sucked.

Even though it had only been a couple weeks, Bowie and I spent every waking moment together for those two weeks. His broody presence at my side grew on me to the point where it gave me comfort, so his absence now became deafening. Tension crackled the air any time we came across one another in the house, and Bowie took to spending the majority of his time in his room with the door locked. When my attempts to draw him out or start a conversation fell on deaf ears, I pulled back, deciding to give him the space to sort through his feelings.

A grace that I still hadn't offered myself. That became all too apparent when Bowie's distant attitude started to annoy me. How dare he drop some vague hint that he might want more from me and then refuse to speak to me? What kind of asshat did that?

Bowie the housemate might've been a thorn in my side, but Bowie the rival contestant only fueled my desire to practice more. We consistently placed just above one another in rankings. Usually only a few votes separated us. The more we sang about true love and heartbreak, with the camera zooming in on the other, the more the viewers at home demanded an update on our relationship status. Fans in the audience had an uncanny ability to notice tiny details, like the way Bowie mouthed along the words when I performed, or the way I always saved his hug for the very end of the show. Sadly, I didn't want to admit that I did it because letting go of him always hurt the most. All of the contestants would hug and congratulate each other at the end of the night.

But with Bowie? That was my only chance to hold onto a fraying thread of whatever there was between us. We both felt it, I'm sure of it. There was always a moment where his deep brown eyes would catch mine, and he'd lean down to murmur in my ear, "Proud of ye, cowgirl."

For some reason, when Bowie said he was proud of you, you truly believed it. His praise grounded a belief in myself that I desperately needed. And he never failed to say it, even on the weeks where he placed higher than I did. Just for that brief moment, where the audience and the cameras melted away, Bowie and I always let our connection happen.

Until some sign of the reality of our situation occurred, like Veronica coming out of the wings to make an announcement, or Billy coming up to congratulate me. Then it was like an icy downpour drenched us both, and the spell was broken. Timing was everything, and right now, it wasn't on our side.

Underneath the Tree

We were at the halfway point of the competition. Jessica had become intolerable as she consistently placed in the middle to bottom of the rankings each week. It wasn't that her performances weren't impressive. Everyone was just that good. Her disappointment turned to frustration, then frustration gave way to anger. An anger that she directed to everyone else.

She became a monster in rehearsals. No matter how many times we ran through the dances or group songs, Jessica wasn't satisfied. Zephyr commented more than once that if a music career didn't pan out, Jessica definitely had a future as the world's scariest drill sergeant. Everyone agreed with her, but we were all too terrified to say anything.

I was always on Jessica's bad side, though. Different people set off her temper for various reasons, yet if I managed to breathe in her vicinity, Jessica was out for blood. Being so mean-spirited was out of character for me. I tried to "kill her with kindness," as my mom always taught me, and it only served to stoke the flames. Jessica outright hated me, that was all there was to it.

Billy saw her ire firsthand the morning after our two hour mid-season special. The network let fans vote online for the theme for the upcoming week, and "A Christmas Calling" won by a landslide. He joined Veronica in the dance studio to share the news.

"We want to sing some non-traditional songs!" Billy announced gleefully. "We can still get America in the holiday spirit even if we aren't singing the same old carols that everyone always sings! And, to top it off, we want to film some interviews with your families about your holiday traditions. Let's show our viewers what things are like for all of you back home!"

I jumped up and down, clapping in excitement. I LOVED Christmas! Carols! Lights! Snowmen! Santa! I'd happily take it all. My mom always worked her tail off to make the holiday season special, even on a preschool teacher's salary. We could give a great interview on all of our traditions.

"Wait—does this mean we're going home?" Miles asked hopefully.

Billy's face fell. "Not just yet," he admitted. "We're going to send crews to talk to your families. But you will remain here."

While Miles and some of the others looked crestfallen, Jessica looked downright pissed. "So then what's the point of including our families? Why get our hopes up in the first place?"

"Why wouldn't we include our families?" I asked incredulously. "Christmas is a time *for* family...to spread cheer with all your loved ones and make beautiful memories."

Jessica rolled her eyes. "Of course Buddy the Elf over here thinks so."

"What's that supposed to mean?" I folded my arms across my chest.

"It means you're exactly the type to get excited over Christmas. You have no idea what it's like for people who have to be alone or can't afford to buy any presents!" Jessica stepped closer so that she was only a few inches away, glaring down her nose at me.

My jaw clenched. While I always had family around me for Christmas, I never had a ton of presents. Sometimes everything I received was handmade. The holidays weren't about how much money you spent.

"Billy, make sure you have this one dress up as the Grinch for the show," I quipped.

Zephyr tried to cover her snicker up with her hand while Joey and Kameron both held fists up to their mouths with a groan. Tessa took a noticeable step back like she wanted to ensure she was outside the ring of fire.

For some reason, I glanced over to Bowie. His eyes remained firmly on the floor, his arms crossed over his chest, as if he couldn't wait for the entire exchange to end.

Jessica's face reddened in fury. "We all know Billy's gonna do whatever you say. You probably slept with him just to get on the show!"

My jaw dropped. The *audacity* of this girl! While it was obvious that Jessica had no respect or enthusiasm for my last minute entry into the competition, I never imagined such a horrible accusation to come my way.

Billy himself stepped forward, coming in between Jessica and me enough that she was forced to take a few paces backward. "You're crossing a line," he said, his voice low and angry. "Let's go outside and talk about this directly." He stalked off, Jessica close behind with her attitude still written all over her face.

I turned to face the rest of my housemates. Tears threatened to spill as I grappled with the idea that people thought I slept my way onto the show. I couldn't even pull off a one night stand! The whole idea was so disgusting and wrong that it left a bitter taste in the back of my throat. "Does everyone think I hooked up with Billy just to be here?"

"Of course not, Fin," Issy said soothingly. "Jessica is just having a hard time. She so badly wants to win, so she's really worried about ranking so low each week."

The rest of the housemates came to huddle around me. Except Bowie. He held back, giving me an unreadable look that made my heart sink. Although I addressed the room, it was Bowie's gaze I held as I swore, "I would *never* do something like that. Billy saw me drunk and singing karaoke. That's *it*."

While everyone else assured me that they believed me and knew Jessica didn't really mean it, Bowie was the one who nodded in understanding. He flashed me a small smirk before sliding out the door unnoticed.

Nicola instructed us to go down the hall to a music room and practice because she didn't want to start dance rehearsals until Jessica returned. Bowie wasn't in any of the music rooms, however, so I whispered to Zephyr that I would go find him. I needed to know what that look was about.

To my surprise, I found Bowie outside at the edge of the property line again. He stood this time, back to the house as he gazed out at the humming city below. Even though it was early morning, it was already too hot to feel comfortable. Sunshine always beat down on you in L.A., which I found to be quite stifling. Since Bowie never bothered to put on a shirt, I guess it wasn't so oppressive.

"Hey," I greeted him.

"Cowgirl," he replied, making me roll my eyes.

"Have we not established yet that I know as much about farm animals as you do?"

He flashed me a small smile before turning his attention to the dirt at his feet. Idly, he toed a small divot in the grass while the awkward silence stretched between us. "I just had to get out of there, yeah? Thinking of ye with Billy, 'tis a bit..."

"Gross?" I supplied, wrinkling my nose in disgust. Billy had to be at least ten years older than me. He was an attractive man, I refused to let my daddy issues manifest like that. I didn't have it in me.

Bowie made a face. "Disappointing," he corrected me. He kept his eyes on the ground rather than gauge my reaction.

What *was* my reaction? On the one hand, hearing Bowie admit that the thought of me being with someone like Billy would disappoint him made my heart race. It was the closest Bowie had come to acknowledging this intense attraction between us in weeks. Weeks that I spent missing his presence.

But our circumstances hadn't changed either. I wanted to focus on winning the competition, or at least building enough of a backup plan that losing didn't mean I was completely destitute. Bowie and I had our whole lives to explore whatever this was between us. Especially when I wasn't still wondering about Luke.

I open and closed my mouth several times and continued to draw a blank. For once, I didn't know what to say.

"We should be getting back," Bowie finally offered. "They're probably waiting fer us."

"Okay," I agreed, my throat tight with emotion. "Is that the only reason you were out here?"

He shrugged. "Not too keen on the plans fer the show next week."

My eyes widened in alarm as I considered the horrific possibility. "Please don't tell me you hate Christmas!"

A dry laugh escaped. "They're meaning to interview our families, yeah?" After a long pause where I didn't follow his train of thought, Bowie added, "Ye reckon they're gonna interview the mother I ran away from? Or the da in America who denied my existence?"

My heart sank as I realized how bad he must feel. Underneath Bowie's rough exterior, he genuinely cared about how his fans viewed him. He didn't want the shame of sharing his murky upbringing on camera. In my own weird way, I could understand that. It's not like I wanted my dad involved with the show in any capacity.

"Hey, we'll figure something out." Gently, I placed a hand on his arm, offering what little comfort I could give.

Vulnerable brown eyes met mine, and suddenly my heart raced for an entirely different reason. My body became hyper aware of how close we were as butterflies fluttered in my stomach. Bowie hadn't looked at me like that in so long...I almost forgot how easy it felt to get lost in him.

Our weird connection reared its head stronger than ever. As our eyes locked and the rest of the world faded away, I couldn't remember a single reason why I hadn't kissed him. His lips looked so damn kissable. And now, with his raw soul exposed to me like that, I found myself inching closer, leaning up so that my face was better angled with his...

"Hey, Nicola's ready for us now!" Riley called from the doorway. He didn't wait for us, but turned immediately to head back towards the dance studio.

"Feckin' Christ!" Bowie swore under his breath. The interruption served to break the spell between us, a spell that I was only too happy to get back.

"No, wait, we can finally do this!" I threw my arms around his neck to pull him closer.

The cocky grin Bowie gave me sent my heart on a zipline. It was both thrilling and terrifying. Both of his hands wrapped around my waist, pulling my lower half tight against his body, where a definite bulge let me know where his thoughts were. He leaned his forehead against mine. "Not until yer ready, cowgirl. This is worth waitin' fer."

With a final tug at my waist, Bowie released me, taking several steps back while fixing me with a stare that made me shudder. He waited a moment before following Riley inside the house.

I was stunned. How was I not ready? I basically threw myself in his arms and begged him to kiss me. Wasn't that enough?

But as the hormones settled and I had time to process everything, I knew Bowie made the right call. I just wasn't sure if I could do the same.

<hr>

ALL THINGS CHRISTMAS made me so stupidly happy. I had the best time of my life over the next couple days, trying on different holiday costumes, rehearsing the carol medley we would open the show with, and filming behind the scenes content about making our Christmas spectacular. After lots of cajoling and threats to sprinkle her with glitter in her sleep, Zephyr found her holiday spirit and started joining in on the fun. We organized a last minute Secret Santa gift exchange with everyone in the house, including Veronica, Billy, Kyle, and some of the other production crew members.

As long as we filmed it all, Billy arranged for us to take a bus together to shop for our gifts and pick up a few decorations. A chain retailer would sponsor the outing in return for some serious ad placement with the show. It was a win-win for everybody.

Imagine my shock when I pulled the name out of the Santa hat to discover my person was none other than Jessica. I seriously doubted the store sponsoring us would have new attitudes for sale, and that was the gift she desperately needed. Still, I refused to let her anti-holiday energy drain my good time. Giving gifts was just as much fun as receiving them!

Zephyr wound up with Ashford. "Would it be too on the nose if I bought him Fashion Stylist Barbie?" she asked with a grin. We both laughed.

The laugh died in my throat when Bowie approached us. Ever since our almost kiss in the backyard, Bowie turned avoidance into an art form. He stayed as far away from me as possible and refused to so much as look at me. This silence hurt more than the last because this one felt hauntingly familiar to my old pal, Rejection. So close proximity now made my lungs seize.

"Sit with me on the bus, yeah?" he asked.

"Uh, sure." His eyes held so much warmth that I couldn't have said no even if I wanted to.

A wide smile, big enough to showcase dimples, spread across his face. "Grand. See ye later." And with that, Bowie swept from the room.

Zephyr's eyebrows stretched to their limit. "What was that

about, and how did you break Bowie Baird?" We both laughed again.

Despite seeing the humor in it, I truly didn't understand Bowie's purpose. Everyone provided a small list of gift ideas, so if he drew my name (unlikely, but not impossible), Bowie didn't need to get more suggestions from me.

The cameras on the bus couldn't dampen my mood. Bowie pulled me into a seat towards the very back while everyone else sat towards the front. Zephyr flashed me an inquiring look, silently asking whether she should sit across from us or not. Minutely, I shook my head. I wanted to see why Bowie was acting this way without her interference.

"So there's an ice cream shop next door to the store," Bowie began, giving me a funny side-eye. "How's about we go there, just the two of us?"

Hesitating, I drew back so that I could clearly see his face. "Like a date...?" I trailed off uncertainly, not wanting to see more into it than what he meant, but also cautious because it was Bowie. He was as mercurial as they came.

Bowie wouldn't make eye contact with me as his ears turned red. Speaking to the ground, he whispered, "I just wanted to spend time with ye away from the fuss of the house."

My heart beat erratically in my chest. This was the closest Bowie had come to admitting his true feelings and intentions. Even with my determination to ignore our attraction and focus on the show, I found myself wanting to say yes. I missed having him around, the silent way he always seemed to know what I needed—even the way he constantly made me blush.

Okay, yes, damn it. It was really nice to be flirted with the way Bowie flirted with me. The whole stonewall thing wasn't working out too well with my feelings.

Slowly, I nodded. "Yeah. I'd like that."

The smile I received in return would have even warmed the Grinch's heart. Bowie's entire face lit up and he laced his fingers through mine. We didn't say another word for the rest of the drive, letting everyone else capture the camera's attention.

When we pulled up in front of the box superstore, everyone clambered off in a rush to get inside. We only had two hours to get all our shopping done. For many of the contestants, it was their first time out in the "real world" since the show started. People needed to shop for more than just their Secret Santas. It was rare for us to have so many crew members included off stage, so everyone quickly broke out into small groups and headed in their own directions. Nobody noticed that Bowie and I hung back, waiting until the cameramen disappeared from view.

The ice cream shop next door was a small place with a lot of neon signs. They all said cute things like, "Scoop, there it is!" along the walls. Bowie ordered a simple chocolate milkshake while I ordered a sundae of cookies n' cream and mint chocolate chip with all the fixings. Chocolate oozed down the sides as the whipped cream collapsed under the weight of all the sprinkles.

"Why in the world d'ye need all that on top of yer ice cream?" Bowie asked, horrified. "Isn't the ice cream itself the treat?"

I performed a happy dance in my seat. "This is even better!" I vowed.

We ate in companionable silence for a while until I finally got up the nerve to ask the question that had been burning through my mind the entire way there. "Why did you ask me out like this?"

Bowie pursed his lips together as if he fought the urge to laugh. "Ye've got chocolate sauce on yer mouth."

In true lady-like fashion, I swiped my tongue along my bottom lip, then my upper one to remove the offensive topping. His eyes darkened with lust as he clocked the movement. It was the only warning I had before Bowie leaned forward over our desserts and kissed me.

The best kinds of kisses are the ones you don't expect. Actually, no, that can't be true. Imagine a prison inmate getting a surprise kiss. That would never go over well.

But this one? This one made me forget my own name. Bowie's lips were so strong and confident, rooting me to my seat in such a way that I could no longer move. Not that I ever wanted to. Stick a pin in me because this was my permanent home.

My lips parted as I forced my lungs to function before my brain short circuited, and he used it to his advantage, his tongue invading my mouth. Making out never appealed to me before, but with Bowie, the act was sexy as hell. I forgot we were in a public place where anyone could see and instead wove my fingers into his hair, drawing him closer.

Bowie was the first one to break. He sank back into his chair, a look of wonder on his face that matched my own. I never experienced a kiss like that with Luke. Not once.

"Wow," I murmured. Subconsciously, my fingers traced along my bottom lip as if my brain couldn't believe what just happened either.

"Wow," agreed Bowie. We both sat there like lovestruck fools, gazing into each other's eyes in rapturous wonder.

Until the melted ice cream from the sundae I knocked over during our kiss dripped into my lap. "Oh, shit!" I cried out. Jumping up, my kneecap accelerated into the table leg with enough force to lift the entire table off the ground, thereby causing it to fall over. Bowie's chocolate milkshake sprayed everywhere. Including the counter and glass display case for the ice cream flavors.

The teenage girl working behind the counter yelped in alarm. She rushed out to assess the damage, shaking her head in disbelief. "You need to leave! Now!" she ordered and pointed to the door.

With ice cream seeping into my jeans and sticking to my legs, I awkwardly shuffled outside. Bowie and I burst into laughter the moment the door closed behind us. A ridiculous first kiss—kind of appropriate for us, all things considered. It took several minutes for our laughter to die down, and the look that we shared made my thighs clench for an entirely different reason. The tether between us felt stronger. Brighter.

His dark eyes held mine as he laced his fingers through mine. "Let's go next door and git ye a new pair o' pants, cowgirl. Ye can't be shoppin' like that."

Rather than lead me into the store where the rest of the contestants shopped, Bowie steered us into a smaller clothing store farther down in the shopping mall. There was only one clerk, whose eyes widened in recognition when she saw us.

Shit.

"*Oh my god oh my god oh my god!*" she chanted in a high voice. Her hands fluttered over her face as if she fought off a panic attack.

Billy wouldn't save me if I accidentally sent a fan to the hospital...probably.

"Honey, it's just us!" I joked. "God has nothing to do with it!"

The clerk broke into a wide smile. She looked to be around my age, with dark skin and a small afro hairstyle. "You two are my absolute favorite! I vote for you every week. OH MY GOD, are you here on a DATE?!"

I quickly glanced at Bowie. If this girl was a superfan of ours, she was probably the kind of girl to spread this all over the internet before I selected a pair of pants to try on.

He must have had the same thought because he gestured to the offensive ice cream splayed across my legs. "No, we had a bit of a wardrobe mishap next door. Just tryin' to be a right honorable gent and git the lady a new pair o' trousers."

The clerk's gaze fell down to my pants and she nodded in understanding. "Of course! Let me get you into a fitting room and I'll bring you some jeans to try on."

"That's so sweet of you! And we'll sign whatever you want when we're done here as long as you don't share it to social media, okay?" I added.

She grinned and clapped her hands in delight. "I won't say a word until later. Can I get a picture, too?"

Bowie shrugged. "If ye make sure we're not disturbed, we'll take all the pics ye want! What's yer name?"

"Jennifer!" the clerk squealed. "I can totally do that! We haven't been busy today at all, so I'll just lock the door until you're done!"

"Perfect." Bowie flashed me a knowing smile that made butterflies erupt in my stomach.

Fitting rooms were in the back corner of the store. Bowie steered me into the large handicap accessible one and put his hand over my mouth when I started to object. "We're the only ones here, cowgirl. Now git in there and take yer pants off."

Why did my skin tingle at those words? There was nothing

sexy about having a sundae's worth of melted ice cream covering your legs, yet the heat rolling off Bowie made me forget why we were even there to begin with. Gently, he shoved me into the fitting room and closed the door.

That's when I hopped on the struggle bus. Everything melted through the jeans and onto my thighs, making it very difficult to peel the already too tight fabric off my skin. Since we were filming today, I had selected a tight pair of jeans that accentuated the curves of my lower half, at Zephyr's suggestion. Now I cursed her decision as I yanked and barely moved it an inch.

"Ye sound like yer battling for yer life in there, cowgirl!" Bowie called.

I huffed in annoyance. "That's because I basically am! Whoever designs women's jeans should be on trial for hate crimes!"

"D'ye need help?" Bowie's voice was closer now, a lower tone, as if he stood just outside the door.

I merely whined in response.

Bowie came inside and the temperature in the small space rose by twenty degrees. I flushed as I realized this was the second time I had been in a state of undress in front of him. Judging from the way his pupils dilated as his eyes roved my predicament, he remembered, too.

Lowering to one knee, Bowie slowly traced his fingers from my waist down to the waistband of my jeans. Goosebumps broke out across my skin in their wake. He never once broke eye contact with me as he wrapped his fists around the fabric and softly wiped his fingers underneath to separate the wet fabric from my thigh. His face was level with my groin area, and I hoped that he couldn't tell how wet my panties were becoming.

Inch by painstaking inch Bowie worked the jeans down until

they pooled at my ankles. Neither of us could move, holding each other's gaze as electricity crackled between us. Tentatively, I reached down to brush my hand along his jaw, finding the hair from his closely cropped goatee to be coarse. I liked the friction it created beneath my fingertips.

Almost as if my touch did something to him, Bowie bit his bottom lip to stifle a moan and pressed his face right into the mound of flesh above my pussy. He inhaled deeply, like the very scent intoxicated him.

Part of me wanted to freeze while the other part wanted to push my hips forward. Luke had only gone down on me once when we were still in high school and our hormones were in overdrive. He claimed he didn't like the taste and refused to do it again after that. I knew there were some men who enjoyed the taste of a woman (at least if romance books could be believed), but that wasn't exactly a conversation I'd had yet with Bowie. He continued to nuzzle his face at my entrance, his callused fingers kneading into the globes of my ass.

When I felt his tongue gently stroke against the seam of my panties, a small whimper escaped, activating the beast within him waiting to be unleashed. Bowie pushed me down onto the small bench of the dressing room and threw both my legs over his shoulder, my knees cradling his ears.

"Don't make a sound," he ordered in a low voice, "or I won't let ye come."

Sliding my thong to the side, Bowie's mouth descended on my pussy with a fervor I hadn't known he possessed. With the first flick of his tongue, I was transcended to heaven. Both my hands shot out to press against the walls of the tiny dressing room to hold myself in place. His tongue speared me as the thumb holding my thong to the side began to work my clit. Only a guitar player would have the dexterity to strum like that. Within minutes, he had me seeing stars and coming harder than I had my entire life.

Bowie drank it down greedily, using my inner thigh like a napkin to wipe his face. My knees were shaking too hard to pull myself upright. He carefully placed my feet on the floor before bracing his arms on the bench next to my hips so that he could look me in the eye. "Ye've got a touch o' Irish magic in ye," Bowie whispered with a smirk. While my pussy throbbed from his mouth, my heart leapt from his words.

The mirror in the dressing room had fogged during our encounter. Discretion was sort of out the window at this point. We had to hope that Jennifer would be satisfied with her photos and autographs and keep this story to herself.

A sinking feeling left me as I realized I was already using my "celebrity" status to expect things from people. The show changed me without even realizing it.

"That's not the face a man likes t'see after a round with his girl," Bowie commented playfully as he helped me to stand up.

I didn't have to force the smile that warmed my face at hearing him call me "his girl."

"Um...sorry to bother you guys, but I have some jeans here for Finley to try on!" Jennifer squeaked from outside the door.

Okay, so now the floor needed to swallow me whole. I didn't really remember my statistics class from high school, but surely there was some kind of possibility that I could die of embarrassment?

Bowie didn't look worried in the least. He smirked at the distress on my face. "Thank ye, Jennifer."

He opened the door just enough to grab the hangers from the hook on the door and handed them to me. "As much as I don't want this day t'end," Bowie admitted, "they've probably noticed we're gone now."

I blanched. Billy would murder us!

Bowie left the dressing room and I settled for the first pair I tried on that fit. They were a different wash than my original pair this morning, but the fit was similar. The only person who would likely notice would be Zephyr, and she and I were gonna have a long chat about the events of the day anyway.

Emerging from the dressing room, I found Bowie and Jennifer at the register area in the middle of the store. They were taking selfies on a cell phone and the clerk appeared ready to swoon. As I approached, her face lit up.

"They look great! Can I get both of you in the pictures now?"

After several more photos, a combination of the three of us, Jennifer with me, and then just Bowie and me, and dozens of autographs (for her friends, she claimed), Jennifer refused to accept money for the jeans. "I'm such a huge fan! I've been trying to get tickets to go see the show live. These are on the house!"

"I'll leave two tickets for you at Will Call next week," I promised. "Just please don't tell anyone what you might have... heard...here today." My face was engulfed in flames as soon as the words left my lips. Bowie snickered.

Note to self: ask Billy how to leave tickets at Will Call for someone.

Bowie and I reached the bus just as the rest of the cast and crew started to filter out through the doors of the store where they had been shopping. Billy approached us with his hands in his pockets, a resigned look on his face that told me he knew we hadn't been inside. I dropped Bowie's hand like I had been electrocuted, and ignored the side eye he gave me in response.

"Why do I get the feeling you're about to ask me for something to cover up another disaster?" Billy asked with a sigh.

"I need two tickets at Will Call for Jennifer at next week's show," I replied.

His head fell back as Billy closed his eyes in defeat. "I'll get it done. Do I want to know why we're so generous?"

"That depends. How does 'accomplice to murder' sound on a resume?"

The aggravated look he seared me with proved he was in no mood for my antics. "I'll be getting on the bus now," I offered.

Billy nodded. "Great idea, now that I don't have a single shot of my two leading contestants on the shopping excursion one of them requested."

"Sorry, Billy," Bowie said without an ounce of sincerity in his tone. "It was worth it, though." He looked directly at me as he said it, causing me to blush a deep shade of scarlet.

Our poor producer looked ready to wring our necks, so we circled around him to get on the bus. I followed Bowie to the very back where we sat on the drive there.

"Shit!" I commented. "Now how do I get a gift for my person?"

Bowie grinned at me. "I already gave a present to mine," he boasted.

"What? How?!" That wasn't fair! Did he con one of the production assistants into taking him shopping late at night?

Stretching up so that he could withdraw a folded piece of paper from the pocket of his black jeans, Bowie fell back in the seat and held it up to show me who he drew from the Secret Santa hat.

Finley Smalls

"Mission accomplished, I'd say." A proud smile etched across his face.

My heart did that weird fluttering thing again as my thighs involuntarily clenched at the memory of that dressing room. A present, indeed.

Never Enough

FIN-LEY!

FIN-LEY!

FIN-LEY!

The screams from the crowd and the adorable signs they were starting to make would never get old. I didn't care how many shows I performed in my lifetime, there would never be enough to make this feeling go away. The spotlights, the adrenaline, the visceral responses from people in the audience—it fed a long-since starved part of my soul.

By the end of the Christmas special, I floated on cloud nine. I placed second, following Miles' impressive rendition of "Every Year, Every Christmas." He absolutely killed it and deserved the top spot. There wasn't a dry eye in the house.

Bowie placed the lowest he ever had, but as he admitted to me afterwards, he hadn't practiced like he usually did because Christmas wasn't as festive and joyous for him as it was for most of the other contestants. Placing in the tenth slot was fine for him.

"Ye'll just have to teach me how to celebrate Christmas properly," he whispered in my ear later that night out at the fire pit.

After the shopping excursion, Bowie and I fell back into our familiar rhythm, seeking each other out at all times. We were as inseparable as two people with an unspoken attraction could be. I refused to discuss our status in favor of living in the moment, and it was working out just fine. Every time Bowie tried to broach the subject, I simply changed it or physically left the area so that we could avoid bursting the bubble. Besides, we snuck outside to the fence line every night after our housemates went to bed to make out like teenagers. It wasn't like he didn't know where my desires lay.

Now, at the end of the holiday special, everyone happily walked backstage, Bowie with his arm around my waist. Zephyr and I chatted animatedly about our performances. She finally cracked the top five, which was her highest placement all season. Jessica managed to round out the top three, and her happy demeanor made it easier for everyone to relax after our performance. I certainly wasn't paying attention when Kameron and Issy, at the front of our loosely grouped herd, came to an abrupt halt.

"Where's Finley?"

That voice alone would be enough to stop me in my tracks. I hadn't thought of him in weeks, and hearing him now made my insides tie themselves in knots.

Bowie kept both hands on my hips as I pushed through the group to find Luke with a bouquet of roses standing in the middle of the hallway that led back to the dressing rooms. He looked exactly as I remembered, his blonde hair slicked to one side with hair gel, and his blue eyes twinkling along with the smile that brightened his face. He wore dark jeans and a gingham print button up under a tan blazer, far nicer clothing than I'd ever seen him in.

Although now I could only see how murky the blue of his eyes was and how his nose was too small to fit his features. Luke no longer appealed to me in that way. Where I once felt the keen sting of love and lust, I only experienced mild curiosity at his appearance backstage. That part of my life seemed so distant and long ago that it was almost like a forgotten dream.

As soon as he saw me, Luke's smile grew, and he thrust the flowers towards me. It just went to show how little he paid attention during our relationship. Roses were my least favorite flower. I always preferred tulips over any other.

Rather than take them, my eyebrows raised. "What are you doing here?"

With an apprehensive glance at Bowie, who stood behind me, his chest at my back and his hands still on my hips, Luke's hand dropped to his side. "Is there somewhere we can go and talk privately?" he asked in a low voice.

Zephyr frowned at my side, crossing her arms across her chest. "And who are you? How did you get back here?"

Luke smiled in an attempt to charm her. Not that it would work with Zephyr. "I'm Luke. Finley's fiancé, if she'll have me."

To my horror, Luke sank down on one knee, dropping the bouquet on the floor to reach into the hidden breast pocket of his blazer and pull out a small velvet box. He opened it to show me a diamond solitaire.

The rest of my housemates circled around with expressions matching the shock written all over my face. I felt Bowie stiffen behind me. His grip was nearly hard enough to bruise. Only

Jessica looked satisfied, a reaction I would examine when I didn't have the worst sight imaginable before my eyes. I had to get Luke out of here before one of the producers noticed and flagged down a cameraman.

"Luke, get up!" I hissed through clenched teeth. "You're embarrassing me!"

My ex shook his head. "Not unless you agree! I'm here to win you back, babe!"

Feeling Bowie's possessive hold on me was only scrambling my brain. I broke apart from him to step closer to Luke. In a fierce whisper, I argued, "I am not talking to you at all unless you get off this floor!"

Grinning as if he won, Luke stood up, once again holding the flowers out to me. I didn't take them, but rather grabbed the wrist of his other arm and dragged him away towards the exit. There was a small storage area for janitorial supplies near the door where we could have some semblance of privacy.

"What the fuck was that?!" I yelled as soon as we were inside.

Luke rolled his eyes. "C'mon, Fin, don't act like you're not happy to see me. I came all this way!"

Physical violence should never be the answer, yet punching him right in the nose sounded like a perfectly reasonable response in this situation.

"I haven't heard from you in months! You broke up with me, and then I found out you were cheating on me!"

"Technically it wasn't cheating if we had broken up," Luke pointed out, then backed up into a stack of mop buckets when he saw my murderous expression. "I made a mistake, alright? Is that what you wanna hear from me?"

"I don't want to hear anything from you, Luke! I didn't ask you to come here!"

He sighed, the fight leaving him. Luke didn't have it in him to be confrontational. "Please, Fin, just hear me out. We were together for four years. You're my first girlfriend—my first everything, really. Of course I panicked a little when you started asking about weddings and babies and stuff! We're too young for all of that right now."

I was going to rip my own hair out. Growling in frustration, I pulled at the roots to ground myself before I appeared on an episode of *Snapped*. "All I asked was *where* you saw our relationship going! I just wanted to know that we were committed to the same outcome in the future."

In the charming way that only Luke could manage, he came forward and grabbed both of my hands in his. "I know that now. It took losing you for me to realize that you were really just asking for what you deserved. We lived together—of course you wanted to know that eventually it would pan out."

Somewhere deep down, a small piece of my heart thawed at his acknowledgement. I wasn't being unreasonable when I wanted to know where we were headed. After growing up together in our very first serious relationship, I had every right to question if my boyfriend saw things long term.

Only now, I didn't really care about his answer. A future with Luke ceased to exist the moment Bowie's lips found mine for the first time. My younger self, who had loved Luke with her whole heart, wanted to get all weepy at the closure this conversation brought. I couldn't help it when a few tears escaped. All of the heartbreak from our breakup came rushing back, dulled and distant, just like the memory of us.

At that moment, Bowie opened the door to the closet. His

jaw clenched and his back went rigid as he took in the tears on my face and Luke's hands holding mine, which I realized belatedly held the jewelry box as well. Betrayal clouded his face before he stomped off.

"Bowie, no—wait!" I called. I started after him, but Luke grabbed my wrist and held me back.

"Look, I've been watching all season. I know there's been something going on between that guy and you," Luke said, "but we can work through it. After all, it's just a tv show, right?"

Yanking my arm out of his grip, I shot him a look of pure hatred. "No, it's not, Luke. Go home!"

I didn't give him a chance to say anything else as I raced down the hallway in search of Bowie. He wasn't in any of the dressing rooms or backstage areas. When I finally found Zephyr and the rest of my housemates outside, lining up to get on the bus, they told me Bowie had a heated exchange with Billy and he had stormed off, out of the parking lot.

"But we have to go after him!" I cried. "This is all my fault!"

"What are we supposed to do? He could be anywhere," Joey pointed out.

My shoulders sank as I realized he was right. Bowie would have caught an Uber by then. Our friends gave me looks of pity as they softly patted my back and got on the bus.

Back at the house, Zephyr let me take the first shower. The hot water did little to soothe my nerves. I tried calling Bowie's cell half a dozen times on the ride back, but after the sixth call, it started going straight to voicemail, like he turned it off rather than talk to me. Even though I knew it wouldn't do any good, I ordered Zephyr to keep trying while I showered.

By the time I scrubbed all the makeup and sweat off, Zephyr had gathered some snacks and settled into my bed. She patted the space beside her and wrapped her willowy arms around me as I rested my head on her shoulder and cried.

"Finley, this is your sign to finally talk to Bowie about your feelings," she gently chided me. "You wouldn't react so strongly if you didn't have very real feelings for him."

"I know!" I sobbed, tears silently streaming down my face until they fell off my chin. "But what if he won't forgive me?"

Zephyr snorted in derision. "Girl, forgive you for what? He walked in and saw you with Luke, then assumed the worst, and took off without talking to you first. He's the one acting a fool!"

Whether her take on the encounter was true or not, I knew I wouldn't feel better until I got to explain the situation to Bowie. It bothered me that I didn't know him well enough to know where he would go while upset. That seemed like the kind of thing I needed to file away for later. Zephyr continued to hold me until my sobs quieted.

"I'm gonna go to bed. Wake me up if you need me, okay? I don't care how late it is." My roommate shot me a meaningful look before crawling out of my bed to slip under the sheets of her own.

Sleep and I would never coexist that night. Once I heard Zephyr settle into her routine and her breathing even out like it did in sleep, I rose and threw a hoodie on over my thin tank top and yoga pants. Creeping down the hallway so as not to wake anyone, I went to the music room farthest from the bedrooms. As long as I shut the door, no one would be able to hear me play, and working through my emotions with music was the only way to dissolve the lump in my throat.

There were three windows in this particular room since it was in the front corner of the house, and enough moonlight filtered in that I didn't need a light. As I rounded the baby grand piano, however, I realized there was already someone in the room...Bowie.

He sat on the floor in the corner, his knees propped up to support his elbows. An unreadable expression crossed his face as his warm brown eyes found mine in the moonlight.

I rushed forward. "Bowie!" His name sounded like a prayer from my lips.

Holding out his hands to stop me, Bowie clambered to his feet, standing an arm's length away. It might as well have been a football field between us. I hated the distance. I hated knowing something I had done led to this moment. We were so rarely alone, and now tension laced the air rather than delight.

"I'm not sure I'm ready to talk to ye just yet," Bowie admitted.

Tears welled in my eyes, blurring his form from view, but I brushed them aside with the sleeve of my hoodie. A hoodie that actually belonged to him, I realized belatedly. He had given it to me several weeks ago when I complained of a chill in one of the music rooms during practice. I was almost ashamed of how many times I'd smelled it just to have his comforting scent, a mixture of black current and tobacco.

"Please, Bowie," I pleaded. "Nothing happened. I swear it! Luke doesn't matter to me anymore...not since you."

There. I laid my heart at his feet. If I wasn't so distraught over his response, I might have been hyperventilating from my own nerve.

So slowly that I almost doubted he moved at all, Bowie closed the distance between us until he stood right in front of me. With a light hand, he tucked my hair behind my ear.

"Say it again," he breathed.

"I just want you." Although my voice was barely above a

whisper, in the deafening silence of the room, they seemed to echo all around us.

"Finally!" he replied before his mouth descended on mine.

This kiss was far hungrier than any we shared before. It was as though Bowie's very soul wanted to weave itself into mine. His hands gripped my face in a way that told me I was the only anchor he had. Our tongues danced, my breasts pressing into his muscular chest, and if I could have climbed him like a tree, I would have. He tasted of all things happy and good.

In what felt far too soon, but was more likely several minutes, Bowie pulled away just enough to end the kiss, but rest his forehead on mine. Our hands clasped, and I couldn't help the joyful sigh that escaped. Offering up my heart to him wasn't nearly as scary as my brain insisted it would be.

"I've been waitin' a long time to hear ye say such a thing, cowgirl," Bowie confessed.

I nodded, smiling tearfully. The chance of being happy loomed on the horizon. It quickly faded from view when he asked the only question that could ruin the moment.

"But what about the show?"

Heart sinking, I drew back, my mouth parted in disappointment. "What *about* the show?" I asked.

Bowie winced at the hurt laced in my tone. "Only one of us can win. And it needs to be ye."

I sputtered. "It could be either of us! The show is almost over anyway, so we can be together—"

"Aye," he agreed. "And I know how important it is for ye to win on yer own merit. I'm not gonna act the maggot and make ye lose that."

"What does that even mean?" I asked in confusion. Tears now spilled over for an entirely different reason.

Bowie sighed heavily and brought our clasped hands up to his lips. "It means that I'm proud of ye, cowgirl, and so all the other stuff can wait. Yer gonna win this thing, d'ye hear me?"

"But what about you? You're just as good! You have just as much of a chance!"

He nodded thoughtfully. "But maybe it's not me dream anymore."

This was an entirely new kind of heartbreak. I finally admitted my feelings for him, only to have Bowie circle back to my original plan: focus on the opportunities *America's Music Star* brought my way. It wasn't fair.

I dropped our hands, backing away towards the door. "Then what is your dream?" I finally asked once my hand found the doorknob.

Even in the pale light from the moon, Bowie's cocky smirk had my stomach doing back flips. "Win the show and I'll tell ye," he promised.

Heartbeat Song

Music was the only thing that kept me sane over the next week. Bowie kept his distance from me again, which eagle-eyed fans noticed on social media. Headlines began to speculate that we had a falling out, with some of the influencers citing the pending season finale as the reason. While they were correct as to the reason, most of them incorrectly postulated that Bowie and I broke up because of the competition where one of us had to win. Nobody knew the truth that we broke up because Bowie wanted out of the competition altogether.

Jessica, on the other hand, seemed particularly interested in our "break up." In a completely uncharacteristic act, she approached me at breakfast one morning and told me that she was always there to listen if I needed someone to talk to. I would no sooner share a bed with a rabid mongoose than relay my feelings to a girl like Jessica Harris. There was something off about her behavior ever since Luke had shown up backstage. We were so busy though, that I never had a chance to confront her about it.

Billy swore up and down he had nothing to do with Luke's arrival. He agreed to provide Luke's name and photo to security so that he would be barred from entering if he showed up to another show.

That didn't stop him from running his mouth all over the internet, however. He was always far more interested in social media than I was, and it turned out being my ex-boyfriend gained him some popularity points. Several of the prominent influencers interviewed him on lives to talk about our history and what Luke suspected of the sudden wall between Bowie and myself. Zephyr had to stop me from throwing my phone down the toilet after we watched a particularly hideous interview where Luke dropped thinly veiled hints at a reconciliation between the two of us. Apparently, my message in the janitor's closest wasn't clear enough for him.

The only silver lining that I could see came when Billy made two major announcements during our week ten house huddle. Now that the finale was well within sight, emotions were running higher than ever. We all desperately wanted to win, Bowie aside, and there was a palpable fear in the air of what would become of the losers. Everyone had to commit to the four week tour, but then what?

"Alright, everyone," Billy began as he called the meeting to order, "let's settle down because I have some exciting news to share. As you all are aware, we are coming up on our season finale. Our ratings have gone up with each episode, so it's truly anyone's game. Use your platforms accordingly and do what you can to lock in as many votes as possible. There's no shame in your hustle if it leads to victory!"

He clapped his hands gleefully, which I knew had far more to do with the ratings than anything else. *America's Music Star* was a global success. Billy finally had some job security with the network.

"So, the big news! I can finally confirm the rumors are true. You all are going to get the opportunity to write and record your own song for the AMS album!"

My friends and I all burst into applause. I used my fingers to wolf whistle as Zephyr jumped up and down beside me. Giving in to temptation, I snuck a glance across the room at Bowie, who shot me the briefest of winks before directing his attention back to Billy at the front of the dance studio.

"To help you with this task, I am delighted to introduce you to Grammy award winning singer/songwriter, Howie Mitch—" At this, Howie walked in to stand beside Billy, a wide smile on his face as he waved to the twelve of us.

Zephyr was on the verge of pissing her pants. Howie had a slew of chart topping singles and could play virtually any instrument. He was rumored to have perfect pitch, a feat that was nearly impossible for the human ear.

Billy continued, "—and Scott Baxter, front man and songwriter for the hit Canadian rock band, Showtime!"

Scott Baxter strolled into the room and this time, my cheers were by far the loudest. I *loved* Showtime! And Scott Baxter's songwriting skills were beyond impressive. He was one of the most prolific songwriters of this century! If I had to choose between Howie and Scott, there was no contest.

"We will have six people working with each of our guest songwriters," Billy explained. "Everyone will have dedicated time in the studio with their mentor to write and record their song for the album. These are meant to be your songs, so I highly suggest you try to create something on your own before you go into the studio. We don't have much time to get this all done before the finale, where you'll be singing your song live for the first time."

At this, chaos erupted. I turned and asked Zephyr to pinch me because it seemed too good to be true. A chance to work with an award winning songwriter AND sing my own song on a live television show? It couldn't get any better than that!

Billy had to wait nearly five whole minutes before the excitement died down enough for him to continue. "That's not the final announcement" was all he had to say before everyone clamped their mouths shut.

He flashed us a wide smile, holding out his arms for emphasis as he declared, "Next week, you'll all get to go home for three days!"

Now that brought whoops of joy. I couldn't wait to see my mom again and thank her for all her faith in me. She had watched religiously every single week. All of the teachers at her school voted for me, and they started wearing t-shirts that read "Smalls Army" in support.

Zephyr and I embraced each other in a hug, our elation over Billy's announcement infectious. It was only after I caught a glimpse of Bowie's crestfallen expression over her shoulder that I realized not everyone wanted to go home.

"What's more, each of you will have a camera crew in tow so that we can film your families, your hometown...really anything that makes you who you are! This is a great way to show the viewers at home your vulnerable sides, so make it count!" Billy finally gave up trying to talk over the din of the room, instead turning to Scott and Howie to shake their hands in thanks.

I couldn't help it. Seeing that brief glimpse of pain on Bowie's face was enough to make me break our vow of silence to check on him. Weaving through the group, I came up beside him and knocked his arm with my shoulder.

"Penny for your thoughts?" I asked.

Bowie offered me a small smile. "It's alright, cowgirl," he assured me. "I'll let America see me dreadful upbringing. I s'pose no one here could imagine life being rough in a country as beautiful as mine. Perhaps I can distract them with all the greenery and rain."

Before I had a chance to respond, Billy sidled up to us with an apologetic smile. "Bowie, we need to talk about next week's home visit. Everyone knows you're from Ireland originally, but the network really can't afford to send you to Europe for three days. Not to mention the time difference, the jet lag, it wouldn't give us what we really need anyway. Are you okay with staying Stateside for your home visit?"

Hope broke out on Bowie's face and he nodded firmly. "Yes. But me da and I don't get on, so there's nothing really here for ye to film."

Remember my impulsive thing? Yeah, that hadn't gone away.

I didn't think at all about the impact my statement would have before I blurted out, "Well, yeah, that's 'cause you're gonna come home to Texas with me."

Dollar signs were actually visible from the gleam that formed in Billy's eyes. "Really?" he asked in delight. "That'll sure make the fans happy!"

"*Finley!*" Bowie hissed in my ear.

I ignored him, heart hammering a mile a minute in my chest. "Yep, it sure will. Bowie's gonna come home with me and see what the Lone Star state has to offer!"

Gleefully, the producer clapped his hands together, resembling a cartoon villain more than I'd ever seen before. "I'll get the whole thing worked out!"

As he scampered away, probably imagining the zeroes that would be added to his new bonus from this development, Bowie grabbed my wrist and pulled me into the corner behind the sound equipment. "Finley, this is not a good idea! We had an agreement."

I frowned at him, pointing a finger in his face. "No, *you* had an agreement! An agreement that is null and void for three days in Texas! Now, we can play the part of good friends while the cameras are rolling if you're too concerned about what people will think, but either way, I'm not letting you stay here in L.A. by yourself."

He rolled his eyes. "If I don't care, there's no reason ye should. What about winning because ye're the best? I don't want ye to secure last minute votes because everyone assumes I'm yer boyfriend."

"And I don't want to go to Texas without you," I countered, determination straightening my spine. "Besides, you have far bigger issues to worry about if we're going to my hometown."

"Oh, yeah? Like what, cattle?" Bowie snorted.

My eyes narrowed at his poor joke. "Like my mom."

———

ONCE DANCE REHEARSALS WERE DONE, Veronica met us all in the kitchen to hand out our songwriting mentor assignments. Glory be, I had been paired up with none other than Scott Baxter! Our first writing session would take place tomorrow evening just after dinner.

Zephyr danced in excitement to be partnered with Howie

Mitch. Her session would take place in the middle of the day tomorrow, so we agreed to work on our songs together that night. As unlikely as it would be, I wanted to wow Scott Baxter. His songs were legendary in the business, and getting his stamp of approval on a song virtually guaranteed me a hit.

Hours flew by and before I knew it, Zephyr and I were heading down to the music room. Zephyr wanted a song that would get people dancing, a pop song that really brought out a smile.

"I've never shown anyone these lyrics before, so please don't laugh at me," she pleaded. Like there was a chance that Zephyr could be bad at something. The girl was literal perfection.

We worked on her lyrics until the darkness fell outside and, in the end, I felt we did a great job in capturing the kind of upbeat message Zephyr wanted to share. She promised to share writing credits with me and I laughed. "Just give me my new favorite dance anthem, please!"

"Damn," muttered Zephyr with a glance at the window. "It's already getting so late! I didn't mean to monopolize all our time!"

I shrugged. "Don't worry about it. I have so many ideas in my notebook, I need to take some quiet time just to sort through them before tomorrow anyway." If there was one thing I'd learned in the past couple months as Zephyr's roommate, it was that the girl needed her eight hours of beauty sleep. Anything less than that and she could rival a dragon in her anger.

"Are you sure? I feel so guilty cutting out on you like this!"

"It's totally fine! I'll play you what I've got first thing tomorrow!" I waved her towards the door where she gave me one last wistful look before disappearing down the hall, allowing the heavy door to close behind her.

Engrossed in my song journal, I flipped back and forth

through the stray lyrics and chord progressions I had written down, occasionally playing the corresponding notes on the piano. One song in particular stuck out at me and I nodded my head along to the beat as I tried to work through the chorus.

The sound of the door moving startled me, but not nearly as much as finding Jessica in the room with me. She firmly pressed the door shut, casting a resentful look my way before she began to circle the piano like a hawk.

"Of course you're already hard at work writing something. I suppose Billy's already buying you a number one placement on the Billboard one hundred charts." Jessica sneered at the ratty notebook that served as my musical diary.

"You know, you're kind of starting to sound like a broken record," I replied smoothly. "Might wanna be careful so they don't throw you away with the trash."

Jessica's frown deepened. "This little plan of yours to steal Bowie away to Texas isn't gonna work. Everyone online thinks you and Luke are getting back together. America loves to forgive the golden boys who apologize. They'd pick him over Bowie for you in a heartbeat."

Her words sparked a fire in me, mostly because I recognized how true they were. Everyone liked Bowie because they viewed him as a bad boy. Women always loved a taste of their forbidden fruit. But nobody actually expected to make the bad boy change his ways. Bowie had a long reputation of hooking up with groupies and getting bras thrown at him on stage. Female fans wanted him for themselves.

I stood up abruptly, snatching my journal so that I could find another music room to work in. Two strides away from the door, Jessica dropped a bomb that stopped me in my tracks.

"I sent for him, you know. Luke. I told him how badly you still wanted him."

Turning on my heel, I observed her in an entirely new light. Jessica was ruthless, and this competition brought out the worst in her.

"Luke's not gonna go down without a fight," Jessica continued. "And since I bribed Kyle to give me all the footage of your little sex tape with Bowie, I suggest you do as I say so that the footage doesn't fall in the wrong hands."

"I can't wait to hear your villain origin story," I quipped. Meanwhile, my dinner threatened to retaliate all over her shoes. Nothing happened that night between Bowie and me, but given our various states of undress, anyone would naturally draw the conclusion that we crossed the line into something more than friendship.

Jessica sauntered past me to the door. "You either blow the competition next week or I release your tape to the media. Luke will be around in Texas to make sure you see things my way, so I'd go ahead and leave the Irish boytoy here."

Did competitions normally make people resort to blackmail or was this just my uncanny ability to get caught up in situations I had no business being in? My mom always used to say my true talent was for landing myself in a lot of avoidable trouble, and boy, was she right. Jessica was simply vile!

"Have a good night!" Jessica said over her shoulder. The door closed behind her, leaving me in an unprecedented state of panic.

How would I get myself out of this one?

People Like Us

The next morning I struggled to get out of bed. Even the prospect of working with Scott Baxter wasn't enough to sway me. Zephyr asked if I felt sick, testing the temperature of my forehead with the back of her hand. I was too anxious to admit the exchange with Jessica the night before, so I told her I had really bad menstrual cramps. Judging from the look on her face, she saw right through my act, but she chose not to say anything.

When Veronica stopped by later, I gave her the same excuse and she said they would excuse me from rehearsals for the day. My meeting with Scott couldn't be postponed however, because he could only be in L.A. for two days a week with Showtime's touring schedule.

Once I was finally left alone, I did the only thing that made sense. I called my mom.

"Finley, what's the matter?" she asked. "You never call during the day."

Starting with good news always worked better with my mother.

If you hit the right note in the beginning, the conversation wouldn't veer too far off course. "I wanted to let you know that I'll be coming home for three days next week!" The enthusiasm in my voice didn't sound natural, but hopefully I could chalk it up to exhaustion.

"Oh, honey, that's great! Now what's the bad news?"

Even though she couldn't see me, my eyes narrowed at the phone. "Who said anything about bad news?"

My mom huffed out a laugh. "Remember me, the woman who raised you for the past twenty-one years? You think I don't know your bag of tricks?"

I frowned as she chuckled over my stunned silence.

"Just spit it out, Finley," Mom instructed.

"Well, Bowie might be coming, too," I hedged. Admitting that there might be a video leaked on the internet that showed me in my underwear next to a seemingly naked, tattooed Irish hunk wasn't exactly something one revealed that often. I didn't have a manual to consult.

My mother surprised me by sounding enthusiastic about the idea. "I hope he can. We'll have fun showing him around."

There was a pregnant pause as I tried to figure out how to tell her. It was like saying the words out loud made them real.

"What is it, Finley? What's really bothering you?"

A lump in my throat made it hard for me to swallow. This was my mother, and I knew she would never judge me, but I also never intended to give her a reason to. Being on *America's Music Star* should make her proud of me. Instead it seemed like I'd done more to worry her than anything else.

"If I did something that could have a really bad outcome, would you still love me?" It wasn't my intention to word it that way, but my filter wasn't working. I needed the reassurance from the woman who mattered most that nothing would be as bad as it seemed.

"In my experience, nothing ever has a truly bad outcome," she said gently, with the kind of patience she normally reserved for her preschool students. "I doubt you've been able to get in that kind of serious trouble at the house. But yes, I will *always* love you!" Mom added with a laugh.

I sniffled. "No, this is pretty bad, Mom."

"Then you face it," she said simply. "Sometimes the only way out is through."

Sage advice from the smartest woman I knew. There really was nothing else I could do other than face the music. Winning the competition meant everything to me, and to Bowie. Jessica didn't have the right to take that from me.

"I love you, Mom," I replied.

"I love you, too, kiddo. I can't wait to see you and meet this new fella of yours."

There's something affirming about a mother's love. They're the only ones who can say it and you genuinely believe them. Despite her advice, I still feared what Jessica would do, though. Anyone who would resort to blackmail to win didn't have much of a moral compass. And since I lived my life with my heart on my sleeve, I had no clue how to reason with someone like that.

I must've fallen asleep because before I knew it, Zephyr shook me awake. "Finley, you have your meeting with Scott Baxter in an hour."

"Thanks." Throwing off the blanket, I pushed myself upright. My roommate handed me a glass of water and placed a bottle of ibuprofen on the nightstand.

"What's going on with you, Fin?" asked Zephyr. "I know you don't have period cramps."

Hesitating, I tried to stall. "Yes, I do. They're super bad."

Zephyr rolled her eyes as she flopped down on her bed. "Girl, please. We share a bathroom and all the hygiene products that go along with it. I know exactly when your period starts! What's going on? Is this about Bowie?"

I wanted to confide in Zephyr, I really did. It had been so long since I had a girlfriend like her, and she had already proved what a great friend she was. But it was for that reason that I had to leave her in the dark. Jessica might retaliate against Zephyr, which was a price I wasn't willing to pay.

"It's nothing," I promised, crossing my fingers under my blanket. "I'm gonna jump in the shower real quick."

Once I was done getting ready, one of the production assistants knocked on the bedroom door to announce that the car was ready to take me to the recording studio so I could meet my mentor. Nerves kicked in, and I battled nausea the entire way there. There was no way I could embarrass myself in front of one of my music idols. Threat or no threat, I wanted—no *needed*—to write a kick ass song with Scott Baxter.

When I walked into the recording studio, Scott already sat on a stool, strumming on an acoustic guitar. He completely zoned in on the task, his reddish-brown hair spiked as his head bobbed along to the beat. Although now in his forties, Scott still looked fantastic and fit as his arm flexed along with the chord he played. His goatee wasn't marred by gray hair like some men his age.

Maybe I just had a thing for guitar players now.

It was my first time ever being inside a studio. Thankfully, it was the perfect sort of thing to record as a behind the scenes reel for social media, so I could always remember the moment. I had my phone out to capture footage of the space, Scott, and then a dozen or so shots of me beaming at the camera. Just for good measure, I reached down and pinched my hip to make sure I was awake.

"Hi, I'm Finley Smalls!" I held out my hand, which he shook with a smile.

"Scott," he replied, like everybody in the music industry didn't already know who he was.

A door to my right opened and a woman exited. She wore a calf length sundress that hugged her curvy figure and square, black glasses that gave off naughty librarian vibes. Clutching a notebook to her chest, she flashed me a small smile before delicately folding her feet under her body as she curled up on a leather couch against the wall.

"You don't need to worry about her," Scott said dismissively. His eyes conveyed a completely different message however, as they continually darted to her.

"What he means to say is, I'm Aniston Sharpe," the woman said, holding out her hand. "I have my own stuff to work on, so just pretend I'm not here."

That didn't explain anything, but it felt awkward to point that out.

"Have a seat," Scott invited, gesturing towards a rolling chair next to him. "You've been the one to watch this season. I've really been looking forward to working with you."

I beamed. Coming from him, it was the highest praise a performer like me could ask for.

"Do you have any material you wanted to work on?"

"Yes!" Eagerly, I pulled my song journal out of the knapsack I carried, flipping it open to the song I hoped to work on. It was a last minute switch I made on the car ride over based on the emotions I currently felt.

Pulling the journal in front of him, Scott started to read the lyrics and cautiously play the chords I jotted down. The music sounded a lot different on guitar than it had on piano, but I heard it as more of a rock ballad in my head anyway. Scott sped the tempo up a bit faster than I intended.

"Um, I hear it a little slower. It's meant to be a love song." Even my ears burned red at the thought of correcting him.

Scott only smiled. "Alright. Can you sing a bit of how you hear it?"

It's just like singing any other song, Finley. Don't freak out.

Yeah, right.

"It's gonna be a bit rough," I admitted. "I haven't really worked out the bridge, and this verse isn't—"

"Finley!" he interrupted. "Songwriting is about storytelling. As long as we're telling your story, it's gonna be great. Don't worry about anything other than that."

If his plan was to calm my nerves, mission accomplished. Scott might be an international rock star, but this was about me. This was my first (and last, depending on how you looked at it) chance to show the world what kind of songs I wanted to perform. I had to make it count.

At least...I could if Scott could manage to stop following Aniston's every movement.

I glanced back at her on the couch, completely oblivious as she scribbled on a notebook before typing something in the laptop balanced on her knees. Leaning in close, I whispered to him, "Do I need to give you a moment?"

Scott jumped in his seat, nearly losing his grip on the guitar. "No, everything's fine." He cleared his throat loudly, shooting Aniston one last look full of longing before directing his attention back to my song journal. "Let's see what you've got, Finley Smalls!"

Honestly

The hours in the recording studio with Scott flew by. I was so happy with the suggestions he made. We made a lot of great progress on the song, more so than any of his other mentees, he said.

Not to toot my own horn or anything.

I still felt on top of the world the next morning when I whizzed into the kitchen, mindlessly humming the melody as I made a cup of a coffee and threw a Pop-tart in the toaster. Jessica, who sat at the table with a bowl of overnight protein oats, frowned at me. Issy, Kameron, and Joey were just about finished with their breakfasts and greeted me with a smile.

"What song is that?" Issy asked. "I really like it!"

I flashed her a proud grin. "It's the one I'm working on with Scott!"

"Hey, what's it like working with Scott Baxter? Is he intense?" Joey asked. Howie was his mentor.

"Oh my gosh, it's so rad!" I gushed. "He totally ran with my lyrics, and then we talked about adding this cool guitar riff, and—"

"Blah frickin' blah!" Jessica cut me off. "God, don't you ever shut up?"

All four of us looked at her in shock.

"Jessica, what is your problem?" Issy asked.

Before she could answer, Bowie strode in, leaning down to kiss me on the forehead as he walked past. "Top o' the morning to ye, cowgirl."

Jessica's face filled with hatred. "Gee, Finley, don't you have something you'd like to say to Bowie?"

All eyes turned to me expectantly, most mirroring the astonishment that I knew was written all over my face. Trying to make me cancel the trip to Texas with Bowie in front of my housemates wasn't part of the deal.

"Not really, no," I replied. "He's welcome to join in on the conversation about working with Scott Baxter."

Her eyes narrowed, but she didn't press any further.

"Aye, Scott's a good lad," Bowie commented.

"Is he your mentor, too?" I asked.

Bowie nodded, then slid into a chair next to Issy with a cup of coffee. I swear, the man never ate anything. No wonder he was so lithe and lanky.

"Howie was amazing!" Kameron admired. "He played like, three different instruments during my session! I could never have his talent! We're gonna write more of a club song so that I can dance to it, too. Think Nicola would help me with choreography?"

"Probably. It's what she gets paid for, after all," Joey replied.

Sliding into a seat across from Bowie, the five of us continued an animated discussion on the merits of our mentors and how well our songwriting sessions had all gone. We were all excited for the different styles of music that would all be represented on the *America's Music Star* album. Each song would reflect how different everyone in the house sounded.

It wasn't until we started shuffling down the hall towards the dance studio for practice that I realized Jessica left the table at some point during our conversation. Given how pissed off she looked, that couldn't have been a good thing.

A theory that was confirmed when Billy and Veronica met us outside the studio wearing matching grim expressions.

"Bowie. Finley. This way, please," Veronica said, holding out her infernal clipboard towards a music room across the hall.

Billy shut the door behind us, which was never a good sign. He stared both of us in the eye for several seconds before asking, "Did either of you know how a sex tape of the two of you got on the internet?"

Bowie burst out laughing. "Aye, and how'd that happen when the lass and I haven't had sex?"

Veronica's eyes widened. "But you're in bed together, and you're naked!"

"I was *not* naked," I grumbled.

"D'ye know about this?" Bowie asked me in alarm.

Ratting Jessica out wouldn't smooth any over with her prickly pear self, but if I didn't tell the truth, Billy and the rest of the producers might start questioning all of the crew. I didn't want anyone to get in trouble for giving Jessica that tape, even if it was a really stupid thing to do. She was pretty intimidating.

"Jessica...might have, sort of...blackmailed me about it." Toddlers made better confessions than that, but the guilt at placing blame made me feel icky.

Billy's eyebrows went up as Veronica started scribbling on her notebook. "What on earth are you talking about, Finley?"

Okay, now I was exasperated. "Jessica said she was the one who called Luke here and told him that I wanted him back. When that didn't sway me off course, she somehow managed to get footage from my bedroom when Bowie spent the night in my room, and told me that she would publish it online unless I agreed to make Bowie stay in L.A. rather than go home with me to Texas and I intentionally performed poorly over the next couple shows so she could win."

Bowie looked incredulous. "But that's...insane. We've been 'shipped' from the start. Fans would love to know we're together! And a feckin' tape of me sleeping next to ye without a shirt on isn't a sex tape. I never wear a shirt around ye 'cause I like slaggin' ye!"

"Okay, I really don't have time to ask Google Translate what you mean right now." I sighed, turning to Billy. "There shouldn't be anything on that tape. It's totally innocent."

Rather than looking relieved, Billy appeared disappointed. "Damn, the network hoped it was real. Imagine the ratings boost from that! Would you all consider making a real one?"

Did you hear that sound? It's the sound of my jaw dropping. What level of the Audacity Game had we entered?

Bowie glared at Billy, extending himself to his full height and folding his arms across his chest. "Makin' love to my girl is my business, mate. Ye and yer network can fuck right off."

A triumphant expression crossed the producer's face. "AHA! So you guys *are* together now! We can use that!"

"Remember what we discussed in the car, Billy?" I asked. "I'm not here for a dating show. Bowie and I aren't together like that anyway." From the corner of my eye, I saw Bowie turn to me with a frown at that statement.

Veronica held up her phone to show us a line graph ascending upwards at an astronomically high rate. "Based on the ratings spike from this so-called sex tape, you might want to consider being like that."

DANCE REHEARSALS WERE the last place I wanted to be. If I saw Jessica again, I might very well rip her hair out, and I'm not really a fighter. It would get ugly just because I wouldn't even know what to do. When Billy and Veronica left the room, Bowie started to say something and I just held up a hand with the firm order, "Don't."

Now I was stuck in my room, going through all of the horrible commentary on social media. In true Finley Smalls fashion, I screwed up on having a sex tape scandal. Fans were disappointed after watching the fifteen minute leaked footage and seeing...nothing. Jessica either hadn't checked or simply expected people to jump to a whole lot of conclusions because the footage only showed a shirtless Bowie spooning me with one arm around me on top of the covers. It was very clear that I had a shirt on, and we were fast asleep.

And for whatever reason, that made the commenters on social media really angry. The comment sections were filled with people complaining that they needed more than that to confirm our relationship, then demanding that Bowie and I actually provide a *real* sex tape. As if fans had a right to that kind of information. I didn't know whether to laugh, cry, or break glass.

My mom sent me a text saying she enjoyed my sex tape

along with a crying laugh emoji. What a supportive parent. When I asked for advice on what I should do, she said to laugh it off because this kind of thing would blow over. And not to be nitpicky or anything, but that's exactly what someone who hasn't ever had a "sex" tape released on the internet during the last two weeks of a reality singing competition would say.

Zephyr, my beautiful bestie, joined me during the lunch break. Plopping on the bed, she nonchalantly ate her salad as I wore a line into the floor from pacing back and forth.

"What do I do?" I begged.

"Finley, it's not even a real tape! Why does this matter?"

"Because fans are mad! They want answers!"

"To what?"

I rolled my eyes. "To know who fathered Rory's baby," I deadpanned. "They want to know if Bowie and I are a couple!"

Slamming down her salad on the bed, Zephyr stood up and grabbed me by the shoulders to look me dead in the eye. "There's. Nothing. On. That. Tape. If you're going to be a celebrity, people are always going to speculate on your love life, Fin. This is never going to go away. Even if you admitted you're a couple, people would question whether you were happy, if you were engaged, if you were pregnant—all of it!"

Nodding, my heart sank at the truth of it. How many times had I read tabloid magazines or watched TMZ online?

"I say you stop moping, stop reading the comments, hell, just stop worrying all together, and focus on the music. We've only got two shows left. And then this all comes to an end." The words caught in Zephyr's throat as I realized she fought back tears.

Immediately, I caught on to what she meant. "And we won't be roommates anymore," I finished. Tears started on both sides as we hugged one another tightly. Zephyr was more of a best friend than I ever had in my life. Going through the experience of *America's Music Star* bonded us in a way that no one else could ever understand.

"Now, you listen here," Zephyr said, drawing back enough to see my face. "If I'm not gonna win, it's gotta be you. That's the only other option I can settle for. So I need you to get your game face on and get back in rehearsals today, okay?"

I gave her a watery smile. "Done."

"Thatta girl." Zephyr fluffed up my hair for me before returning back to her salad. I realized how loudly my stomach growled and went down to the kitchen to grab something quick to eat.

Riley sat at the table with a laptop open while Issy, Kameron, Tessa, and Miles all sat with plates in front of them. They turned to greet me with tentative smiles, clearly unsure of what to say or do, given the circumstances.

"It's fine, y'all. I'll be okay," I assured them.

"Actually, I've gotten most of the videos taken down now," Riley said. We all whipped our heads in his direction.

"You did what, now?" Miles asked.

Riley shrugged. "I can't take all of it down because, you know, the internet is forever and all that, but I was able to triangulate the sites of origin and take the footage off those sites, so it'll be harder for people to find the tape now."

I stared at him in disbelief, a look I shared with all of my housemates.

"How do you know how to do that?" Kameron asked in awe.

Riley shrugged again. "My friends and I usually spend our summers hacking into things. Once you know how code works, it's not hard."

Miles raised his eyebrows. "Only slightly illegal."

A faint tinge of pink crossed Riley's cheeks. "Maybe."

"The important thing is, we're with you, Finley!" Issy gave me a bright smile and a thumbs up. Our housemates joined in.

"Yeah, I'm so sorry this happened to you," Miles added. "Do you know who would leak something like this?"

I wasn't sure how to answer, and at that exact moment, Jessica and Tessa walked into the kitchen. Happiness quickly drained from Jessica's face when she saw me, and she hung her head as she circled around to the other side of the kitchen to pull a water bottle out of the refrigerator.

"No, I don't know who would leak a tape of me sleeping," I replied loudly.

What Jessica did was wrong. But she could ride the highway to Hell on her own. I refused to get on myself.

I swore I could feel her judgmental eyes burning a hole into the back of my head. This wasn't over yet. I might have saved our housemates' opinions of her, but Jessica was still determined to win at all costs. Sleeping with one eye open and a boobytrapped door might be in my future.

Don't Rush

"And in the top place AGAIN...Finley Smalls!" Enid's voice could barely be heard above the roar from the crowd.

Yeah, I slayed the Golden Oldies night with my rendition of "Respect" by Aretha Franklin. It took a lot out of me vocally. But it was worth for cinching the top spot on the third to last week of the show.

Next week's show would feature the footage from our hometown visits. We were going to sing songs relating to where we're from. Then it was the finale, and I could hardly breathe just thinking about it.

Now, as I accepted a hug onstage from Enid and all my housemates, I tried to simply bask in the glow of the moment. Looking out into the crowd, I saw several girls who had chunky purple highlights like mine. Signs with the phrase *You're killing it, Smalls!* had become incredibly popular, to the point where the network licensed them and sold them at the doors for people to buy when they walked in. A group of people online dedicated themselves as my biggest fans and called themselves "The

Smalls Army" after seeing the shots of my mom's friends. Hey, I love a good word pun as much as the rest of them. It was cute and super flattering.

Tonight would be filled with travel hustling as everyone boarded red eyes for their journey home. After Jessica's stunt with the tape, even though it didn't count as a sex tape, Bowie and I agreed that he would stay behind in L.A. There was too much gossip about our relationship again, and it definitely dragged the spotlight away from our performances. As much as I wanted to celebrate tonight's top place spot, a small voice in the back of my mind questioned if it was authentic.

To even further keep our relationship status out of everyone's mouths, Bowie did not come over to celebrate the win with me at the end like he usually did. It hurt far more than I cared to admit. Somehow hearing Bowie's praise always made it seem real, like it gave me permission to be proud of myself.

He smirked at me with a quick tilt of the head from across the stage and then disappeared into the throng. Jessica placed fourth, and despite the cameras still being on, she looked like she was on the war path. Her hands fisted at her hips as she glared up at the leaderboard, where Bowie ranked third and Joey ranked second. It was Joey's highest rank of the season and I couldn't stop congratulating him.

A sentiment Jessica couldn't share. "You were lip syncing!" she screamed at Joey. "I've heard you in rehearsals all week! There's no way you sounded that good tonight!"

My eyes widened as I glanced out at the devotees who still sat in the audience, determined to see us until the very end. I tried to brace my arms around the two of them to guide them off stage, but Jessica threw my arm off so she could continue to hurl accusations at Joey.

"Admit it! You cheated! You're fake!" Jessica threw a finger in his face accusatorially.

Joey held up his hands in surrender. "I've been working really hard in one of the practice rooms at night. That was me singing, I swear!"

"AND NOW YOU'RE LYING TO ME!" Jessica bellowed.

"Okay, now, that's all, folks!" I grabbed both of them by the sleeves of their shirts and shoved them off stage. There were already people holding up cell phones, meaning their entire exchange would have gone viral by now.

Jessica seethed as she slapped my hand away again. "Why are you covering for him?!" she shrieked. "Joey faked his song and you're DEFENDING him?!"

"Joey, get out of here!" I threw the command over my shoulder at him and Joey immediately took off for the dressing rooms. Jesscia made to follow him. I caught her around the waist and held her back, where she started thrashing like a wounded bear.

"Get your hands off me!" she commanded.

This is the part where a smooth narrator voice over would occur in a movie. Someone like Morgan Freeman who would explain that I, in fact, did not take my hands off Jessica.

I hugged her.

My arms pinned her own to her sides, and she struggled against my hold for several minutes. For a minute, I thought she might headbutt me, so I started humming a soothing lullaby right in Jessica's ear in the hopes that it might make her calm down.

Guess what? After five minutes of struggle, Jessica let out the heaviest sigh I'd ever heard and melted into my arms. Her head rested on my shoulder and it wasn't until I felt her body vibrate with the sniffles that I realized she was crying. Slowly, her arms came around my midsection and hugged me back.

"Jessica, it's all gonna be okay," I whispered into her hair. "This show doesn't define your worth."

"But I want to win!" she wailed into my shoulder.

My heart broke for her. "Whether you win or lose, this won't be the end of your music career. You have way too much talent for that."

"Really?" Plaintively, Jessica pulled away from me and wiped the tears off her cheeks with the back of her hand. Her blonde hair was now plastered to one side with sweat and tears, the metallic gold jacket she wore dulled in the poor lighting off stage. Yet to me, she resembled a child, a lost child who wanted nothing more than for a caregiver to approve of her.

"Without a shadow of a doubt," I swore. "I just know that big things are waiting for you."

After collecting herself for a bit, pushing the hair out of her face and swiping the globs of mascara from the corners of her eyes, Jessica gave me an apologetic smile. "I feel really bad about what I did to you," she admitted.

I shrugged. "Every good celebrity has one scandal. If that's the worst that ever happens to me, I'll consider myself lucky."

Jessica reddened, keeping her attention focused on her shoes. "I didn't watch it beforehand. I didn't realize you two weren't together."

As messed up as it was, I believed her. What's more, I could forgive her. Even though I didn't know much about Jessica's home life, I read enough between the lines to gather that her parents weren't there for her very much.

"Can we just start over?" I suggested. Holding out my hand, I said, "Hi, I'm Finley Smalls and I'm from Texas! Now you try."

She rolled her eyes, but still accepted the handshake anyway. "Hi, Finley. I'm Jessica Harris and I'm from Miami, Florida."

I grinned at her, pleased with the personal growth she'd displayed in such a short time.

The rest of our housemates surrounded us, hope shining in their faces.

"Does this mean y'all buried the hatchet?" asked Cooper.

Not wanting to embarrass Jessica, I hollered, "This means it's time to celebrate at the fire pit!"

They all laughed and whooped in agreement, but it was Gretchen who pointed out, "We can't. We've all gotta pack so we can head home. I've only got two hours to shower and get ready before I'll be heading out to the airport."

With a maniacal laugh I didn't know I possessed, I grinned at them all. "You know what that means?"

"What?" asked Jessica.

"Shots, baby!"

Joey and Kameron, ever the party animals, clapped with glee. "That's what I'm talking about! To the house!"

Shots weren't necessarily the best decision. Since it was my idea and I was running on the high of finally breaking through to the human underneath Jessica's brand of cyborg, I might have had a few too many. By the time I stumbled back to my room to throw my freshly laundered clothes in a bag, I was a bit wobbly.

Somehow without Zephyr, the room didn't offer the same comfort it usually did. Since she had a longer flight out to New York City, she left earlier in the night. My flight out to Texas was the last one heading out for the night. The poor shuttle driver had a constant loop back and forth between our house and LAX for most of the night. Zephyr left her Himalayan salt lamp on for me, so I didn't bother to turn on the lamp before I lurched inside.

Only after I dropped down on my bed did I realize there was already a person in it.

"Oy, cowgirl! D'ye drink with yer eyes closed?" Bowie sat upright, both arms holding his stomach where I had once again knocked the wind out of him by using him as a couch cushion.

"What are you doing in my bed anyhow?" The words were only slightly slurred. I was just drunk enough to have all my inhibitions disappear, but not drunk enough to where I wouldn't remember anything the next morning. That was drinking responsibly as far as I was concerned.

He settled back down, turning on his side to make more room for me. "I had to see ye before yer off." Dark brown eyes softened as they found mine.

"Oh, okay." Drunk people never question anything. Everything sounds logical and reasonable when you're three sheets to the wind.

After I successfully plucked my sneakers off, I slid further back onto the bed so that there was only a few inches between us. Our heads shared the pillow, and I couldn't figure out if I tangled my legs in his or he in mine, but the drunk devil on my shoulder liked the feeling either way.

"Ye be careful out there in the Lone Star state." Bowie bopped a finger on the tip of my nose, smirking at me in the dangerous way that made my pussy clench with need.

"Just shut up and kiss me already," I slurred, crashing my lips down on his.

God, even the strength of his kiss turned my body into putty. With a groan, Bowie bit down on my lower lip, then pulled away from me. He lay on his back, staring up at the ceiling, with an arm thrown across his forehead. I stayed tucked into his side, perfectly content where I was.

"This is not what we agreed on, Finley," Bowie murmured quietly.

I hated the way his words stung. It was ten times worse because of the tequila lining my system.

"I know," I agreed. "I'll be leaving soon anyway."

Bowie snorted. "Yeah, off to yer gobshite of an ex. I feel worlds better."

Leaning up on one arm, I tried to hide my smile as I peered down at his face. "Are you jealous?"

He rolled his eyes, but smiled up at me just the same. "I'd have to be jealous of the whole world. Ye've no idea how much ye light up a room, do ye? The stars be lookin' to ye for guidance, cowgirl. That's how bright ye shine."

This definitely wasn't the tequila doing my thinking. It was my own heart doing backflips at Bowie's estimation of me. I couldn't be held accountable for the way I pulled him close and planted my lips firmly on his once more.

Tip of My Tongue

"Miss?" A hand shook my shoulder. "Miss? You have to deboard the plane now."

Slowly, as if someone used glue to well them shut, my eyelids opened to reveal a slightly flustered flight attendant crouched at my side. Passengers tried to brush past her as she folded herself in as much as possible while attempting to wake me up.

"Where am I?" I muttered groggily. Those shots were coming back in full force.

"We've landed at the Dallas-Fort Worth airport, miss," the flight attendant explained. "Everyone is deboarding now."

My head throbbed as I sat up straighter, the sunlight filtering in through the windows with the brightness setting on high. I left LAX around two a.m. California time, meaning I was now in another time zone and the sun had just come up in Dallas. The problem was I had no recollection of getting on the plane in the first place, just that I passed out as soon as my butt hit the seat.

That was a question to answer at another time, I guessed. The last of the passengers trickled out to the gate. In a rush, I stood up and grabbed the knapsack that served as my carry on so I could follow them.

Mom, ever loving, dependable Mom, stood at baggage claim holding a large poster board that read *I get my baby back today!* For some reason, seeing that show of support sent my emotions into orbit, and I couldn't hold back the tears. I barreled into her hug like a bull escaping the pen at a rodeo.

"Oof, this is quite a greeting!" my mom laughed into my hair.

I only squeezed harder. "I missed you so much!"

"Well I've only got this one day with you to myself," she said. "Let's go make it count."

The camera crew would arrive tomorrow and stay overnight in a hotel before we all flew out together the day after. One day alone with our families was all the network would allow.

Driving to our favorite breakfast spot felt surreal in the craziest way. Nothing had changed in my hometown, and yet nothing felt the same. The same shops operated with the same employees, the traffic on 820 still moved at a snail's pace during the morning rush hour, and all of the billboards contained the same cheesy advertisements. I saw everything in a whole new light, though. Home hadn't changed; I had.

Cheers greeted us when we walked inside Wally's, a mom-and-pop style diner that we had gone to since I was a child. The place was still family owned and operated, so all of the waitresses there had watched me grow up. Now there was a sign hanging behind the counter that measured roughly four feet wide, stating:

HOME OF AMERICA'S MUSIC STAR WINNER, FINLEY SMALLS

"You guys!" I drawled, equal parts flattered, exasperated, and nervous. It suddenly dawned on me that winning wasn't just about me. My win meant my vocal coaches succeeded. That all of our family friends and neighbors who pitched in to help raise me so my mother didn't have to do it alone won, too. Everybody in my community would benefit from the win.

"Get on over here and give an old lady a hug!" cried Darlene, Wally's wife and our most frequent waitress. She came around the corner with her arms spread wide. One of my ribs might have broken from her embrace.

I backed out of it quickly. A little too quickly, so that I bumped into a table behind me and sent a man's hot mug of coffee down to his lap. He jumped up with a howl, steam actually billowing from his crotch where the coffee stained. In my haste to make it right, I snatched the nearest rag I could and tried to wipe up the offensive liquid and end the man's agony.

It was only after several other patrons started wolf whistling as they held up cell phones that I considered where exactly I was wiping. The definitive bulge in his pants would have been a better indicator for someone who paid more attention than me.

Spinning on my heel, my mom had a hand clamped over her face while Darlene fought back a laughing fit.

"That was bad, right?"

Darlene lost her fight with the giggles.

It only took an hour for the gif of my crotch clean up to go viral. Billy sent me a text that read,

> THIS IS NOT WHAT I HAD IN MIND WHEN I
> SENT YOU HOME FOR THREE DAYS.

Shoving the phone across the table to my mom, I laid my forehead down on table. We were just finishing up breakfast and one text from him was enough for me to spew it back up. I no longer wanted to do anything other than go home and hide on my mom's couch.

My phone beeped again. This time, it was a text from Bowie.

> I don't think much of my replacement, cowgirl.

"It was just an accident," my mom replied, pushing the phone back to me. "No one will remember this in a few days."

"That's your comfort?" My head snapped up as I looked at her incredulously. "I'm now an internet meme and all you've got is that 'at some point people will forget'?"

"'Fraid so." She waved Darlene down and asked for the check.

Darlene scoffed. "For Finley Smalls, it's on the house. You just go on back to L.A. and win that competition, ya hear?"

I was beginning to think coming back home had been a mistake. I was going to crumble under the pressure from everyone. They already acted as if I won the damn thing, plus Bowie expected me to win if we were going to explore something between us. That was a lot to process.

Which was probably why I was now staring at Lou, the local bartender at my favorite watering hole, about three pomegranate mojitos deep at eleven o'clock at night. Except Lou didn't know how to properly make a pomegranate mojito, so it was mostly vodka.

My mom and I made a day out of shopping and getting our nails done, something we'd never been able to afford before. That part of my day was amazing. Getting to slap my card on the counter and tell her, "Don't worry. It's on me."

But she always followed up with a statement about how nice

things would be for us after I won the competition. Like it was a sure thing. Then the swirling thoughts would start as I journeyed down the mental rabbit hole of "what if"?

Thank God for Lou and his piss poor pomegranate mojitos.

"Finley! There's my girl!"

Bloody hell, please tell me he's not here about to test my gangster!

An arm hooked around my waist, drawing me up against a man's chest. I fixed a glare over my shoulder at none other than Luke Davenport. His breath smelled faintly of beer—definitely not enough to call him wasted—and his group of friends that I always despised circled behind him like leeches. He would invite them over to play games and they would all expect me to wait on them, as if being a female automatically meant I was a maid.

I squirmed out of his grip, turning in the seat so that I faced him head on. "I am *not* your girl, Luke. How did you even find me?"

Placing both hands on my shoulders, Luke scrunched down so he could look directly in my eyes. "C'mon, Fin, we were together for four years. You really think I don't know where you like to hang out?"

Alright, fine, that might be a fair point. It wasn't like Luke was the world's worst boyfriend. He had *some* admirable qualities...sort of. But right now he was acting like a snot rag and I was not in the mood.

"Please leave me alone," I said wearily, swiveling my seat around to face the bar and taking the straw of my drink between my teeth.

Instead of leaving, Luke slid into the empty seat on my right.

"Baby, I know you've seen all the shit on social media. You have to believe how sorry I am."

I rolled my eyes. "I never doubted the sincerity of your apology, Luke. I just no longer want it."

His eyebrows gathered into a deep V on his forehead, his blue eyes turning stormy. "You're really gonna throw away all our history? Everything we've been through?"

"In the landfill down the street," I confirmed. He might have been my first love, but that didn't mean he was my forever love. I knew that now. And that wasn't even my romantic heart yearning for Bowie to be the forever one. I just literally saw how quickly life could change. Mine had, in the best way possible, my feelings right along with it.

"When Jessica Harris contacted me on Instagram, she swore up and down that you talked about me all the time. That you missed me." Luke's voice reminded me of one of my mother's whining preschool students.

I sighed. How many times did I need to rip off this Band-aid?

"Then you were grossly misinformed," I replied. "None of that ever happened. I don't miss you or our relationship. It's over, Luke."

"No." Luke shook his head. "I refuse to believe that. You just need a reminder." Both his hands shot out to grip my face and pull my lips to his.

I floundered like a damn fish. Waving my arms frantically, I tried to break away, but his grip was too strong. Lou, being the benign human being he was, would never intercede in a physical altercation like that.

Suddenly Luke jerked back like someone yanked him off the barstool by his shirt collar. Which I realized is exactly what happened when I watched Bowie throw Luke to the ground like a rag doll. Several tables went flying and glass shattered on the floor as my ex scrambled to get up.

"The lass said 'no,' mate," Bowie sneered. "Back where I come from, langers like yerself would get a right beatin'."

Never before had I heard a sentence so confusing, yet so sexy.

Bowie stood in between Luke and me, his posture rigid and his fists clenched. His long hair was pulled up in the man bun that only he could pull off, and I had never been so turned on in my life.

"What are you doing here?" I hissed at his back.

Luke managed to get back to his feet and got right in Bowie's face. "Just because she slept with you doesn't mean you're her boyfriend. Finley wanted to get back at me and I forgive her for it. So piss off, 'mate'!"

I charged around Bowie, ready to drop kick Luke's balls with my shin. "You're a rotten person!" Now that I had long acrylic nails, my hands were like weapons that I sliced through the air.

They would have sliced Luke's face if Bowie hadn't grabbed me around the middle. "Stand down, cowgirl, I got this shit fer brains!" he thundered, placing me back on the barstool.

He turned around to face Luke again, right as Luke threw a punch into Bowie's jaw. A sickening crack echoed throughout the bar as his hand went slack and Bowie's face popped to the side. He snapped back immediately, and the snarl on his face made me wince in fear. I'd never seen Bowie angry before.

"Don't they teach culchies how to fight in America?" Bowie threw an upper cut into the bottom of Luke's jaw as his other arm punched Luke in the solar plexus. My ex-boyfriend folded like a dollar store lawn chair. All of his friends jumped back with their hands up in surrender, a comical sight that I would greatly enjoy when I thought back on this moment later. The other patrons didn't give us a second thought. This was Texas—it wasn't a real bar unless a fight broke out.

"C'mon." Bowie laced his fingers through mine, leading me out of the bar. I had to step over Luke to reach the exit. "Add the lass's drinks to that gobshite's tab!" Bowie instructed the bartender on the way out.

"And that serves you right, Luke!" I added.

Sober

An Uber waited at the curb and Bowie shoved me inside. "Take us back to the hotel," Bowie said to the driver. His breathing was labored, and he kept his gaze trained on the window rather than looking at me. The grip from his hand was starting to hurt my fingers, but I was too scared to say anything. I had never seen Bowie act like this before. Normally everything rolled off him.

It was a short ride back to a hotel located only a few blocks from my mom's house. Bowie didn't say a word, just paid the driver and led me inside to the elevators. We rode up to the top floor in tense silence.

Bowie's room was at the very end of the hall, a suite with a king size bed. The room offered a wonderful view of a parking lot at the Hulen Mall. Peak luxury and all that.

I gingerly sat on the bed as Bowie went into the bathroom and washed his hands. A thin layer of sweat lined his face and neck, so I wasn't too surprised when he pulled off his shirt and tossed it into a corner of the room. He came to stand in the doorway of the bathroom, simply staring at me, both arms braced against the doorframe. The veins in his arms throbbed, making his muscles appear more formidable.

"Why are you here?" I finally asked.

"Yer efforts to clean up an oul fella's britches made me lose me marbles," Bowie admitted. It was more truthful than I expected.

"Sorry." I flashed him a sheepish grin that he didn't return, wiping the smile from my face. "How did you know where I was?"

"Yer ma. I called her first so's I wasn't wakin' anybody up and makin' a bad impression."

Wow, was I really that predictable? Did everyone know my favorite bar?

"I didn't know Luke would be there." I was pretty sure Bowie knew that, but it wouldn't hurt to remind him.

He nodded. "None of it's yer fault."

Slowly, like I faced a dangerous animal escaping a zoo, I rose from the bed and walked towards Bowie, stopping when I was only an arm's length away from him. His pupils were blown, darkened with rage, but he didn't try to stop me. He stayed silent, simply watching my every move.

"A-are you angry with me?" I managed to stammer out in a whisper. I just wanted to calm him down. I hated seeing him so volatile in his temper. That wasn't the Bowie Baird I knew.

Bowie expelled a long breath of air, some of the rage in him finally deflating. "I'm angry that spanner's mouth was the last thing you tasted."

Oh.

Based on the context, I had to assume "spanner" meant something bad. "It didn't mean anything. You can kiss me instead." I definitely wouldn't say no to that.

His muscles flexed as the arms bracketing the doorway went rigid. Now his eyes darkened in a completely different way. "Finley, we're finally alone in a bedroom with no cameras," Bowie said, his voice low. "If I kiss you, there won't be any stopping what comes next."

Could he hear the way my heart pounded in my chest? It felt loud enough for it to echo throughout the room. I wanted Bowie more than I'd ever wanted anything. Given the hungry look in his eye as he watched me, if I had to choose between him or winning *America's Music Star* in that moment, Bowie would win by a landslide. I no longer cared about how fans saw us, or if our votes were earned based on fans shipping us. None of it mattered anymore.

Carefully, I slid out of my flip flops and pushed them to the side as I slipped the strap of my knapsack over my head. Dropping it at the end of the bed, I held Bowie's sultry gaze as I slowly backed towards the bed, laying back once my knees hit the edge. I spread my legs, allowing the short sundress I wore to ride up and reveal more of my thigh.

The spell cast its intended effect as Bowie's breathing grew harder and his jaw clenched, a purple bruise just starting to blossom. He looked ready to swallow me whole.

"Whatever you say," I replied coyly, arching my back to accentuate the deep cut of my sundress. A wanton goddess, somewhere in the unknown portion of my brain purred in delight.

In three...two...one...

"Ah, fuck it," Bowie growled and lunged.

The thin band of stubble lining his jaw burned so good as he attacked my mouth with a ferocity that made my knees weak. Pinning my wrists to the bed over my head, Bowie lavished my mouth with his tongue. He needed to possess me in every way possible. Kissing me wasn't enough.

With a flick of his tongue, Bowie worked his way up to my earlobe. "I've waited for this for so long, cowgirl," he murmured. "Ye better buckle up because tonight this feckin' arse is mine!"

I moaned as his words triggered the arousal building between my legs. "That's the hottest thing ever that I don't understand!" My eyelids fluttered as Bowie's tongue sucked along the edge of my collarbone.

As he moved lower, he let go of my wrists. I immediately wound my fingers through his hair and pulled out the hairband holding it back. Long, dark waves cascaded down and tickled my skin as Bowie found the swell of my breasts. The feather light touch oddly contrasted the harsh kisses he dragged along the collar of my sundress.

"Yep." He suddenly stood up, taking all the heat with him. "That dress has to come off. Ye either help me or I rip it down the middle. Yer choice."

Was he serious right now? Luke and I had passion, but it was never like this. The wildest we ever got was the one time we had sex in the shower. He twisted an ankle and we never tried again. To be fair, I'd never seen the kind of ravenous longing on Luke that I now saw on Bowie's face.

My hesitation was too much for Bowie. Leaning down, he gripped the collar and heaved. The fabric split down my chest, parting all the way down to my belly button before he yanked again, and it completely separated. I would send Zephyr a fruit basket tomorrow to thank her for her foresight in matching all my bras to my panties. The set today was a rich blue that set off the color of my eyes. I think they might have made Bowie forget how to breathe because he reached a preternatural stillness I assumed only animals could achieve.

I leaned forward to let the fabric slip from my shoulders. Grabbing the waist of Bowie's jeans, I tugged him closer so that he stood between my legs. The ache there only compounded as I slowly inched down the zipper to free his bulge.

Holy shit, Bowie was *huge*. It defied the laws of nature. Now I understood what all the fuss was about with his groupies.

Unfurling his erection from his boxer briefs vaguely reminded me of staring down a python at the Dallas zoo. I knew both had the power to hurt me. But unlike the snake, I also knew that if I didn't handle it for myself, I would regret it for the rest of my life.

"Good. God." Blinking rapidly, I pinched myself to make sure I wasn't dreaming.

Bowie smirked.

I couldn't help myself. I licked up the length of his cock, tracing his vein with my tongue. His moan sent a ripple of desire through me as if he had a direct line to my pussy. Taking his cock in my mouth, a hum of approval crawled up my throat. Bowie grabbed onto my ponytail to hold me in place as his hips thrust forward. Saliva gathered in the back of my throat, but I couldn't swallow with how far back Bowie reached. He pumped savagely as I willed my gag reflex to settle. Strangling on his cock was obviously the best way to leave this world.

"No!" Bowie withdrew himself. I pouted, making him laugh. "Ye first, cowgirl. I can't even enjoy me self if I haven't gotten ye off."

This man was going to ruin me.

Rest in peace, Finley Smalls. You had a good run.

He wrapped an arm around my waist, and in a single throw,

had my head resting on the pillows. Settling between my thighs, Bowie used his teeth to pull down my panties. Inhaling deeply, he peppered kisses around my entrance until he slid one finger through my slit.

"Is this what I do to ye, cowgirl?" He grinned up at me from between my legs. "Do I make ye ruin yer knickers?"

The blush crept all the way from my toes to my hairline. Bowie had such a filthy mouth, and I found I actually liked it. This kind of dirty talk was foreign to me, but if this was what I had been missing out on, consider me a changed woman.

I whimpered in response.

One finger slipped inside and I saw stars. He pumped tentatively, stretching my walls, before he lowered his mouth to my clit and sucked. My knees shook so hard that my teeth rattled. I had to clench my jaw shut to prevent their clacking from ruining the moment.

Bowie groaned in satisfaction, settling between my legs to add a second finger. Even the rough calluses felt sensational. He curved his fingers inside to reach the G spot I'd read about in magazines and let me tell you, *Cosmopolitan* is not lying. That is a magic button capable of making my entire chest rise off the bed.

Within seconds, Bowie had me coming harder than I thought possible. Ripples of pleasure waved through me endlessly, the moans escaping my mouth in a crescendo with each one. He grinned up at me with a cocky smile. "I always knew yer screams would be worth it, cowgirl."

"Get. Inside. Me. *Now*," I heaved. Leaning up, I gathered his long hair in my hands and all but yanked him on top of me. Feeling his weight over me sent a shiver of thrills down my spine.

It felt right. Perfect. All the satisfaction of clicking two Lego pieces together.

With another cheeky grin, he pecked a brief kiss on my lips before hugging the edge of the bed to snag his jeans. In one swift move, Bowie had the condom opened and on, pushing up on his forearms to guide himself into my entrance. Once he was properly lined up, both hands went to my breasts, freeing them from the cups of my bra. At the same time that he twisted my nipples, sending a biting shockwave through my overstimulated system, Bowie thrust himself deep enough inside to rearrange my organs.

I cried out in ecstasy, having never experienced that kind of pain mixed with pleasure before. I loved it.

Before I could say as much, Bowie flipped onto his back, his hands gripping onto my waist to lock me in place. I straddled him, my knees no longer weakly shaking but tucked in tight at his hips.

"Show me how cowgirls ride," Bowie taunted, his tongue poking out to touch the top of his lip.

That was all the challenge I needed. Rolling my hips, all of my inhibitions went out the window as I treated his rigid cock like a pogo stick. Bowie was there for *my* pleasure, and no amount of orgasms would ever be enough.

He reached up to grope my tits again, giving each nipple another brief pinch. I leaned both my arms back to hold onto his ankles, which Bowie used as leverage to take back control, pistoning his hips faster as he chased his own high. One of his hands dropped down to my clit, circling the swollen bud, as I threw my head back with a scream.

"Ye better not be coddin' me, Finley Smalls," panted Bowie. "I need a second one from ye!"

"FUCK YES!" My voice no longer sounded like my own as I climaxed even harder. Black spots flickered across my vision.

And with the caress of an Irish prayer, Bowie cried out my name as he achieved his own release, jerking upwards until his hips stilled.

I fell forward on his chest, both of us coated in sweat. He didn't seem to mind and fiercely wrapped his arms around me to hold me in place. Glancing up at him between my lashes, Bowie pulled me upward to crash his mouth onto mine. There was more passion in that kiss than most people experienced in a lifetime, like he needed to solidify the entire encounter was real.

As Bowie drew back to stare at me, brown eyes filled with hunger and awe, I realized something.

I loved him.

This wasn't at all like the baby love I felt for Luke, which turned out to be a paltry imitation. This was a real, all-consuming kind of love. The sort of thing that could leave a person broken and shattered if they weren't careful. Yet here I was, ready, willing, and eager to give Bowie everything I had and then some.

"Finley...that was..." Bowie whispered.

"Yeah," I breathed in agreement.

"Ye definitely have a touch of Irish magic in ye now." He waggled his eyebrows proudly.

I burst out laughing, rolling off him enough so that I could curl up at his side.

"We need to clean up," I suggested lightly.

He nodded, but neither of us made to move. Bowie kept an arm around me, pinning me to his side, as we both stared up at the ceiling in rapture. I never wanted this moment to end. It was the happiest I'd felt in a long time.

Already Gone

I wasn't entirely sure how much time passed as we laid in each other's arms. Eventually the need to pee drove me into the bathroom and Bowie offered to order food through Uber Eats. After taking a brief shower to clean myself up, I realized I didn't have any clothes to put on. Bowie ripped through my dress.

The hotel had a threadbare robe hanging from the back of the door, so I donned that instead. When I exited the bathroom, I found Bowie standing by the bed, cell phone in hand, and he cast me a look so wistful that my knees nearly buckled.

"Where is this going?" I asked. Déjà vu struck me hard. This was exactly how everything with Luke spiraled out of control, and I couldn't shake the feeling that I just triggered another catastrophe by saying the words out loud.

A sensation that only amplified when Bowie sighed and sat down on the edge of the bed, fingers sliding through his hair. "Everything is complicated for us, yeah?" His brown eyes looked sullen, downcast to the tacky green carpet rather than looking at me. "We knew that going in."

I nodded. "The show's almost over, though. After that, it won't matter."

"Won't it?" Bowie asked. "Ye'll be a huge megastar and touring the world. Ye won't want to set yer sights on a bum like me."

My heart broke. My poor Irishman had no idea how special he was, thanks to the awful family that raised him. I could tell from the conviction in his voice that he truly believed what he said.

"Bowie." As gently as I could, so that I wouldn't startle him, I sat down next to him on the edge of the bed. "That's not how feelings work. Not for me, anyway." Once again, the filter on my mouth disappeared as I admitted. "And I feel deeply for you."

His eyes darted to mine with a look I recognized. Hope. It highlighted every feature of his angular face. "D'ye mean it? None of my back story or reputation changes that?"

I frowned, having never considered his bad boy persona. Zephyr, Tessa, and the rest of the girls in the house talked about it as if Bowie himself had already confirmed he had a rap sheet a mile long of groupies he'd banged. Fucking like it was a sport and he needed the practice to remain captain.

"I mean, I'm not exactly happy that you've slept with most women in the Los Angeles area," I admitted sheepishly. "But you've never given me a reason to question your motives with me."

He hadn't. If sleeping with fans mattered to Bowie, he sure missed out on a lot of opportunities over the past three months. Women hung around before and after every show. Their faces were always full of longing, eyebrows raised in a silent offer. Bowie could have had any pick of them.

That had to count for something, right?

Bowie chuckled, but it was an empty sound, like his heart wasn't in it. "I haven't slept with all the women in L.A.," he promised. "Hell, I've barely slept with anyone. None of the lasses could hold a candle to ye."

Pride glowed from my very pores. "Really?"

But he wasn't looking at me. Bowie shook his head in disbelief, eyes back on the carpet. "That gobshite did such a number on ye, cowgirl, that ye don't even realize how amazing ye are. Nothing I've shared with anyone before compares to what we just did. That was so...I mean..." His voice trailed off as he rubbed his hands together.

The sinking feeling returned to my gut, because while he was saying all the right things, Bowie still wouldn't look at me.

I clasped his hand in mine, gently squeezing. "It was for me, too," I assured him.

A tortured look crossed Bowie's face as his eyes finally met mine. "But we can't be together, Finley. Not yet, anyway," he added.

Opening my mouth to protest, Bowie brought a hand up to cover it.

"No, please listen to me. Just listen, before that brash brain o'yers starts talkin' nonsense again." His tone was pleading, begging, for me to pause long enough for him to get the words out. "I know in me bones that yer gonna win. Ye have to win, Finley! Ye have to! I don't want to stand in the way of any of what comes after. They're always gonna watch us. We'll always be in the news, and never have a moment's peace. Is that the life ye want?"

Pointedly, I glanced down at the hand that still covered my mouth. He removed it and settled back to give me his full attention.

"Bowie." Both of my hands found his, and I pulled them into my lap. Just the touch of his skin on mine grounded me in a way that I knew no one else could. Billy's words from all those weeks ago floated around in the back of my mind. "If that's the life I'm gonna have, I want to share it with someone who makes it bearable. And that's *you*. We will make it work."

He sighed heavily again and withdrew my hands from his. "I'll make ye a deal," Bowie offered. "Ye win this thing. Ye g'wan and make yer hit records, and world tours, and every other thing that only Finley Smalls could do, and in five years, if ye still believe that o' me, we'll give it a go. Magazine covers and all."

Resolution rang out through his voice. Nothing I said or did was going to change his mind.

"Why me?" I finally settled on. "Why did you even approach me on that first day?"

Bowie shrugged. "I-I just looked at ye and...knew," he finished lamely, a hint of a smile dancing across his features.

"Knew what?" I pressed.

"That ye were gonna mean more to me than anyone else has before."

I swallowed thickly as I tried to keep the tears from filling my eyes. "Then let's have tonight. I'll give you your five years as long as you give me tonight."

A wicked grin presented itself, and before I knew it, I was flat on my back again, Bowie hovering over me.

"Ye drive a hard bargain, cowgirl." Bowie nuzzled his face into my chest, pushing open the loosely-tied robe enough to expose one breast to him. With a flick of his tongue, he took the nipple into his mouth, all while gazing up at me expectantly.

There seemed to be a problem with my lungs as they no

longer drew oxygen into my body. "No wonder Irish families are so big," I commented. "Y'all really know what you're doing!"

"Nah, love, that's all me." Bowie gave me a roguish wink and pulled the belt of the robe so that the entire thing opened to him.

It wasn't until the wee hours of the morning, when a sleeping Bowie nestled against my back, holding my body tightly as if he couldn't bear the thought of letting go, that I realized he used the word "love" with me for the first time.

Beautiful Disaster

I had been fortunate in my young life to never experience a walk of shame. Not that anyone should feel shameful after a good hook up, but as I tried to figure out how to gracefully leave Bowie's hotel room the next morning in the thin robe provided by the hotel, the concept did become easier to understand. I was also running on only a few hours' worth of sleep because when a man as luscious and virile as Bowie Baird agrees to make one night count for the next five years, Lord did he mean it. Was there some sort of Celtic god of stamina that he could have prayed to? I was deliciously sore in the best way possible.

But I also needed to sneak back into my mom's house before the film crew from the show arrived or things would really escalate. Leaving the warmth of Bowie's arms around me and his soft snores in my ear proved to be far more difficult than I anticipated. Did it really matter that people knew about us? What if neither of us won the show and this was all for nothing anyway?

There was so much pressure to win. Too much, really. I longed for the days where I could hide under the covers and all the bad stuff magically went away. That's what I wanted to do right now, although hiding under these covers would be a far more exciting time. I wonder if Bowie had ever been woken up by a blow job before.

Only one way to find out.

Nestling under the covers, where his naked body in all its tattooed glory lay on display, I tentatively traced a single finger along the vein on the bottom of his semi-hard cock. It grew harder under my touch, sending a trill of delight through me. Boldy, I scooted down farther to take him in my mouth.

My lips had only just closed around the base of his shaft when Bowie's gravelly voice permeated the air. "Don't start something ye can't finish, cowgirl."

Cold air captured me as he whipped the covers off to look at me with a cheeky grin. "As lovely as the sight of ye with me in yer mouth is, we need t'get ye back home."

Ugh, I hated that he was right. The sun had already risen in the sky, and I wouldn't have much time to get ready as it was. I desperately needed a full shower...one that didn't lead to Bowie licking every inch of my skin dry. That man saw sides of me last night that had never been seen by the naked eye before.

"How am I supposed to get home?" I whined. "You ruined my only option for clothing!"

He grinned before getting up and going to his open suitcase on the floor. Chucking a black t-shirt and gray sweatpants at me, Bowie said, "Put that on. It'll be enough to get you home."

The clothes weren't as loose on me as I wanted them to be, but the heat from Bowie's gaze as I donned his clothing drove that thought from my mind. "Don't start something you can't finish!" I reminded him with a smile.

Bowie grinned again before his smile grew sad. "Our night's over, Finley. Just focus on winning this yoke."

My eyebrows rose. "One more time, in English, please."

It looked ridiculous, but the only shoes I had to put on were my platform sandals from last night. Neither of us wanted the bliss from our hotel room to end, so we both lingered by the door, doing an awkward foot shuffle to try and stall.

"I'll get an Uber," I announced flatly.

Bowie nodded, his lips pursed in a thin line. "Text me when ye make it home safe."

Nodding, my eyes darted around the room. Anywhere but his face.

He leaned down and kissed my forehead. "I'll see ye back in L.A." Our fingers wove together as he opened the door just enough for me to slip out, his bare chest gloriously displaying all the tattoos. Tattoos I was now very familiar with, having traced them with my tongue for most of the night.

A camera flashed. Then another. And another. Dozens more as I stumbled backward, blinded by the flash.

"Finley, over here!" a man called.

"Bowie, what do you have to say?" another cried.

Paparazzi filled the hallway, their cameras capturing my exit and turning a walk of shame into an execution. Bowie immediately jumped out in front of me, trying to block their view. "Go, Finley, GO!" he yelled.

Bowie's hotel room was at the very end of the hall. The only way out was through the emergency exit behind me. According to the sign, an alarm would be triggered upon opening the door, but that seemed like a far better alternative than allowing the paparazzi to continue photographing me leaving my housemate's hotel room.

There was no contest. I dove for the door, bracketing my ears with my hands as the shrill cry of the fire alarm erupted.

By the time I reached the bottom stair (and I panted a *lot* more than I cared to admit, at that point), all of the people staying in the hotel had been evacuated to the parking lot. A fire truck screeched to a halt at the front door as an assembly of firemen filed out, masks and suits on. Dozens of guests had followed me down the emergency stairs.

"Oh my god, it's Finley Smalls!" someone yelled. A few people stepped forward, outright pointing at me. Many others had their mouths open as they gawked. Indistinct murmuring broke out through the crowd.

Is that Finley Smalls?

I think it is!

Guys, that's the *Finley Smalls!*

The whole scenario seemed like a really bad Saturday Night Live parody. All of the paparazzi from upstairs had to evacuate, too, so they resumed their obnoxious catcalls as more cameras flashed. This time there were even more as hotel guests began to whip out their cell phones. Bowie pushed his way through, grabbing my hand to lead me away from the cluster of onlookers. Running away proved to be difficult in my sandals, which definitely weren't designed for any kind of physical activity, and I tried not to feel excited over the prospect of Bowie's hand in mine. If we were going to Hell in a handbasket, at least I had good company.

Bowie led us down for a few more blocks before slowing his pace. He whipped out his phone to call an Uber, both of our hands shaking.

"There's one only a minute from here," he managed to get

out. Sweat trickled down in rivulets between his abs, and his long hair plastered to the sides of his face.

"Welcome to Texas," I stated blankly.

It took a moment for the quip to sink in, but suddenly neither of us could stop laughing. Bowie's voice boomed out loudly, making me laugh even harder. We laughed until my sides ached, right up until the Uber driver pulled up.

Bowie sobered up long enough to lean into the driver's open passenger window and ask, "D'ye watch *America's Music Star?*"

The driver, a beady-eyed man in his late forties, peered at Bowie suspiciously. "Television is the government's way of controlling us. I haven't watched anything on that box in over thirty years!"

With a smirk, Bowie nodded and slapped the window frame. "Yep, this is our guy."

My mom was already up, anxiously watching the news in a robe and slippers from the couch. Thankfully she had already removed the rollers from her hair or I never would've heard the end of it. Once I entered, Bowie trying to cower behind me, Mom abruptly jumped up in alarm.

The news anchor announced that I had been involved in a practical joke involving the fire alarm at a popular area hotel. It cut to a scene in the parking lot, with all the bedlam between the paparazzi and the crowd of guests. That was the last thing I saw before my mom's bushy curls flew into my face as she enveloped me in a fierce hug.

"Finley! I've been *so* worried about you!"

Adrenaline finally crashed, and I sank gratefully into my mother's arms. My wonderful mom, who got up early on her day off because she had to watch the news and make sure I was okay. I didn't deserve her.

"Mom, I can explain—" I began, but she cut me off.

"You must be Bowie," she said, letting go of me to pull him into a hug. "I'm Jeanne. It's so great to finally meet you!"

Bowie stared at me with wide eyes over my mom's shoulder. I shrugged, indicating he should just go with it.

"How did you know to turn on the news, Mom?" I asked suddenly. An ominous feeling crept up the back of my neck, goosebumps breaking out along my arms.

"Billy called as soon as your whereabouts were leaked online. He's been trying to reach both of you," she added pointedly. I pulled my cell phone out of my pocket and realized there were close to fifty text messages and close to two dozen missed calls.

Aghast, I turned to Bowie. "Did he try your cell, too?"

With a sheepish grin, he shrugged. "I didn't want to waste any of our time together."

My mom went into the kitchen and came back out with a tray full of steaming coffee mugs. "Oh, now, isn't that just sweet, Finley? All the good men know the right things to say."

If the world could just chew me up and spit me out, that would be great. Any kind of sinkhole would do, really.

At least my mom had the good sense to provide me with the elixir of life. Coffee was the only way to have this conversation. Just the smell alone gave me a sense of relief.

"Honey, the cameras are gonna be here in a few minutes, so you might wanna go put some clothes on." My mom plopped down onto the sofa, coffee mug in hand.

I rolled my eyes. "You already know they're going to give me clothes to wear anyway."

"Oh, yes, dear, but I was talkin' to your fella there. Or did you want to be shirtless again, Bowie?"

Bowie and I exchanged a look, mine full of mortification, his trying to suppress a laugh. I'm sure my mother was very amusing when you weren't facing the gallows, otherwise known as a television crew.

"Where's the toilet?" Bowie asked.

"Just down the hall. First door on the right." My mom's eyes followed him as he strolled towards the bathroom.

"Mom, he-he doesn't have any—clothes," I finished lamely as I alternated between sitting on the edge of the chair and trying to show him where to go. It was like my legs couldn't decide to sit or stand.

"Finley, you need to calm down. This is all gonna blow over." More of her sage advice that didn't actually seem to help.

I gulped down more of the coffee, enjoying how it burned on the way down. "You said that yesterday, and look at how that turned out!"

She waved off my dramatics. "Oh, that incident at Wally's has already blown over! Just like I said it would."

"It didn't 'blow over,' Mom! I just fucked up all over again by having the press follow me to Bowie's hotel room!" I hung my head in my hands, feeling the weight of the world press down between my shoulder blades. "God, it's like I'm trying to set a record for the number of scandals in a single season of a reality show!"

"Well, that means your name will be in the books for something!" My mom's eager optimism normally made me feel a lot better. We were silver linings kind of people.

But this seemed particularly bad.

"Everyone is gonna assume that Bowie and I slept together," I told her.

She chuckled under her breath. "That's not really an

assumption, is it?" Dropping a lump of sugar into her coffee, Mom stirred loudly, the metal clanking against the ceramic mug. "You know, I like him for you. A lot better than Luke."

Declaring me to be part vampire would have been no less surprising. "But you always said he looks like a criminal."

"And he does! But that's just the old fuddy-duddy in me." She waved off my concerns like they were gnats hanging around the fruit platter.

I stood up to glance down the hall, satisfied when I heard the shower still running. Turning back to her, I tried to hush her. "Mom, what if he hears you?!"

"Fine." She held up her hands in surrender. "But just know, Bowie Baird might look like a hooligan, and he might have a bad reputation. That doesn't mean he isn't right for you."

Sighing in defeat, I sank down onto the seat next to her. "Yeah, well tell him that."

Casting a furtive glance over my shoulder, she leaned in close to whisper, "Mission accomplished."

I looked up and Bowie's brown eyes met mine. They radiated warmth, not fear. He heard what my mom said and didn't mind one bit.

"Yer ma's a bit of a genius." He sent a roguish wink my mom's way, and I swear, the woman swooned like a cartoon character.

A loud knock came from the front door, and my mom jumped up to answer it. "That'll be the TV folks, so you might wanna go change, Finley!"

Magic

"The boss wants to talk to you." Veronica held out her cell phone as soon as I stepped back into the living room after the world's fastest shower.

I tried to hide my surprise that they sent Veronica, of all people, but seeing as she looked mutinous, shock was probably the least of my problems.

Billy was on a video call and his expression mirrored the murderous intent of the production manager's. "WHAT THE HELL IS GOING ON DOWN THERE, FINLEY?" he boomed.

It was so loud that I jerked back, making the towel wrapped around the wet hair on top of my head fall down. "Um, that was rude!" I scolded him.

"Do you seriously want to compare notes on who's being RUDE right now?" Billy roared. "The network has me on a chopping block because of the stunts you've pulled so far on this trip! They're ready to fire me unless I put a leash on you!"

Now, I'm not proud to admit this, but when Billy spoke of

me wearing leashes, my mind instantly went back to the hotel last night where Bowie educated me on the sexual pleasure of choking. Apparently, they're called "hand necklaces"?

I'm a big fan.

My producer wasn't thrilled to see the dreamy look in my eye while yelling at me, however. "FINLEY! Are you even listening to me?!"

"Um, yes, sir! Sorry, Billy!" I squeaked. "What do you want me to do?"

"You have no choice—you either feed America a love story so romantic that the stars align for you or I will personally kick your ass from here to kingdom come!" A vein started to throb in his forehead as he glared into the phone.

"Wow, so you're like, *mad* mad," I theorized. I kept my tone light and thoughtful in hopes of calming Billy down.

It didn't work.

The death glare he tasered me with actually made my body break out in a cold sweat. I offered him a sheepish grin that was really more of a grimace. The screen went black, so I handed it back to Veronica, who wore a look that clearly showed her lack of amusement at my replies, too.

"It was a perfectly reasonable conclusion!" I insisted.

Veronica just shook her head and jerked a thumb over her shoulder. "The stylists are setting up for you in the kitchen. Your mom is force-feeding them omelets."

Since everyone I met from L.A. so far only ate a vegan, locally sourced, organic diet, the thought of my sweet and sassy mom trying to feed them processed food from the last chance aisle at Tom Thumb's was actually kind of funny. It could also result in a fight worthy of the World Wrestling Federation. That would hardly help get me back in Billy's good graces.

My mom's tiny kitchen looked like a Sephora bomb went off. There were makeup containers everywhere along with all kinds of different hair products. A makeup ring light had been set up in the corner behind the kitchen table, and Bowie sat in a director's style chair while one of the artists attempted to cover the bags under his eyes. She sounded frustrated at how much concealer she needed to apply.

"Have you slept at all in the past week?" the stylist asked furiously as she dabbed another layer of makeup on.

Bowie smirked at me. "I had a busy night."

My mom, God rest her soul, dropped the frying pan in her hand, splattering eggs all over the floor. "I like you, young man, but let's not push it," she told him pointedly.

He apologized to her, but shot me a cheeky wink as soon as her back was turned. The makeup stylist rolled her eyes. Someone had given him a pair of dark wash jeans and a tight black t-shirt that rolled up at the sleeves. It helped give Bowie a lot of bicep definition, and I wasn't mad about it. His long, dark hair was semi-pulled back so that it was half down, but revealed more of his face. A few stray wisps framed his face.

Maybe it was the lingering endorphins from last night, but he had never looked so sexy to me. Having him in my mom's kitchen almost seemed like a surreal experience from a dream.

"C'mon, Finley, let's do something with that hair of yours," the other stylist said. She sat at the table and pushed the food around on her plate to make it look as though she ate it. Little did she know my mom would see right through that trick.

I climbed into a second chair, perpendicular to Bowie, so that he looked at my back. As soon as I sat down, his hand reached over and rubbed soothing circles along my lower back.

"How bad was it with Billy?" Bowie asked.

Shrugging, I gave a half chuckle, half wail. "Oh, you know… he's thinking twenty-five to life looks pretty tempting after how badly I screwed this up."

Even from behind, I could sense Bowie's exasperation. "Ye didn't do anything wrong, cowgirl. We're consenting adults!"

I hesitated because I knew Bowie would not like Billy's solution. "Well, he seems pretty determined to push our love story narrative now."

The chair creaked dangerously as Bowie shot out of his chair to look me in the eye. "They can't make us do that!"

"But if that's what it takes…" my voice trailed off as I shrugged, looking at anything but Bowie. In a weird way, it might almost be a relief to just live my life out in the open. Yeah, fans were gonna speculate, but they were gonna do that regardless.

My mom sank into a chair at the kitchen table across from us. She raised an eyebrow at the hairstylist who worked on braiding my long mane of hair, then glanced meaningfully at the woman's full plate. Her con hadn't worked on Jeanne Smalls. "I don't understand. What's all the fuss about if you two get together?"

I sighed. "I just wanted to win based on my actual voice. I don't want people to vote for me just because they like my relationship."

There was a blank pause for several seconds before my mom roared with laughter. After another brief pause, the stylists joined in. Bowie and I glanced at each other, an eyebrow raised in question.

They're all a bunch of lunatics!

"Um, what am I missing?" I asked my mom incredulously.

She wiped actual tears from her cheeks as she tried to calm

down enough to answer. "Honey," Mom began, "people are gonna vote for you for all kinds of different reasons! It's a television show!"

Rolling my eyes, I settled back into my chair. "Well I know that, obviously, but—"

"No, Finley, there's no 'but' here," my mom insisted. "It's like voting for president. Sometimes you just gotta pick the lesser of two evils! Besides, if you think for one second that everyone in America cares more about who you're dating than the sound of your voice, you're crazy! People like happy. And baby girl, Bowie makes you happy. Doesn't take a reality show to see that." More laughter burst forth from both the stylists.

I was dumbfounded. My jaw actually fell open. Wasn't my mother the one who warned me that reputations had a way of lingering? And now she was basically telling me to ignore her own advice?

"Mom, how can you say that? Don't you want me to win because of my voice?"

She stood up, taking the plates over to the sink. "Finley, you are more than just your voice. Have you ever stopped to consider maybe people are just voting for *you*?" Casting me a pointed look over her shoulder as she started washing the dishes by hand, my mom continued. "If they want you to win, that means they want you to win. It's that simple."

"C'mon, everyone! Look alive! We're on a tight schedule!" Veronica swept into the kitchen, clipboard in hand, and snapped her fingers in the stylists' direction.

Bowie's presence at my back felt like a magnet. Was I really overthinking it? Could it be as simple as Mom said? He and I needed to talk, but I wanted privacy for that conversation. It wasn't something we could talk about in present company.

I wanted to believe she was right. I wanted to believe that I could have it all. That there was some version of this story where I came out on top with Bowie *and* won the competition. But me winning meant all of my friends would lose, including Bowie. He deserved it just as much as I did.

Could I take that away from him?

The Trouble With Love

Bowie and I spent the day with my mom and the camera crew. We visited all of my favorite places at home, plus went to some of my old stomping grounds. Bowie couldn't get over what my high school looked like, and asked if all American schools resembled prisons. We even got the chance to go inside and talk with some of my old music teachers. I had a hard time keeping the tears at bay when they interviewed my old choir teacher, Mrs. Firkus, and she did nothing but sing my praises. She always believed in me.

I didn't want to let her down now.

The marching band along with some of the student clubs led a small parade down the street closest to my high school. Bowie and I got to sit in a convertible, only we sat on the back of the car where we would be visible. There was a far larger crowd lining the streets than I expected, including all of the staff from Wally's and Lou, the bartender. Everyone shouted my name as they held up signs declaring me *America's Music Star*. I had so much more support than I imagined, and it made me really emotional. If I didn't have Bowie's hand to squeeze, I doubt I would have made it through the event without succumbing to blubbering hysteria.

All of these people wanted to see me win, many of them total strangers. Appearing on the show was so much bigger than I originally thought it would be. I just wanted to sing for a living, but I never really let myself imagine what that would actually look like at this level. America got to know me over the course of three months. They not only voted for me, they cheered for me. Many of them were already buying tickets to our national tour. If I won, they might get tickets to the headlining world tour that came afterwards.

There might be a little girl in the crowd right now who wanted to be a singer someday *because* of me.

Towards late afternoon, Veronica set up chairs in front of the high school's sign so that we could do a "candid" interview. She would ask us questions, although her portion would be edited out later for the show so that it just looked as if Bowie and I were discussing things on our own. I was a bit nervous about it; although he and I hadn't done anything to hide our affection, we hadn't been overt with it either.

"So," Veronica said from her own chair next to the camera, "how does it feel to be back home now, Finley?"

Grinning, I gushed, "Oh, it's so rad! I can't believe how much support everyone here is giving me. Definitely makes me want to give it my all in the finale. I don't want to let anybody down."

"What about you, Bowie?" Veronica asked. "What do you think of Finley's hometown?"

"I can see how it made a mark on our Finley," he replied smoothly, tossing me a quick wink. "Everyone's been warm and inviting, just like her."

"It doesn't make you nervous to meet Finley's mom?" Veronica pressed.

If I wasn't on camera, I would shoot laser beams at her from my eyeballs.

Bowie shrugged good-naturedly. "Finley's ma is important to her, which makes her important to me. Nothing to be nervous about."

My heart skipped a beat at how natural the words sounded leaving his lips. Like he meant every bit of it. From behind the cameraman, I saw my mother, who stood watching, clutch her hands to her chest as though he won her over just from that answer alone.

Love really didn't have a good timeframe. It could strike at any time, whether you were ready for it or not. And as I sat there, watching Bowie comfortably answer question after question where he put me on a pedestal, making my mother practically melt, and indicate I was the one America should vote for, I realized something.

It didn't matter if the viewers knew it or not. I loved Bowie, regardless of the show, and that was unlikely to change. My feelings couldn't detract from a win and they would definitely cushion the blow if I lost. There were other ways to pursue a music career. I had certainly learned enough from this experience to know that staying in L.A. to chase my dreams was the right call, no matter what. Hell, Bowie and I could do it together.

I loved Bowie Baird. And he deserved to hear that from me, so none of the voices in his head could convince him that his stepfather was right.

Having long since tuned Veronica out, I had no idea what she was saying or who was supposed to answer her latest question. I simply leaned over the arm of my chair and planted my lips on Bowie's.

They were as strong and steadfast as always, providing the same kind of comfort and assurance I had come to rely on from him. Kissing Bowie felt like coming home. Wasn't that the whole point of the visit?

Bowie's callused fingers grazed my cheek as he held me close for a moment to extend the kiss before slowly pulling away on an exhale. "What'd I do t'deserve a kiss like that?" he whispered.

"I-I love you, Bowie," I breathed.

For the first time ever, it didn't feel scary to say the words out loud.

I remembered saying them for the first time to Luke. A jackhammer had taken up residence in my stomach, to the point where I thought I might vomit rather than get the words out. We had been dating for over a year before I said them out loud, and his careless response had been to shrug and go, "Cool. I love you, too, I guess."

But just like all things, Bowie was different. Saying the words out loud only solidified their existence, and as sure as I was that the sun would set in the sky as the night crossed the horizon, I knew he felt it, too.

Sure enough, a smile so pure and golden stretched across his face. Both dimples appeared in his cheeks, and his brown eyes swam with joy as they drank in every detail of my face. "It's about time ye said it, cowgirl."

His hands cradled my face as he returned his lips to mine once more. In my girlish fantasy, fireworks erupted behind us.

Only it wasn't fireworks. It was the cheer of the production crew and my mother, making my face go beet red. The entire thing had been recorded.

"FINALLY!" my mother cried. Her hands and gaze were raised upward as though Jesus himself would call down to agree with her.

Bowie and I both burst out laughing. Mine continued until my ribs hurt and tears streamed down my face. After a while, when we were all calm enough to talk, the interview resumed. We alternated answers, and I was lighter than air.

Probably because Bowie's hand remained firmly clasped in mine the entire time.

Walk Away

My mother would not hear of Bowie staying at the hotel another night. We would have to catch another red eye back to L.A., and Veronica pulled some strings so that we could be on the same flight and sit together. Apparently, the network was very appreciative of our on-screen declaration of love as it would guarantee them certain ad placements. Love was lucrative in Hollywood.

Once I moved out after graduation, my bedroom turned into my mother's office/craft space, so there wasn't really anywhere for Bowie to sleep. She insisted we take her bed, waving off our protests until we were nearly exhausted. "But there better not be any funny business," Mom said firmly, turning into Teacher Mode and pointing a stern finger in both our faces. "That door is to remain open and my daughter unsullied."

She knew it was a bit too late for that, but I had to admire Mom's denial.

I was ready to crash after a long day of filming outside and greeting everyone at my high school. The network didn't want either of us to sing because they didn't want to risk our voices so close to the finale, so instead we held a mini-singing contest for other people in the community where Bowie and I were the judges. Flasks started popping up in the crowd and the contestants became consistently drunker as time went on. All in all, it was a lot of fun and not much different than the fateful night of karaoke that started me on this journey in the first place.

I readily agreed to keep my hands to myself in my mom's bed because even my bone marrow felt tired. Veronica and the team dropped Bowie and I off long after the sun had set with a harsh reminder that she would be back around two a.m. to take us to the airport. My eyelids could barely stay open long enough to promise her that I would be ready.

Judging by her pursed lips and skeptical eyebrows, Veronica didn't believe me.

I swear, there's no faith in the world anymore.

Bowie let me lean on him as I stumbled up the walkway, pushing past the overgrown shrubs and kicking mulch out of the way. He stifled a laugh when I tripped stepping into the house and apologized to the door frame. My mom had waited up for us on the couch.

"I love you so much, Finley," she whispered as she hugged me once more. I told her she didn't need to get up early to see us off, so this would have to do as our final goodbye. "Win or lose, I'm proud of you."

Despite my exhaustion, I squeezed her tighter, a lump forming in my throat. I needed to hear those words from her. Being this close to the finale was sort of like looking down the barrel of a gun for Russian Roulette. The anticipation could make you pee yourself if you really thought about it. Mom was the only person I knew who could keep me grounded.

"You're gonna come in for the finale show, right?"

She nodded. "Wouldn't miss it for the world. I already bought my ticket and got my hotel information from Frowny Face."

"Frowny Face?" I repeated, one eyebrow raised.

"That production manager of yours!" my mom whispered conspiratorially, as if she expected there to be a live feed somewhere in the room. "She's scary!"

Laughing, I nodded and stumbled down the hall. "That she is. G'night, Mom!"

Falling onto the bed, I took a deep inhale of the sheets, the comforting smell of my mom's favorite fabric softener reminding me that I was home and loved. Bowie came into the room a minute later, and in my exhausted daze, I could have sworn he only covered me with a blanket. It was impossible to know because within seconds of hitting the pillow, sleep came.

***

COFFEE. Freshly brewed, hot coffee. The only scent strong enough to pull a sleeping Finley Smalls from the dead.

The clink of a ceramic mug being set down along with the heavenly aroma made me blearily open one eye. Sure enough, there was a steaming hot cup on the nightstand beside me. The other eye shot open and I sat upright. Bowie leaned on the windowsill, watching me with a bemused expression as he drank from his own mug.

"I wasn't sure if ye'd wake up or not," he mused. "Ye slept like a bleedin' Disney princess!"

It was pitch black outside, save for the orange glow of the solitary street light. According to the time on the clock radio sitting on the nightstand, I had approximately ten minutes until Veronica and the crew showed up to take us to the airport. Just enough time to drink coffee, brush my teeth and hair, and throw all my toiletries into a bag.

For some reason, Bowie looked like he hadn't slept at all. There were noticeable circles under his eyes and he yawned into his mug as he took another drink. Before I could ask about it, though, he tipped his head back to drain the mug and crossed the room to the door.

"We've only got a few minutes," he reminded me. "Veronica likes to be early." A few seconds later I heard the muffled sounds of the water running in the bathroom as he finished getting ready himself.

I'd like to commemorate that for once I was actually on time. Waking me up with a strong cup of coffee is the way to go. Bowie waited for me at the front door, just barely visible from the light filtering in through the living room window. My mom slept soundly on the couch, the quilt rising and falling evenly with her breaths. Her kindness to Bowie and the crew over the past couple days had been just what we needed. She deserved so much more than the hard life she had lived thus far.

Right then and there, I made a vow to buy her the nicest house in the neighborhood as soon as I won. She needed this victory as much as I did.

Bowie took the duffel bag from me and slung it over his shoulder along with his own. Lacing his fingers through mine, I could just make out the soft hint of a smile as he led me outside. Veronica's car pulled up in front of the house.

Except...I was able to easily walk down the cement pavers to get there. All of the overgrown shrubs and weeds were gone, my mother's flower beds neatly arranged once more. It gave the house a facelift.

I stopped, mouth gaping as I turned in a circle to take it all in. I looked back at Bowie in wonder.

He lifted a shoulder, eyes determinedly staying off my own. "Don't make it into something," he said quietly.

"Bowie..." my voice trailed off as I tried to find the words. "Did you do this? In the middle of the night?"

His hand went to the back of his neck, squeezing as if he needed to rid the tension there. "I just figured yer poor ma had been so nice and didn't want it to look like she had a manky gaff, so it's best to just help. Plus, then she didn't have t'worry about the sleeping arrangements. I don't want her thinkin' o' me as a tool just out to ruin her daughter's purity."

Even though there were tears lining them, I rolled my eyes at his assessment. "Bowie, I lived with Luke for almost three years. The purity ship has already sailed."

Bowie stepped closer so that I could feel his minty breath on my face. "Yeah, but I'm a right side better than that eejit. I want her to like me."

I smiled warmly. "She does. Trust me, she wouldn't have let you stay here if she didn't. Now you're gonna be exhausted all day."

He shrugged as if it were no big deal. Lacing his fingers through mine once more, we walked towards the waiting SUV. "I can sleep on the plane. Yer worth it, Finley Smalls."

Basking in the glow of his praise, I barely even noticed the ride to the airport. There was hardly any traffic on the roads with it being the middle of the night, and we pulled up to the departures entrance in record time.

What I wasn't expecting was to see Luke there waiting.

He stood forlornly in front of the glass doors, watching us exit the car with a puppy dog look of sadness. Guilt tore through me as I spotted the red mark on his face from where Bowie clocked him.

Clearly, he wanted to see me, so we might as well get it over with.

"What are you doing here, Luke?" I asked him. Bowie hovered a few feet away, just inside my peripheral.

"I guess I just wanted to apologize. And ask one last time if there's any chance for us," he added sadly. Glancing at Bowie's glaring form, it was obvious that Luke already knew the answer to that question.

Part of me almost felt sorry for him because of it. "Luke, this is getting really old. You know I'm with Bowie now. I love Bowie. I'm sorry if that hurts you, but there's nothing you can say or do that's gonna change my mind."

He nodded sadly, kicking an imaginary pebble with his shoe. "I knew you'd say that. I really made a mess of things with us, huh?"

I leaned back on one foot to quizzically look him up and down. "Maybe. Or maybe it was supposed to happen this way, you know? I never would have gone to L.A. and had this opportunity if we were still together. My life kinda fell into place as soon as you fell out of it."

Luke winced as though I smacked him.

"So I think it's time you walk away and let go," I finished.

"Yeah." Luke scrubbed a hand down his face before stuffing his hands into his hoodie pocket. "Good luck, I guess."

Smiling, I gently patted his shoulder as I passed. Bowie's arm wound around my waist as soon as we stepped away, and although he cast an angry look back at Luke over our shoulders, I didn't need to.

Any residual feelings I had for Luke Davenport died out a long time ago.

Long Shot

"Ooh, Finley Smalls, you are about to make me a *very* rich man!" Billy gleefully rubbed his hands together as he greeted me. We had just arrived back at the house in time to begin a long day of rehearsals. Nicola demanded an extra two hours of practice time with us to make up for our trips, and even with coffee and a good nap on the plane, I didn't think I would be functional by the end of the day. This kind of greeting from Billy only served as a reminder for how precious my time at home had been.

"And why is that, Billy?" I asked, my voice a dull monotone.

He gleamed. "I just saw the rough footage of your little declaration to Bowie! The audience is gonna eat this up like candy!"

"I'll post your address so they know where to send the dental bill," I quipped, turning on my heel to go into the dance studio. Billy sputtered behind me, but I tuned him out.

"FINLEY!" Zephyr pulled me into a fierce hug. I missed her bright energy so much.

"Please don't leave me again," I muttered into her hair,

which was now straightened into long caramel waves down her back.

She laughed. "Seems like you found ways to entertain yourself without me. First that crotch shot on an old man, and then sneaking out of Bowie Baird's hotel room, half naked?! What has gotten into you, girl? I mean, other than Bowie, of course!" She elbowed me playfully as we both burst out laughing.

"I'm just ready to get back in the swing of things here," I admitted. Having the structure of the show, despite how long and demanding it was, had somehow become comforting to me. I actually thrived under that kind of schedule. Hopefully that boded well for a future in the industry. I needed to always stay busy and have a dozen projects to focus on.

Nicola called us all to order, ending the reunions taking place across the studio. Jessica gave me a small smile from across the room, which was tremendous progress for her. Maybe the time apart did everyone some good. Now we could all put our efforts into making the finale larger than life.

DID I say larger than life? I meant finding a way to off our dance instructor without anybody noticing.

Nicola was ruthless in the studio. Rather than make the choreography a little easier on us since we had less time to practice, she decided we were going to have two main group dance numbers. Our finale would feature other recording artists' performances along with a song from each of us, plus our new original. The network intended for it to be a three hour broadcast, but the live footage from the app and website would start an hour prior. Viewers could buy a membership to be able to access that content early, which had already brought in over a million dollars.

I swear, people needed to doublecheck the kinds of things they spent their money on.

Since one of the dance routines would be part of the subscriber content, Nicola demanded sheer perfection. Which would have been great if we had more than three days to learn and rehearse both routines. And if we were professional dancers. Some of the ways in which she expected my body to move just weren't natural!

To top it all off, we had to record our song with our mentors this week. Each one of us would randomly get pulled out for two hours at a time so that we could meet our mentor at the recording studio, put the final touches on our original song, and then get the track laid. Even though it had been less than a week, I could barely recall the song Scott and I worked on, let alone sing it. The finale was going to be a disaster if I didn't pull it together.

Actually, scratch that. The finale would be a disaster either way.

All I could picture were the faces in the crowd at the parade back home. How could I disappoint them? Could I even go back there again with my tail between my legs? Being on *America's Music Star* was no small feat, but did it even mean anything if I didn't earn the top spot? History rarely remembered the losers.

As I looked around at all of the strangers who became friends who became family, it dawned on me that it wasn't just my own future at stake. If I won this show, it meant Gretchen couldn't leave her abusive husband. It meant Riley's mom wouldn't have enough money to put him through college. I didn't even want to consider what God would do to me if Miles didn't get the money for his church. Was there some sort of Divine retribution involved in that?

Every performer in this room deserved that victory. So how could I reconcile taking away their moment just so I could selfishly have my own?

How could I look my mother in the eye if I didn't?

It was the strangest position to be in. I didn't want to hurt anybody, but there was only ever going to be one winner. Knowing Billy, there was already some sort of crazy scheme in place on the off chance there was a tie in the votes.

"Okay, c'mon," Bowie said, startling me out of my musings. "Git outta that head of yers." He held out a hand to help me up from where I sat on the ground, having flopped down on the five minute break Nicola granted us.

If only it were that simple. Flashing him a look to show him my irritation, I accepted his hand and rose to stand. "How do you know what I was even thinking about?"

He snorted. "Because ye get this look on yer face like yer trying to solve a math problem with goldfish. Whatever's on loop in that brain o' yers can shove off, alright? It's all gonna be fine."

Bowie could say that. He didn't feel the weight of the world on his shoulders over winning the competition.

Veronica saved me from having to answer by popping her head in the door and calling for me. "The car's out front. It's your time with Scott."

I flashed Bowie what I intended to be a reassuring smile, but it only made frown lines appear in his forehead. Rather than have Veronica's head explode from throwing her schedule a minute behind, I waved and left the room.

This time when I arrived at the recording studio only Aniston was present. She sat at a makeshift desk, typing a mile a minute on her laptop. She didn't bother greeting me, and with her noise canceling headphones on, I was too intimidated to ask her where Scott was. Crossing over to the actual recording area, Aniston made no move to stop me, so I let myself inside.

The recording booth felt like hallowed ground, and despite my anxiety over the finale, being inside the booth made me giddy with excitement. Just to warm up, I sat down at the grand piano in the center of the space and started playing a melody. Messing around, really. I didn't have any of the chords written down or any lyrics yet. Still, I hummed along, mindlessly plugging in words here or there. Whatever it was, it sounded nostalgic. Hopeful, even.

"YES!" A booming voice from behind sent me skyrocketing off the bench.

Clutching my chest, I turned to find Scott Baxter standing in the doorway, both hands triumphantly raised over his head. His blonde hair wasn't gelled to perfection like I was used to, and he wore a plain t-shirt and loose sweatpants—far more casual attire than I had ever seen him wear before.

"THAT'S the song we should be recording!" Scott continued. "What's it called? Do you have the bridge worked out yet?"

My eyes widened in surprise. "That was just me goofing around. It's nothing."

Scott shook his head. "No, Finley, that's a hit song."

The urge to check for earwax made my fingers twitch. I had to have misheard him though, because it sounded like he said the errant music I played while lost in thought sounded like a hit song.

Instead, I chuckled awkwardly, pointing a finger gun at him to complete the insanity. "You're a funny guy, Mr. Scott Baxter. Funny, funny, *funny*."

"I'm telling you! Play it again and I'll show you."

Even though I knew it was crazy, I figured it would only benefit me in the long run to humor a songwriting legend. I sat back down at the piano and started playing the notes again. This time through I noticed the chord progression on my own. Scott picked up a guitar and roughly played a riff over the notes, adding an edge that I really liked.

"Sing along, Finley," he instructed.

"I don't have any lyrics for it!"

He rolled his eyes. "Then just sing whatever comes to mind!"

My brow furrowed in concentration. I had no idea what to say. Yeah, I wrote the odd thing down here or there in my song journal, but I never wrote a full song, beginning to end. It was all a random mix.

I thought of Bowie and the anticipation of what was to come.

I thought of Zephyr and the warmth of her smile.

I thought of all of my housemates and how much they made me want to be a better person.

I thought of my father, who never thought I would be good enough.

I thought of my mom and her unending light.

So much waiting at the top,
I know I need it all to stop.
It's all just spinning in my head.
Listen to the laugh instead.
It's just a carousel.
Round and round
Like a carousel.
Only time will tell,

Can I make it off?
Or will I drown?
On this carousel.

THERE WAS an electric charge to the air as the final note died out. A reverence, if you will. I couldn't tell where those lyrics came from or why I sang them, but I oddly felt lighter now. Like just giving them a voice took a burden off my shoulders.

Scott grinned in satisfaction. "Now that's what I'm talking about!"

I couldn't help smiling back. "But I only have ninety minutes left. How are we gonna finish writing and recording an entire song in an hour and a half?"

"If we go over, we go over. Sometimes that's just how it goes." He shrugged as if it didn't really matter. Which I'm sure to him, it didn't.

"You can't give me special treatment or else my song will be forfeited from the competition," I protested. "I *need* to win this thing!"

"No, you need to keep making music," Scott corrected me. His fingers idly played more riffs on his guitar as he spoke, a move so similar to Bowie that I smiled. It must be a guitarist thing. "Trust me, whether you win or lose this show, you're gonna be making music. You've got 'it,' Finley, whatever 'it' is. I see a long career ahead of you."

Okay, nobody warned me that I needed to bring tissues with me!

"Really?" I asked in a weak, watery voice. It would be so uncool to cry in front of Scott Baxter, but then again, if he scanned social media at all in the past seventy-two hours, he saw me half naked, running from a hotel room. Would a few tears actually ruin that kind of street cred?

Scott gave me a soft smile. "It's time to start believing in yourself, Finley. If you can't believe in yourself, the audience won't either. Start living each day as if you're meant to be number one."

I let his wisdom seep in, willing myself to commit the advice to memory.

"C'mon," he said. "We've got a lot of work to do and not much time to get it done."

Couldn't Be Better

As unlikely as it sounded, Scott's advice took root. Over the next few days, I really started to believe that I could win. Early polls showed that I was in the lead. Bowie was a close second, with Miles right on his tail. That meant that a good performance could make or break America's votes.

A great performance? Well, you might as well put the champagne on ice now.

That was why I kicked it into high gear. Most of my housemates battled burnout; going home and seeing their families again had only reinforced how homesick they felt. So while they used their spare time to make plans to return home and solidify their next steps, I only focused on the finale. I needed it to be the best performance I ever gave. The eyes of the world would be on me.

While Bowie definitely noticed the increase in my determination, he never said a word. Every night he came to find me in one of the music rooms I snuck in just to steal a kiss and wish me luck.

Although we hadn't actually made the promises out loud, I assumed that after everything that happened back in Texas, his five year promise was out the window. We were basically a couple now anyway. I only sank into bed long enough to get in a decent nap, but whenever that happened, I joined him in his room. Bowie had a room to himself since Riley stayed at a hotel with his mom. That meant I could come and go freely without disturbing anyone.

After careful consideration of the finale's theme, "The Greatest Inspiration," I chose my favorite song by my favorite female vocalist of all time. In my twisted mind, that meant I had even more of an obligation to blow everyone away while singing it. My inspirational song choice and my original song would ultimately pave the way to victory and the $2.5 million contract, or I would move into a small apartment in L.A. with Bowie. We could find gigs together and work the music scene until someone noticed us.

But on the day before the finale, my fragile plan disintegrated when Billy and Veronica arrived to group rehearsals and asked for Bowie to join them. Both of their faces held somber, thoughtful expressions, which were completely out of character. It made the hairs on the back of my neck stand up.

Bowie was gone for close to an hour. By the time he came back, we were breaking briefly for lunch. I tried to catch him as everyone headed into the kitchen, but Zephyr snagged me first. She and I promised each other to have lunch together since it was our last one in the house. I still hadn't managed to reconcile my status quo with the next chapter that didn't include sharing a bedroom with Zephyr. She was my soul sister.

"What do you think they wanted with Bowie?" I whispered to her. With my tight schedule, I only wanted to spend fifteen to twenty minutes eating, so I shoveled ramen noodles in my mouth like they would disappear if I didn't eat them fast enough.

Zephyr shrugged. "They've been pulling everybody in one by one. I'm sure we'll each have a turn."

"Really?" Was I that self-involved now that I only noticed things that happened to my (possible) boyfriend and me?

She nodded.

For some reason, the gesture brought on the waterworks. It hit me like a truck that I would no longer spend my days rehearsing dance routines before sharing nightly stories with Zephyr. As much as I wanted to move on to whatever came next, I hated the thought of losing our time together.

"Promise that we'll bunk next to one another on the bus during the tour?" I suddenly asked her, dabbing tears from my eyes.

Zephyr rolled her eyes. "You honestly thought I'd do it any other way?" She pulled me into a fierce hug, rubbing soothing circles on my back. "You can't lose my friendship, Finley Smalls. You're stuck with me for life."

I grinned into her hair.

"Finley, come with me," Veronica said from the doorway. The somber look was back, as if she had to transport me to a funeral.

"But...my ramen..." I whimpered. I held up the cup of noodles as if that would change her mind, but Veronica merely glanced at her watch. Passive aggressive much?

We walked down the hall to a practice room where Billy and a few other people sat at a folding banquet table. They all wore expensive looking suits like him, but I didn't recognize any of them. I wasn't sure if they could be from the network.

"Finley!" Billy beamed at me, holding his arms wide in greeting. "So nice of you to join us! Have a seat."

A lone chair sat on the opposite side of the table. All eyes zeroed in on me as the light conversation stopped the moment my butt hit the seat. Even though I had no reason to be nervous, a small shiver trailed down my spine.

"Do people have to be read their rights before the torture begins?" I joked.

Billy snorted, but the rest remained impassive. Not my toughest crowd yet, but I'd win them over.

"Finley, allow me to introduce C.D. Weiss from Ragamuffin Records, Belle Burroughs from Cali Records, Vince Paducah from the Paducah Entertainment Group, and Bishop King from Albatross Studios."

Each one of them nodded towards me as Billy said their name. None of them offered me a smile. This had to be what zoo animals felt like as people watched them through glass everyday.

"Bishop King, huh?" I asked. "Your parents had high hopes for you!"

...Crickets. Jesus, did these people know *how* to smile?

"They're here today to talk to you about your future," Billy continued. He had gotten used to ignoring my ill-timed humor, after all. "Obviously there can only be one winner on the show, but that doesn't mean you don't have a future in the entertainment industry. All four of these companies are eager to work with you."

A gasp escaped. That wasn't what I expected him to say.

"What are your goals, Finley?" the man on Billy's left, C.D. Weiss, asked. "We all think you're born to perform. You've got what it takes."

I warmed from this praise, even if it was delivered by

someone who couldn't smile. "Thank you, sir. Singing is all I've ever really wanted to do."

They all nodded. Belle spoke next. "If you don't win *America's Music Star*, we are each prepared to offer you contracts for a recording deal. They won't be equivalent to what Billy can offer, but we wanted to meet with you and throw our hats in the ring, so to speak." She cocked her head as she assessed my reaction.

Which was for my jaw to fully drop open like it could catch flies. "All of you," I repeated slowly, "want to work with me? Y'all want me to record more music?"

Billy leaned back in his chair, a smug expression on his face. "I told you, Finley, you were meant to be on this show. I know talent when I see it. Even if you don't win tonight, this is not going to be the end of your career in music."

All five of them watched me expectantly as I gaped at them like a damn fish. I didn't know what to say. The urge to burst into tears crossed my mind.

But then I pictured my mother's face and knew the sage advice she would give me if she were in the room with me. "Let me talk to that entertainment lawyer first," I replied. He had negotiated a great contract with me for the Avalon hair care commercials.

Judging from the satisfied look Billy wore, consulting an entertainment attorney was the right thing to do. "I'll get him here after the show for you," he promised.

Veronica came up from behind, tapping on her watch to indicate our time was running out. Billy nodded to her and gestured towards the door. "Good luck tonight, Finley," he said.

The rest of the assembled group echoed the sentiment.

"Don't tell any of your cast mates about this meeting. Not everyone will have the same opportunities you do." Billy grimaced, likely disappointed that he couldn't offer everyone the same kind of deal. Billy might be drama-hungry, but he was a decent person underneath it all.

I nodded, my throat too thick with emotion to respond. No matter what, I could keep making music. Obviously, I wanted to win the show. Even the record people themselves admitted *America's Music Star* was a better deal. But they had thrown me a lifeline that removed a substantial amount of pressure for tonight. I could actually *enjoy* the finale, knowing my career was only just getting started.

I was more than ready.

"Finley, have we not established by now that I know what I'm doing?!" Ashford barked at my side. Using a pin, the waist of my dress pulled in tighter, accentuating more of my figure than I liked.

I rolled my eyes in the mirror. "This isn't me questioning your artistry! This is me telling you, I already want to throw up so putting me in a dress that doubles as a body condom isn't going to help!"

This was what I got for allowing Ashford to create my final look of the night without any of my input. I should've known better.

"Well, it's my name in the credits as the head costume designer, so this is what's happening!" he snapped back, viciously stabbing more pins into the fabric. "You've lost so much weight since I first started on this dress, it's not my fault that I have to tuck it in!"

Okay, maybe he wasn't so bad.

"Aw, Ash, you sure know how to win a girl over!"

He shot me a look of annoyance that bordered on violence. "Do not call me 'Ash.' You know the rules!"

Even though the man drove me crazy with all the sparkles and high heels he required me to wear each week, I would miss Ashford after this. His ire had become oddly comforting. He was a snobby little thing, but I loved that about him.

"C'mon, Ashy, bring it in!" I threw my arms around him before he could run away.

His sputtered protests made it hard to hold back my laughter. "What? Unhand me! You Americans and your incessant hugging!"

I only squeezed tighter. After a few seconds, he relaxed and loosely wrapped his arms around me.

"Fine," Ashford admitted in a begrudging tone. "I might actually miss you after this."

"What was that?!" I shouted, making my housemate's heads pop up from various points of the costume closet, where they were all looking at their own outfits and accessories for the night. "Did you just admit that you love me, Ashford?!"

"Unhand me, you little minx!" Ashford pushed away from me, but there was a distinct twinkle in his eye as he said it. "You cannot soil this blazer. Stella McCartney herself gave it to me."

Zephyr and Tessa came around the corner, both of them already dressed, hair and makeup flawless. Zephyr wore a fuchsia mini dress that showcased her endless legs. Her long hair hung pencil straight down her back. Tessa had on an emerald green dress that fanned out in a A-line skirt, Chiffon stretched up to her neck, creating something that reminded me of the looks at the high school dance in *Grease*. She wore her hair in an elaborate twist on the back of her head to complete the musical movie comparison.

"C'mon, Finley!" Tessa held out her hand. "Our families are starting to arrive!"

Since today was the big finale, all the contestants were allowed to invite their family members to sit in the audience. They were given special seats where the cameras could capture their reactions to our performances. We would only have five minutes or so to see them before the bonus content streaming started, and even though I had just seen my mother, I needed her to ground me on what could very well be the most important night of my life. In just a few short hours, my entire world would change. You kinda wanted your mom there when that happened.

Accepting Tessa's offered hand, Zephyr wrapped an arm around my waist as we headed down to the green room together. I had come to learn from my time on the show that green rooms didn't necessarily have to be green in color, but were primarily just used as an area backstage where people could go to relax and wait before a show began. Billy and Veronica hardly ever gave us a chance to use the one here since they were such sticklers for punctual rehearsals.

There were quite a few people gathered inside already. It made me happy to see two people who strongly resembled Jessica talking to her with smiles on their faces. She flashed me a soft smile over her shoulder as we passed and I winked at her.

Craning my head to look around, Tessa broke off with a squeal as soon as she spotted her fiancé. He was a handsome man with dark brown hair and a wide smile. Good for Tessa.

"Hey, there's my family!" Zephyr pointed to a corner where a large cluster of people waited, all of them different ages, sporting t-shirts with Zephyr's face on them. Underneath they read, *Our Music Star!* in bold letters.

I laughed. "Oh, they definitely claimed you! Go-I'll catch ya later!"

Turning in a slow circle again as Zephyr ran off to greet her family, it only took a moment for me to find my mom in the crowd. But what nearly made me faint was that my dad and stepmom stood with her. Both Mom and Deborah had big grins on their faces, pride filtering out of every pore, while my father merely looked uncomfortable.

"Mom!" I allowed her to envelope me in a tight hug, giving myself a moment to gather comfort and courage from her embrace. Underneath it all, I was still a little girl who needed her mother for strength. "I'm so glad you came!"

"Oh, Finley, sweetheart, we're just so proud of you!" Deborah gushed. She pulled me in for another hug as soon as my mother let me go.

I kept my eyes on my dad over Deborah's shoulder. "What are you guys doing here?" I asked, though my question was directed at him.

He casually slid his hands in his pockets to indicate that he would not be hugging me like my mothers did. "Your mother invited us," Dad replied with a shrug. As if it didn't really matter to him.

Which, I reminded myself, it probably didn't.

"John, isn't there something you'd like to say to Finley?" Deborah prompted him. Both she and my mother watched him expectantly. I wondered how many times they rehearsed this conversation before coming here.

"Yeah, we're real proud of you," he tacked on. Except he couldn't even look at me while he said it. His eyes continued to dart around the room, watching all of the other happy reunions my housemates had with their families.

I scoffed. "Right. I can tell you're just brimming with joy over my performance tonight."

My dad shuffled awkwardly, his eyes still looking anywhere but me. "You're my daughter, of course I'm proud of you."

Nope, he wasn't going to get off the hook that easily.

"That's funny because the last time we spoke, I seem to recall you not even remembering how old I am. Does the little bit of success I've had suddenly change that?"

My mother blanched, stepping forward to come between us like she needed to play mediator. Which was the role she always played. Why would today be any different for her?

"No, Mom, you can stand down for once." I glared at my father, refusing to let it go. It was high time my mother recognized that he and I could never have a relationship. They're not meant to be one sided, and I had zero incentive to continue chasing my father in hopes he would change.

"I appreciate that you came with Deborah to show me support tonight," I said. "But if I win tonight, that's a direct reflection on my hard work and my mother's sacrifices. She's my parent, not you. You're the one who taught me to question myself, to doubt my worth. But I don't do that anymore." I looked at him in disgust, finally recognizing him for the pitiful excuse of a human being that he was. After all, what kind of grown man abandons his only daughter? "I am enough. I always have been. You're just the idiot too blind to see it. After tonight, I don't ever want to see you again."

"Finley!" My mother's reprimand fell on deaf ears because when my father finally looked in my eyes, the hardened, angry expression told me everything I needed to know. He didn't care and never really had.

Tears sprung to my eyes, but I refused to let them fall for

him. "Enjoy the show," I mumbled to my mom and Deborah, both of them aghast at what I'd said. I spun on my heel, running from the room as quickly as I could in the ridiculous heels Ashford made me wear with my dress. A security guard at the stage entrance stopped my mothers from following me beyond the green room. It was only once I rounded the corner that I allowed the tears to fall.

And then I walked into a solid wall.

"What's this, cowgirl?"

Okay, so it wasn't a solid wall as much as it was a solid wall of Irish muscle and sexiness, but same thing, really.

"My dad came," I admitted tearfully, "and I finally told him off."

"Bet it felt good, yeah?" Bowie asked quietly.

I nodded because I didn't trust myself to speak. My tears had undoubtedly already ruined my makeup and I needed to go get it fixed pronto.

A gentle hand titled my chin up until warm brown eyes found mine. Bowie had on a tight black Henley with the sleeves rolled up to show off his muscly, tattooed forearms and black leather pants. His long hair created a curtain around his face, accentuating his high cheekbones. My Irish angel.

"Yer da's not worth losing this competition," reminded Bowie. "Pull yerself together and git yer head in it. I'm bettin' on ye, cowgirl."

I flashed him a watery smile.

"A steak dinner worthy o' Texas is on me after ye win tonight," he added, breaking through my tears so that I laughed instead of cried.

"Deal," I agreed, "so long as you keep your promise to me."

One dark eyebrow arched up in question.

"If I win, you have to tell me what your new dream is." It seemed like lifetimes passed since that day in the music room when we made our vows to one another, yet it also felt like just yesterday. Time was hard to measure when you lived so fully in the present.

Bowie smirked at me, promising mischief and pleasure all in one look. "I keep my promises, lass, don't ye worry."

Go High

The cheering sounded thunderous tonight. Or maybe it was just the bigger soundstage since we moved to a larger venue in favor of the network selling more tickets. Or maybe it was simply my nerves rattling me because this was my final show on *America's Music Star*.

Somehow, we managed to simultaneously move at light-speed and slow motion. Things were unfolding as naturally as they did for any other show, yet the clarity of each minor detail stuck out clearly. Had I been looking at the world around me through a filter this entire time? I would have questioned the emotional tension running high through The Pen, except it was all of my housemates, not just me.

Our opening performance went perfectly. We all absolutely nailed it, an upbeat dance version of "I'll Be There For You" by The Rembrandts. Bowie, as my dance partner, of course, whirled me around like a professional, and I struggled to hide my delighted giggle. Smiles were contagious because we were all so happy to be on stage together for the last time.

As soon as Bowie twirled me off, I threw my arms around his neck. "How did you learn to do that so well?" I cried.

"Ach, cowgirl, ye wound me!" he replied playfully, clutching his heart. "D'ye think ye're the only one spending every free second in a practice room? I wanted to surprise ye!"

I didn't get a chance to tell him how much my toes appreciated the practice because Zephyr whizzed by and snatched my hand in the process.

"Come on, Finley!" she urged. "It's time for our all access interviews!"

Since fans could subscribe in for an extra hour, they were allowed to submit questions for Enid to ask us. Billy claimed they were randomly selected, but I couldn't imagine them allowing a question that might paint the show or any of the contestants in a bad light. My gut told me that my questions would have more to do with Bowie than anything with my music. Not that I minded that anymore.

The contestants all sat on hard stools on a drop step display. Boys behind on an elevated step with us girls in front, level with Enid's chair, which was far more comfortable, I noted wryly. We were somewhat organized into alphabetical order, putting me at the head of the girls' row. Bowie sat behind me, and even the act of feeling his knees between my shoulder blades helped me relax. If I played my cards right, this wouldn't be my last interview. I could do this.

"Oh my gosh, you guys, we are at the FINALE!" Enid screamed the last word, making the audience erupt. I could just make out my mother's face in the audience. Tears streamed down her cheeks, which she made no attempt to wipe away. My stepmom sat next to her with an equally awestruck expression on her face. Dear ol' dad was nowhere to be found.

Good.

"I don't know about you, but I am so excited to be here!" Enid gushed. More cheers followed. "We've really been through it this season, haven't we? Jessica, what do you think has been your favorite part of appearing on *America's Music Star* this season?"

All eyes turned expectantly to Jessica, who sat almost dead center in the group, and she waved to the cameras and crowd. "Everything about this show has been wonderful," Jessica replied smoothly, "but I honestly have to say that my favorite part has been the friendships I formed. I wasn't expecting to make friends here, but they made me a better person." Jessica looked at me and flashed me a wink.

My heart melted.

"That's so amazing!" Enid agreed. "What kinds of things did you enjoy about the show, Riley?"

Riley blushed, like he always did whenever attention came his way. Unless that boy had a full DJ setup or computer in front of him, the poor kid struggled to speak. After so many months of watching it happen, I actually found the behavior a little endearing. Riley was like the little brother I never got to have.

"Um, I'd say getting to perform so many different kinds of music," Riley answered. "There were a lot of songs I sung on this stage that I never would have attempted for any other reason." The audience laughed and he let out a weak chuckle, glancing their way with apprehension before turning back to Enid. "It's good to get outside of your comfort zone."

Enid nodded vigorously. "Right?! There's been a lot of growth like that this season! Speaking of growth, we have to talk to our resident lovebirds! Bowie and Finley, how has this entire process been for you as you're falling in love while competing for the same prize?"

Even though I expected some form of the question, hearing Enid Wexler speak so candidly about my love life felt a bit jarring. My smile tightened on my face and I paused to gather my wits.

Bowie saved the day, like always. "I'd have to say I already won a prize," he admitted. "Nobody goes on a singing show expecting to find a lass like Finley Smalls. I'm a lucky fella!"

All of the women in the audience collectively sighed with stars in their eyes. Damn Bowie for always saying the perfect thing! It took a lot of work on my part to keep my face dry.

Enid looked between us like she wanted to announce us as husband and wife right then and there. "That is the sweetest thing I've ever heard! Finley, how does that make you feel?"

Oh dear God. Now all eyes were on me, expecting some sort of witty, adorable comeback. It wasn't like I could follow up with my signature sarcasm.

I settled for raw honesty. "Meeting Bowie Baird was a stroke of Fate. Somehow, someone upstairs knew I needed him, and whether we win or lose tonight, I'm just incredibly grateful for that."

Bowie's tattooed hand reached down to massage my shoulder before I snaked my free hand up to meet it, lacing my fingers firmly through his. The grip on my microphone was turning my knuckles white. But I didn't care. I hoped Bowie and every person watching could read my sincerity because I meant every word. Whether we walked away with the grand prize or not, Bowie and I had each other.

Enid dabbed at her eyes, her bright red smile positively simpering over my response. "You guys are just the cutest couple! I hope you don't mind me saying that all of us here tonight, and I'm sure everyone at home, can't wait to see what happens next for you two!" She leaned forward slightly, as if she expected us to announce an engagement or something.

"We can't wait either," Bowie agreed. "Relationships take time and work, and we have a lot of changes coming. Finley and I just want to enjoy every moment we can together."

Okay, so that was another perfect answer that just made me want to jump his bones as soon as we got off stage.

"So Issy, what's it like sharing a house with two people as in love as Bowie and Finley?" Enid asked, shuffling a small deck of cue cards in her hands.

What a gross question. Issy didn't need to speculate on us during her own time to shine. I glared at Enid, disappointed with the tabloid fodder spin the interview took.

Issy, who sat next to me, blinked at Enid for a moment before answering. "We were all focused on our own performances, so I don't think I really spent a lot of time thinking about Bowie and Finley."

Judging by the red hue brightening Enid's face, she recognized that Issy wanted to politely put her in her place. "Of course! Your performances this whole season have been so moving! Can you tell us more about your classical song choices?"

And so the interview went. Thankfully, Enid never circled back to Bowie and me and I never had to go back in the hotseat. When it came time for the fan questions, my question was actually a good one that had nothing to do with my relationship. Something told me Billy had more to do with that than an algorithm that "randomly selected" from submitted questions. He stood just offstage and gave me a small smile when my turn came.

"Alright, Finley Smalls, let's see what America wants to know about you!" Enid flipped to the next card in her deck and grinned. "What singer would you say has had the most profound impact on you?"

Oof, that was such a tough question.

"Honestly, it's hard to narrow it down to just one artist," I admitted. "Probably Kelly Clarkson. She's a woman after my own heart, you know? We're both from roughly the same area, and she was such an inspiration to me growing up. If I could be one tenth of a performer that she is, I'd consider myself a success."

The audience roared in approval.

"Yeah, Kelly Clarkson set the bar pretty high, didn't she?" Enid agreed, looking out to the audience, which prompted them to cheer again. "Plus, she was the original singing competition winner! Maybe you could follow in her footsteps!"

"Now that would be a dream come true!" I smiled out at my mom, who loved Kelly just as much as I did.

Enid nodded emphatically. "And now, our final viewer submitted question is for Bowie Baird! Bowie, @CamillaIRL27 wants to know about any culture shock you experienced when you came over from Ireland."

As the audience oohed in agreement, Enid looked out in their direction and encouraged them to keep going. "Right? Isn't this such a great question?! So how about it, Bowie?" She turned in her seat again so that she faced his direction. "What kind of culture shock have you experienced?"

It was a loaded question that even I didn't know the answer to. While I was certain of Bowie's feelings for me in a way that defied logic or reason, he still shared very little of his past with me. I knew how much it pained him to talk about Ireland and the life he escaped with his horrible stepdad. Turning in my seat, I gently placed a hand on his knee, hoping he drew strength from my touch the same way I did from his.

Our gazes locked, and I saw a split second of hesitation. I realized how easy it was for him to talk about me because it deflected the attention off him. Bowie didn't want to be vulnerable about his past, but he sure wanted to be hopeful about his future. In its own weird way, having feeling develop between the two of us for the world to see saved him from having to examine his childhood. Lord knew his stepfather didn't deserve any sort of recognition in Bowie's story, and ultimately, the media would turn it into a circus of some kind. Once you had any level of celebrity, your entire life story became ripe for anyone to pick.

As infinitesimally as possible, I nodded, letting Bowie know that it was okay to turn it all back on me. I didn't mind if he continued to hide his darkness behind me. I had more than enough light for the both of us.

A brief prickle of relief dotted his features, gone before anyone but me could have noticed.

"The only culture shock I've had is when I went to Texas with Finley," Bowie informed the audience. "Everything really is bigger there!"

Laughter broke out across the room and a lot of our cast-mates joined in. Enid giggled appreciatively. "What was your favorite thing about Texas? And you can't say Finley because we all obviously know it's Finley!" She rolled her eyes in a goofy way to the audience, inciting more laughter.

Bowie shrugged. "Every place I've been in America has been amazing. I'm looking forward to more of what the country has to offer!"

He had such a natural way of ending interviews on a good

note so that people were happy. I needed him to teach me how to do that.

"Well there you have it, folks!" Enid found her mark with the camera. "Our pre-show special is over, but you can tune into the U.S. Broadcasting Network now to watch the live finale of *America's Music Star!* Voting officially opens...NOW!"

With that, the theme music came on through the speakers, cueing the segue to commercial. Lights flashed shortly thereafter to signify everyone could get up and move around since we were no longer actively filming.

"Alright, y'all," Miles, ever the hype man, crowed. "It's show time!"

Behind These Hazel Eyes

Either Billy had an uncanny sense of humor or he was just downright mean, but I was the last contestant to sing on the show tonight. Everyone got to sing their cover song and then we would circle back to the beginning of the line to sing our originals. The show would announce the *America's Music Star* soundtrack at the tail end. People from the network were already working overtime behind the scenes to have the songs uploaded to the major music streaming services. A CD and vinyl would hit stores next week.

It was entirely possible that by this time tomorrow I could claim to have a top selling song on iTunes or Spotify. That scared the shit out of me.

Is this how my life would be from now on? Always rapid fire, with a dozen balls dangling in the air above me, threatening to drop at the same time? An entire season of a reality singing competition passed in the blink of an eye. Would the rest of it move just as swiftly?

Oddly enough, Bowie was the first person to sing tonight. I

expected Billy to put us back to back again, but maybe he thought it would sway too many votes. Bowie and I still hadn't had a chance to discuss my offers for record deals outside of winning the competition. Since he was called into a room with Billy and Veronica, too, I had to believe he received a similar offer. And while that was great in theory, where did that leave our relationship when all of this ended?

There were too many questions buzzing around in my head. I needed to focus, but how could I? Everyone's futures were at stake.

I started to pace back and forth along the back of The Pen. While it probably would have been better for me to be out front, letting the crowd see me, I couldn't bring myself out of hiding. Ashford and some of the other stylists watched me apprehensively. Pacing wasn't doing much to turn my mind off, but it prevented me from turning into one of those unhinged rage monsters on *Snapped!* so I figured it was the right call.

Even when Ashford notified Kyle, who almost immediately reappeared with Billy, I couldn't stop pacing. There was too much at stake and I was going to crumble under the pressure. Maybe I was a loser like my dad said. I never won anything in my life—why would the show be any different? Had I been deluding myself this whole time into thinking I was somebody special? Someone worth hearing on the radio?

"Finley." Billy's voice was firm as he grabbed me by the shoulders, squatting down slightly so he could look me in the eye. "Win or lose tonight, it's all going to be okay."

"I know that." I nodded, painfully swallowing the lump in my throat. "But it's also all going to change."

He pulled me into a hug, wrapping his arm tightly around my shoulders. "Change is a good thing. Change is what led me to find you. Change is what brought you on this show. Let the change happen."

Let the change happen, Finley. Just let it happen. It's that simple. Welcome The Change. Be The Change.

I could do this. I didn't have any other choice.

I resumed pacing, this time with my new mantra floating around in my head. Only two songs stood between me and a life changing moment. Knocking out two songs was easy. A total cakewalk. They might as well add some tigers and raw meat to at least make it challenging for me, right?

Except, when Kyle tapped on my shoulder and pointed towards the stage, I could barely remember what song I selected, let alone the words. Where was my mark? Were the stage lights always so bright? How the hell had I sung it in rehearsals?

One by the one, as the contestants sang their final song, they all returned back to a dressing room to switch into their next outfit and have their makeup redone. Bowie hadn't returned yet by the time I was due to arrive onstage, only amplifying my growing anxiety.

Performing on stage never bothered me before. Then again, I never had so much hanging in the balance of two songs.

The lights were still dimmed as I made my way over to center stage. A prop master tied a garland of dark flowers around the microphone stand as an ode to the original song, my favorite Kelly Clarkson hit, "Behind These Hazel Eyes."

Like a magnet drew me straight to her, I somehow found my mother sitting in the audience. People were still shuffling around to return to their seats as the lights flickered a warning. Filming was about to start. In mere moments, I could change our lives forever.

But my strong, hardworking mom only mouthed the words,

"I love you" to me. It was like a beacon straight to my heart. I had never been so grateful for her presence before.

Everything went black except for a lone spotlight shining on Enid Wexler, who stood next to the judges' panel. My mind was so far gone in that moment that I couldn't even remember or recognize a single person sitting at the table. And really, what did it matter? They couldn't vote for a winner. Only the people at home counted.

I pictured the crew at Wally's, who already had banners and shirts ready.

I pictured all my choir teachers and vocal coaches who helped me become the singer I was today.

I pictured Zephyr. And Tessa. And Kameron. Even Jessica. All of my housemates who became my closest friends, who now felt like family. They lifted me up in the ways I needed most.

Even though I knew he would never see my performance or care, I pictured my dad's face, the anger in his eyes as he realized I no longer cared whether I earned his approval or not. His words were empty—fleeting—and didn't get to define me anymore.

Lastly, I imagined Bowie, his knowing smirk and the way his Irish accent would lilt around the words "I'm so proud of ye." I would believe him because only Bowie managed to make them sound real.

The raunchy guitar chord opened the song as a peace settled over me. My brain shut itself off as I felt the lyrics with every fiber of my being. Like Kelly herself, I let the emotions take over so that you could feel it in the song.

This was my moment. And the only thing my own hazel eyes would reveal was hope.

Carousel

I've never undressed as fast as I did after that performance. Bowie's original song would be up next and I didn't want to miss it. Rather than wasting time by going back to a dressing room, Ashford humored me with a privacy screen backstage and helped me change in a corner. By now we were familiar enough with one another that it didn't even bother me that he saw me in my skivvies. Just one more thing about my privacy that drastically changed from the show.

Two hair stylists worked on creating wild curls as I stood off stage to listen to Bowie's song. His new outfit consisted of a black leather vest, exposing his toned, tattooed chest, and a pair of ripped up black jeans that hung suggestively off his hips. They dipped so low that I could see the V leading down to what I knew to be a particularly impressive package. Bowie was raw sex appeal veiled in temptation and smoke.

Contestants had the option of performing their song with their mentors, so Bowie took his place on stage beside Scott Baxter, both of them with acoustic guitars. They kept it simple, sitting on black stools next to one another under a solitary spotlight. Dark green lights flooded the empty stage behind them. There was no band back there and I frowned. I didn't remember him saying anything about it being an acoustic only set.

Just the first few notes told me Bowie's song would be a hit single. It oozed rock star bad boy. Plus, hot damn, did he look sexy singing it. Even while seated his body had a way of moving to the rhythm of the song that made my heart skip a beat or two. It was almost unfair that the Universe made a man that talented *and* gorgeous. Leave some for the rest of us mere mortals, okay?

Bowie's voice sounded so sultry and smooth. I couldn't help but beam as I pulled my new dress straps over my shoulders and listened to his song...except, what were those lyrics he sang...?

I'm cavin' in
Letting my heart out
Only you can matter right now
You're my new dream
You're my new dream
And now I can't wake up
Just be my new dream
Don't ever let me wake up

Bowie's lyrics washed over me and a warmth settled in my chest. He used his chance to write and perform an original song to keep his promise to me. If there was ever a grand, romantic gesture, my guy killed it.

With a final chord, the song ended to pyrotechnics and flashing green lights.

"Doll, this was waterproof makeup! How did you manage to

ruin it?" Ashford scolded me as he came around to remove the screen.

Surprised, I swiped at my cheeks and realized they were coated in tears. The emotion of hearing Bowie's promise to me, something that only the two of us could know, turned me into a human faucet. I wouldn't change a damn thing.

"If Michael Jackson can sing as a zombie, so can I," I deadpanned. Ashford did not look amused.

"Cami, Ava, get over here and fix this disaster!" He snapped his fingers at two of our makeup artists and stomped off in a huff. I only had eyes for Bowie, though.

It sounded like the audience converted into thousands of teenage girls. Their high-pitched screams made me laugh and jump for joy for him. I know Bowie wanted me to win, but he honestly deserved it just as much. I'd never met someone else who was so clearly destined to make music.

"I don't think you have a dry eye in the house after that!" Enid told him as she joined him on stage in her new bubble gum pink evening gown. The girl really was morphing into a modern day Barbie. "Scott, what was it like working with our resident rock star?"

Scott smiled and waved out at the audience when they cheered louder at his name. "Bowie came into the studio ready to work every time. He knew exactly what kind of song he wanted to perform and wrote the entire thing himself. I really acted as more of a producer than anything. The kid's got talent," Scott added with a shrug.

The audience ate it up, taking their applause up a notch in volume.

Sheer pride ran through my veins. Ignoring the two women who just wanted to make me presentable, I jumped up and down and hollered with the rest of them. Bowie took my breath away, and I could not be prouder of him.

"Wow, that's high praise from someone like Scott Baxter!" Enid replied, turning to the audience with a grin. "What do you have to say to that, Bowie?"

Through the small gap between my makeup artists as they dabbed new foundation on my face, Bowie locked eyes with me. The whole world faded away. Even though he was on stage for an interview, I knew his response was meant for me.

"I just have a really great muse," Bowie replied smoothly.

Yep, there went my ovaries. I was so head over heels in love with Bowie Baird.

"I'm sure I look rad, y'all!" I didn't want to be rude, but I was tired of the girls fluttering around me. This was one of those significant moments where Bowie deserved all of my attention.

Both Cami and Ava frowned at me, but walked away grumbling under their breath. I assumed that meant I looked presentable enough that they would let me go out on stage.

The audience clapped and shouted more as Scott and Bowie waved one last time before walking off stage. It was too hard not to beam at my Irishman as he strode purposefully towards me, guitar strapped to his back, before wrapping both arms around my waist to do the romantic lift-twirl thing.

My lips found his as I firmly planted a kiss that I hoped conveyed the blissful pride radiating through me. He eagerly opened his mouth to invite me in, tongue swiping through my mouth in a way that made my panties wet. I planned to put that tongue to good use tonight.

A man let out an exaggerated cough beside us, making Bowie break apart with a laugh. "Can ye blame me for wantin' to celebrate with me girl?" he asked.

It might have been nothing, but I swore I saw Scott Baxter's eyes dart to the right, where Aniston Sharpe stood at the wall, waiting for him.

"Yeah, you're a lucky man, Bowie." Scott held out his hand to shake Bowie's.

Bowie gracefully set me down, one arm tucking me neatly into his side, as he shook his mentor's hand. "'Twas an honor to work with ye," he replied.

Scott nodded to me. "I'll be seeing you real soon, Finley." He sauntered off towards Aniston, and I turned back to Bowie to finish what we started.

Until Ashford stuck his hand in between our faces. "We need to fix your lipstick *again!*" he cried in anguish. "Have you no respect for artistry?!"

"Oh, Ashy, I have the utmost respect for you and the Shining Twins." Cami and Ava both stood behind him with stoic glares on their faces, makeup brushes in hand.

Bowie snorted. "I'm gonna return to The Pen. Finish up here and join me." He pecked another quick kiss on my lips, smirking at Ashford afterwards, then ambled away to hand off his guitar.

Ashford's gaze drifted up to the ceiling. "What have I done to deserve this?"

"You didn't embrace the nickname," I quipped.

Despite himself, Ashford let out a chuckle. "And to think, I actually thought I would miss you." Still, he fondly pulled me in for a quick hug before snapping Cami and Ava to attention. They descended on me like ravenous vampires at a blood bank.

By the time they deemed me ready, I missed three more of my housemates' performances. I made it back to The Pen just in time for the commercial break before Zephyr's song. For once, she looked ready to vomit. Even Bowie stood there trying to calm her.

"Good Lord, Zeph, what is wrong with you right now?" I reached out to rub her shoulders as she bent down to brace her hands on her knees. She inhaled deeply through her nose, then exhaled through her mouth.

"I've never sung an original song before, Finley!" Zephyr whispered. "I don't know if I can do this!"

Well knock me over with a feather. I didn't think cool, calm, collected Zephyr had it in her to be nervous. For some reason, I automatically went into tough love mode, like my brain just knew that was what my best friend needed.

"Okay, then suck it up, damn it! Everybody here tonight has to sing an original song! You are Zephyr-I'm-so-cool-I-only-need-one-name. Nobody's got time for your pity party, and I'll pop all the damn balloons!" Fisting my hands on my hips, I stared down at her with what I hoped was a firm but loving expression.

Bowie's eyebrows went up in shock and some of our housemates gathered around to watch.

Zephyr took another deep, shuddering breath as she looked up at me, hands still on her knees. After a long pause, she asked, "Do you seriously think I would decorate a pity party with *balloons*? What am I, five years old?"

We both burst out laughing, and I grabbed her hand to yank her into a hug. Kameron, Cooper, and Joey watched us, shaking their heads.

"And people say men are weird with their feelings," Joey muttered.

I swatted at him rather than reply, keeping my attention focused on Zephyr. The lights flashed, signaling that she needed to find her mark on stage. Placing both my hands on her cheeks, I leveled her with a look straight out of my mother's playbook. "You got this, Zephyr. I believe in you."

Tearfully, my friend nodded. I saw the resolve steel her spine as she drew herself to her full height and headed on stage. Once I started cheering for her, the rest of my castmates joined in. Bowie wrapped an arm around my waist, and we watched Zephyr like proud parents from the back of The Pen.

Zephyr's song was a fun pop track. Howie joined her on stage halfway through and they both busted out dance moves worthy of a K-pop band. Everyone roared in excitement. Bowie and I cheered along with them.

All too soon, the song came to an end. It was by far my favorite performance of Zephyr's from the entire season.

Before I knew it, the night was winding down. My original song was up next.

Bowie turned to me with his signature smirk, placing a gentle kiss on my forehead. "Git out there and win this thing, cowgirl."

I smiled at him even though my legs felt like jelly and an entire hive of bees had taken up residence in my stomach. It was now or never.

Lights flashed to signify the people needed to return to their seats. I needed to find my mark on stage. The stage crew had worked to transform the set during the commercial break so that it resembled a carnival. Once the song started, an image of a spinning carousel would shine along the stage behind me.

Scott wouldn't be visible to the audience until the first chorus. We planned on him executing a rad guitar riff during the bridge, but he wasn't going to sing with me. Somehow this song felt too personal, like sharing a diary entry with the world, and it didn't feel right to have someone else sing it.

The stage remained dark as I took my place behind the microphone stand. As I inhaled a deep breath in to settle my nerves, I experienced the kind of clarity that doesn't normally exist in the real world. Time actually froze for a moment as I became hyper-aware of everything and everyone around me. There were my mom and stepmom out in the audience, smiling at me as if I were being crowned queen. All of my friends were in The Pen to cheer for me. I didn't even have to check to know that Zephyr would be the loudest of the bunch. Bowie was the proudest, though. His love radiated through me like an electromagnetic pulse. Billy, Veronica, Ashford, Kyle...all the people who had become a part of my world were just off stage, waiting to hear my song. This was a moment I could never—*would* never forget.

The overhead lights flashed one more time to signify to the audience that filming resumed. A camera zoomed in on Enid's face as she stood out on the stairs in the audience. "And now, the song we've all been waiting for," she smiled. "Please give it up for Finley Smalls!"

Roughly two dozen signs waved frantically out in the audience. *You're killing it, Smalls!*

Proud member of Smalls Army!

Finley Smalls: My American Music Star!

I couldn't believe how lucky I was to say that I had fans. Hopefully this song resonated with them the way it did with my soul. That was why I needed to sing this song, I realized. This was never about winning. This song served as my declaration, to my fans, my haters, and myself, of who I am and what my music was all about. I sang for me, and that was the only thing that mattered.

Taking another breath, this one full of relief and acceptance, I let the words flow out of me.

There's so much waiting at the top,
I know I need it all to stop.
It's all just spinning round in my head.
I choose to laugh it off instead.

It's just a carousel.
Round and round
Like a carousel.
Only time will tell,
Can I make it off?
Or will I drown?
On this carousel.

Don't wanna let you down.
Don't wanna say goodbye.
When it comes to an end,
I can't run and hide.

It's just a carousel.
Round and round
Like a carousel.
Can I make it off?
Or will I drown?
On this carousel.

I never expected this
Whirlwind surprise.
But now that I see love

Shining in your eyes.
I know I'm enough.
I know I'm enough.
For you...

It's just a carousel.
Round and round
Like a carousel.
I'm so glad I fell,
Don't wanna make it off.
We'll go round and round.
On this carousel.

Except, when I sang the bridge of the song, it wasn't Scott Baxter who played the guitar at my side. It was Bowie.

You would have thought we were playing in a sold out stadium from the pandemonium that broke out. As I sang the lyrics about finally feeling like I was enough, I recognized I meant them for Bowie. Somehow, without even meaning to, he healed a part of me that felt restless for most of my life. I wasn't crazy for wanting to sing. My determination to give my all to every song I performed seemed understandable to him. Bowie never once made me feel less than, and actually built me up in a way I never knew I needed.

I had no idea when he found the time to learn my song in addition to his own, but the smirk he flashed me let me know that he understood the tears of delight streaming down my face were for him. We both smiled out at the crowd, and as I ended the final chorus to the decrescendo of his guitar, happiness like I had never experienced washed over me.

Fans were going in nuclear orbit out in the audience. My

mother looked like she was outright sobbing into a wad of tissues. We received a standing ovation from everyone in the room, even the stage hands and production assistants I saw just offstage.

Now was as good a time as any to throw caution to the wind. When your whole life is about to change, you want to share it with the people who matter most.

"I love you, Bowie Baird!" I said and wound my arms around his neck. He grinned at me like that was the best thing he had heard all day before wrapping an arm around my waist. Our kiss contained all the magic of my favorite childhood princess movies combined. This was my forever. I didn't even need to win the competition to get it. There were only two things I now wanted out of life.

Playing music and Bowie.

Second Wind

I chose to believe it was my song that made the audience so wild that Enid couldn't ask me any questions at the end of my performance, although it was obviously everyone losing their mind over Bowie and I kissing on stage. Who could blame them? He's a great kisser.

There was a quick commercial break where people could cast their final votes and the stage could be reset. All of my castmates joined me on stage, and you would be hard pressed to find a dry eye in the house. We all hugged one another, whispering words of encouragement and luck, and promising that no matter who won, we were all in this together.

Jessica timidly approached me, hesitating for a moment before embracing me tightly. "You deserve to win, Finley," she admitted. I noted only a hint of disdain in her eyes as she said it. "Thank you for giving me some real competition this season."

I rolled my eyes, but we both laughed.

Even though we all knew this wasn't really goodbye, especially before the month long tour the network would send us on, this was the end of an era. *America's Music Star* and everyone associated with it had been our tight-knit family for the past three months. We spent virtually every waking moment together. That was a bond you didn't come back from lightly. I loved every single one of the people on stage with me.

Suddenly, all of us watched as Issy straightened her shoulders, her spine going ramrod straight. Her hands fisted at her sides as she walked determinedly towards Kameron, parting the group like the Red Sea. His eyes widened in alarm as she stopped directly in front of him.

"Kameron Potts, I love you!" she declared before cupping her hands around his jaw and pulling his lips to hers. Kameron froze for only a second, then gripped her so fiercely that there was no room for air between them. Passion blazed around them like an inferno.

We all stood, shell shocked, before I cried out, "I KNEW IT!"

The rest of the group broke out in a mixture of laughter, congratulations, and shock as we all tried to process what just happened. Issy broke apart from Kameron with a shit eating grin while he looked outright dazed. Cupid struck him hard.

"Sorry, Finley. I saw what you and Bowie went through and I didn't want anything like that to happen to me," Issy confessed. A faint blush of embarrassment crept across her cheeks.

Well, I certainly couldn't blame her for that. "Girl, get over here and give me a hug!" I said. "This is so rad!"

Relief washed over her thin face and we wrapped one another in a hug. I could hear Bowie behind me reach around to slap Kameron on the shoulder in congratulations.

None of us bothered to look out at the audience and see if anyone recorded Issy's announcement, but in the heat of the moment, none of us really cared. If this was really going to be my life, I simply had to accept that there would always be someone wanting to record a piece of it. That was just the dark side of fame.

Lights flashed to signify the end of the commercial break. Bowie and I stood center stage next to Enid, who changed into yet another evening gown, this one a satin blue number with enough glittery rhinestones to turn herself into a human disco ball. Zephyr stood to my right. Another six contestants stood on Enid's other side so that we fanned out across the stage with her in the middle. All the cameras zoomed in on her as the audience lights dimmed to announce filming had started.

"Welcome back, everyone, to the season finale of *America's Music Star!*" Enid's words were drowned out by a sea of applause. There was a collective hum of anticipation in the room, as if every single person held their breath to hear her announcement.

"This has been such an amazing season with some of the most talented group of people I've ever seen. Let's not waste any time—let's see who you chose as *America's Music Star!*"

Drum rolls echoed from the band and all of the lights panned over to Enid so that she glowed under a huge spotlight. Bowie's fingers laced through mine. I hadn't realized the way my knees shook until he gently squeezed to comfort me.

Here it was, my new future barreling forward based on Enid's next breath.

"And the winner is...*Zephyr!*" Enid bellowed excitedly.

Joy, pride, excitement, and relief shot through me all at once in a heady rush that rattled my bones. Zephyr's face had gone slack, almost like she went into shock from hearing her name. The screams coming out of my mouth were inhuman, and I might have crushed a bone or two with the way I squashed my bestie to my chest.

Zephyr deserved this so much. I could barely contain my happiness for her. There wasn't a single ounce of regret or remorse that I lost. As far as I was concerned, my best friend's successes were my successes. She and I were never really competitors, only supporters.

All of the castmates descended on Zephyr in a heap of tears, more hugs, and delight. Large confetti pieces rained down on us from the rafters as her original song played over the audio system. Fans cheered loudly out in the audience, making it nearly impossible to hear one another.

In the end, Veronica had to come on stage and shoo us off because we couldn't stop celebrating. Everyone in the audience had already left. Zephyr still couldn't believe it, with big, fat tears running into her wide smile. Her whole body trembled when she hugged me again to scream, "I did it, Finley, I did it!"

"I know you did, honey, and I'm so happy for you!" I said.

We moved as a group into the green room. Bowie remained firmly planted at my side, both of us ducking down to hug my mom as soon as we found her amongst the chaos. Zephyr's family enveloped her in a group hug so big and powerful that they all collapsed into a dogpile on the floor together.

"Finley, you are still a winner to me! Don't let this get you down!" my mom crooned, lovingly brushing my cheek. "Your song was absolutely beautiful."

More tears came as I glowed from her praise. I would probably be dehydrated after this.

"Thanks, Mom. I never could have done any of this without you."

Bowie winked at me before asking, "What about me, Jeanne? I think my song was pretty great, too."

She playfully smacked his arm. "You better ask my permission before you marry my girl, you hear? And I expect lots of grandbabies...*after* the wedding!"

Panic surged through my body at the thought of weddings and babies. Bowie and I hadn't even been official long enough for milk to expire. "MOM!"

Bowie outright grinned, his dimples briefly appearing as he took in my alarm. "What, cowgirl? Yer ma recognizes a good thing when she sees it. A wise woman, this is."

The green room wasn't big enough for this man's ego.

"But really," my mom continued, "what are you both gonna do now? You go on this tour, and then what?"

Bowie's gaze locked with mine as he gave me a knowing smile. "Oh, we'll think of something."

Don't You Wanna Stay?

"Okay, your mic is set and I'll cue you through the earpiece when it's time to walk out." Veronica waited for me to nod that I heard her before sweeping from the room. My hair and makeup team still fluttered around me like chirping birds, all of us buzzing with excited nerves over our big day.

And this was a *big* day. Probably the biggest of my career.

Once they declared me ready to go, I slowly walked down the long hallway to the green room. The walls were lined with framed commemorations of my various diamond and multi-platinum albums throughout the years, and as silly as it seemed, my fingers traced along their frames in comfort.

You can do this, Finley Smalls. Look at what you've already accomplished! Just set your mind to it, and you can do anything!

Giggling echoed from the green room and I smiled in anticipation. As soon as I entered, a small body barreled into my legs, just hard enough to make me teeter in the high heels on my feet.

"Dash, you are getting so fast!" With a laugh, I scooped my son up and tossed him in the air. He was three and getting to the size and age where I wouldn't be able to do this anymore.

I reveled in these moments, where his raw, unfiltered delight shone through. Becoming a mom had been so scary with how busy my career kept me, but Dash made me want to slow down. His birth had been what made me realize I needed to hit the pause button so that my life wasn't entirely focused on work. It made me put a new kind of plan in motion, and today was the day when I would finally learn if it paid off or not.

"Don't get him riled up or I won't be able to manage him!" My mom walked over to take Dash from my arms. She loved being a grandma and traveled everywhere with us so that I always had a spare pair of hands and didn't have to rely on a nanny. That lessened the guilt somewhat to know that Dash was always surrounded by family. Not that he didn't charm the pants off everyone he met. He had my entire crew wrapped around his finger.

"Are you nervous, sweetie?" she asked. All these years later and the woman still read my emotions like she had a built in radar.

I swallowed thickly. "A bit," I admitted. "Although I don't know why. It's not like I've never done an interview before!" With all the practice over the years, I had actually become quite good at them.

"Yeah, but these aren't the kind of interviews you're used to," my mom pointed out. "It's okay to be nervous. Keeps you on your toes."

Always the sage advice.

"Finley, you're on in two," Veronica told me through the earpiece.

I frowned, looking around for the one familiar face I needed right now. "Where is...?"

My mom shrugged. "He'll be here, don't worry."

Another stern reminder from Veronica came through the earpiece and let me know she was aware I hadn't made it to my mark yet. She was lucky she was the best stage manager in the business or I wouldn't have hired her again. Except that was a lie because deep down I knew that Veronica's neurotic need for structure, timeliness, and order was what would make us successful today.

"I've gotta go, Mom, they're summoning me." I shot her an apologetic smile. "I love you. And I love you, Dashy-washy!" I sang it playfully, tickling my son's ribs as he roared with laughter on my mom's hip.

"Good luck, Mama!" Dash cried.

No matter how many times I heard him say it, those three little words had the power to bolster my nerves. It was one of the first phrases Dash learned. I guess having musicians for parents was bound to rub off on him at some point.

I left the room to follow the corridor around to the hidden stage entrance. Just as I stepped up to the X Veronica had ordered the production crew to paint on the floor for me, the enthusiastic chatter of the audience reached my ears. Their voices thrummed ahead before quieting as Veronica indicated filming was about to start.

In three...two...one...

"Welcome to the Finley Smalls Show, everyone!" The

catchy narrator's voice came over the audio system while Veronica hissed in my ear to walk out.

Today was the first episode of my brand new talk show, a highly anticipated event that sold out instantly. Two hundred people filled the studio audience chairs and their bright, happy faces were all I could see as I walked out on set, waving both hands. They cheered animatedly, ignoring my gestures for them to calm down.

My fans honestly were the best out there.

"Thank you! Thank you!" I called to them. "Thank you so much for coming to the first Finley Smalls Show, y'all! As soon as I got the green light from U.S. Broadcasting Network to do this, I knew I wanted to start at the very beginning. So I hope everyone's ready for a little trip down Memory Lane!"

Everyone in the audience roared their approval.

"Please help me welcome our first guest, Emmy awarding winning actress and singer, Zephyr!" I waved my arms to the side like a game show host as my best friend glided out on stage to join me. She still moved with the grace of a model on the runway and looked just as incredible. Long legs went on for days until they reached her denim mini-skirt. As far as I was concerned, Zephyr hadn't aged since the day I met her.

She beamed at me before kissing me on both cheeks. We settled into the cushy armchairs across from one another, and she waved out to the audience again.

"Oh my gosh, it's so great to see you!" I gushed. "Wow, how long has it been now? Two years maybe?"

Zephyr nodded. "Yeah, I think the last time we saw each other was at the Oscars after party. Little Dash had only just had his first birthday!"

Although both our careers took off after the *America's Music Star* tour ended, Zephyr and I always tried to stay in touch over the years. Despite her debut album going platinum, featuring two singles that both cracked the top ten of the Billboard charts, Zephyr no longer recorded music. She moved on to acting shortly after that and never looked back. In the fifteen years since our time on the show, Zephyr starred in more than thirty-eight feature films, and was arguably one of the busiest women I knew.

We spent the rest of her segment reminiscing over our time on *America's Music Star*, more than a little awestruck over the realization of how far we had both come. Our friendship remained as strong as ever. This woman saw me through all the ups and downs of my career, my family, and everything in between. Sitting in front of a studio audience to gab over our antics through the years honestly felt like an intimate gathering between friends. I forgot the cameras were even rolling.

"Wrap it up, you're running out of time," prompted Veronica in my earpiece.

"Wow, Zephyr, I am so grateful you came on the show. Thank you for being nostalgic with me!" I stood up to hug her.

"No, thank *you!* A talk show is just what you needed. Isn't this the perfect job for Finley?" Zephyr asked the audience, who cheered in response. She beamed at me and the cameras before Veronica lifted a fist in the air to signify they cut to commercial.

Zephyr's smile faded so that it wasn't so painful for her cheeks. That was something you never realized until you were suddenly dealing with fame. There was a difference between your regular smile and the smile you kept on your face in front of the cameras. The latter tended to make your facial muscles a little sore.

"I really am so happy I could be here for you," she said, her voice low so that no one else could hear. The microphones clipped to both our shirts had been turned off remotely by one of the production members.

"Thanks, Zeph," I replied. "I'm so glad you could take a break from filming to come out here. Do you have to fly out right away or can you come over for dinner later?"

Her lips drooped in a playful pout. "I wish I could, but I'm literally getting into the car now to head straight back to London. This movie isn't gonna make itself!"

Zephyr had finally taken the leap of faith to become an executive producer as well as the lead actress on her current film, something that I knew she would knock out of the park. Naturally, Zephyr didn't buy into my giddy optimism, but that was okay because I had enough faith for the both of us. I even wrote the titular song for the soundtrack.

"You give my godson that present I left in your dressing room, okay?" Zephyr shot me a pointed look, knowing I hadn't given Dash her last gift. But honestly, what mother alive let her three year old son have a monogrammed golf cart, even if it was kid sized? "And give my love to all the family."

I pulled her into another hug. "You know I will. Love you!"

"I love you, too, babe. Good luck!" Zephyr skipped around the seat in time for a makeup artists and hair stylist to dart forward and fix my stray hairs and touch up my tinted lip balm. Gone were the days that I needed bright purple streaks in my hair for people to notice me, and maybe it was just talking so much about my time on *America's Music Star*, but I found myself wishing I still had the colorful pieces.

"Okay, Bowie's at his mark. We're live in three...two...one..." Veronica instructed in my ear.

"Alright, y'all, welcome back to the Finley Smalls Show," I said to the camera in front of the audience. "My next guest needs no introduction, but I'm gonna do it anyway. Y'all give it up for my husband, Bowie Baird!"

Considering ninety-eight percent of my audience consisted of women around the age of thirty-five, it was no surprise that they all sounded like rabid teenage girls at the sight of my Irishman walking. Time had been generous with Bowie's looks, and although he cut his long locks in favor of a spiky undercut, he had also become very well acquainted with the weight room of our home gym. His physique rivaled those of men half his age. The hard muscles and a great moisturizing routine kept his tattoos in excellent condition. Tattoos that now featured a prominent arm design of our son's name on the left and the lyrics to *Carousel* and *My Dream*, our first number one singles, intertwined on the right.

Rock star eye candy, through and through.

"Hey, baby!" I greeted him. Bowie smirked at me before kissing me lightly on the lips and making the women watching us fan themselves.

"Hi, cowgirl." Brown eyes filled with mirth, I shot him a look that was half glare, half laughter. He loved how much it still rattled me when he called me that.

"Isn't this amazing? Look at how great our audience is!" I gestured out to everyone in the stands watching, making Bowie wave again to their applause.

"Yeah, I'm right proud of ye." Despite living here in the United States all this time, Bowie still hadn't lost his Irish accent, though I loved to tease him about how much it had softened through the years.

I tried not to whimper under his praise. No matter how long

we had been together, Bowie's compliments still felt like precious jewels to me. I had only started to believe in myself because of it.

"Since we're traveling down Memory Lane for the show today," I replied, "what do you remember most about our time on *America's Music Star?*"

Bowie's smolder told me I would regret asking that question in front of a live studio audience. "I remember seeing ye for the first time. My first thought was something akin to 'Jesus, they let angels walk around here, now, do they?'" He paused so that we could all laugh. "Truly, ye were the most gorgeous creature I'd ever set eyes on."

It was a story I had heard before and often, but it still made me want to giggle like a schoolgirl with a crush. The way Bowie made me feel loved and cherished was the stuff of romance book level fantasies.

"Ye know, I've always wondered, how did it come to be ye on the show?" Bowie asked. "I don't think we ever talked about it. How did Billy—the producer, for those of you who don't know—come to pick ye?"

A crimson blush fanned out across my face as I recalled that fateful day. Oh, to be young, dumb, and drunk again.

"It's actually kind of funny. Billy found me at a karaoke bar in Hollywood. We were just talking about random things, nothing at all to do with music, and I had one too many cocktails and decided the best thing I could do was go up to sing a Madonna song."

Even I roared with laughter at the randomness of the memory. The audience joined in.

"I always wanted to be a singer, so going to a karaoke bar

wasn't really my scene, do you know what I mean? Those participants tended to be more...enthusiastic than talented."

Everyone laughed again.

"So yeah, I just decided I was gonna go up there and show them what's what, and I think I made Billy's day."

Bowie snorted. "Ye certainly did. Billy struck gold when he discovered ye. Pretty sure all he ever saw was dollar signs when ye were around."

I nodded in agreement, making the audience laugh even harder. "No, y'all don't understand, he definitely wanted to wring my neck half the time, but yeah, I think it all sort of worked out in my favor!"

And it had. Once they announced Zephyr as the winner, Bowie and I immediately called up Zach Muñoz, the entertainment lawyer I had hired to negotiate my contract with Avalon Hair Care. He came to the set right then and there to represent both of us in negotiations with Ragamuffin Records. Ultimately, Bowie and I each walked away with a contract for three records worth a million dollars each. But most importantly, we each had more of a say in the selected songs, the writing, and the creative process as a whole.

Zach also signed on as our manager and served as the best man at our wedding seven years later.

"We really have come a long way since the show, haven't we?" Bowie mused.

I couldn't help but glance out at the crowd of two hundred people who admired me enough to buy tickets to my very first talk show without even knowing if I could do it or not. My mom held Dash on her hip, standing in the back behind Veronica and all the camera monitors. I couldn't hear what they were saying, but I saw Dash's face light up when she pointed at the screen. It was a toss up between whether it was the sight of Bowie or me that brought out his smile. As much as I wanted a mama's boy, Dash was definitely Daddy's BFF.

We might have come a long way, but it was the *best* way. I loved my life. I loved all the people who connected to my songs. I loved how rewarding it felt to see and hear their reactions when I was on stage.

And then I found the most incredible life partner to share it with. Someone who really understood the drive it took to be successful as a recording artist. Bowie never blamed me for it because he was doing it, too. We had wildly successful co-headlining tours for four years in a row. Our mantel proudly displayed the awards we both won over the years, but more importantly, our walls shared the photographs of all the memories we'd made along the way.

Now I had the opportunity to keep us all in one place so that we could spend more quality time with Dash. Bowie booked some time to produce a few albums with other up and coming rock bands, and at the end of our segment today, we could announce his next gig as a celebrity judge on a new singing competition. It was the perfect fit for him and I couldn't wait to see him act as a mentor to other young kids just out there chasing their dreams.

"Okay, coming up on commercial break. What's next, Finley?" Veronica said in my ear.

I arched an eyebrow at Bowie, then crossed my legs to cover the aching need my body instantly felt when he winked knowingly at me in response.

I saw my future full of movies, world tours, and more music. Once I had a sense of how Bowie's celebrity judge thing went, maybe I'd go on the show next season. It would be really cool to dip my hand into acting...hell, maybe I'd even write a book! My road to success was a little unorthodox, after all. Fans would probably enjoy that. As cliche as it sounded, the sky really was the limit. As long as I had my family with me, I'd be alright.

What was next, indeed.

THE END

Acknowledgments

First and foremost, I have to thank the G.O.A.T. herself, Kelly Clarkson. I am so grateful to live in a world where your music exists. Thank you for inspiring me throughout all the stages of my life.

A giant thanks to my editor, Lea Froelich, and beta reader, Sarah Guzak. This book is a direct reflection of your commitment to my dreams. I love you both for it. Thank you for making me a better writer, but thank you even more for being an amazing friend.

I am so lucky to have such incredible support from bookish friends. My book club girlies, Toni, Sarah, Heather, Chantel, Madie, Janessa, Morgan, Felicia, and Renee continue to show up and show out for me with everything I do, and I could not be more grateful.

My fantastic cover designer deserves all the praise in the world. Kate, I am in awe of your talent and creativity. Thank you for continuing to share your gift with me.

Thank you to my parents for always allowing me to explore different music. I never would have gone down the Kelly Clarkson rabbit hole without that freedom. You might've created a monster, but at least now we know it's a monster that paid off!

To my readers who continue to ride the waves with me, I appreciate your support. I wish I could tell you that I will find a rhythm to the different genres I write in, but we all know that wouldn't be me. Thank you for reading my books, no matter the genre.

Jack, Tristan, and Cael, I love you. I love being your mom. All I want to do is make you proud. Every book takes us one step closer.

And even though he is no longer with us, thank you to my grandpa who always told me I would be a great writer someday. I always find myself ruminating over those words as I finish a book, and this is the first time where I actually believe them. I miss you so much, Grandpa.

Spread kindness like confetti, y'all.

-SG

About the Author

Samantha Gail is a former Probation Parole Officer who supervised sex offenders before deciding she needed something with happy endings and chose to write books instead. Her work falls into multiple genres, primarily thriller, romance, and fantasy. She currently manages a bookstore and writes when she's not spending time with her three children and three fur babies.

Also by Samantha Gail

Epoch: Book One of The Hourglass Saga

Full Circle

Number One Fan

Check out this preview of Samantha Gail's bestselling small town romance!

Full Circle
Prologue

Celeste

Mama always used to say that life comes full circle. Some of my earliest memories are of her explaining that what goes around comes around because my mama believed in the power of karma. It made her feel better to imagine rude customers at The Comfy Cushion, our family's restaurant, stubbing their toe or having an umbrella turn inside out than for her to reply in kind. Poor manners were inexcusable, according to Mama.

She didn't live long enough to explain the concept of soul-mates to me, but I'd like to think that she and Daddy were destined to be together. They used to turn up the old jukebox at closing time after all the customers left and slow dance right there in the middle of the dining area.

I know it devastated him when Mama passed, called too soon by the good Lord. At least, that's what the preacher said. Daddy didn't abide much by the church, but my nana said her daughter wasn't a heathen and wouldn't be buried like one, so the preacher man came out and said his piece. Daddy was a blubbering mess by the end of it, so who's to say really? I was twelve years old when Mama died, too angry at the world for taking her away from me to care one way or another what the preacher said. He would forevermore represent the day we buried my mother's body in the ground, and it was a grudge I felt I'd hold til my last breath.

"We've still got each other, sugar bee," Daddy said that night as he cuddled my sob-wracked body to sleep. His words comforted me, my child naivete convincing me that my daddy could never leave me like my mama did. Boy, how wrong I was.

It would be years before I ever felt the kind of eternal love Mama gave me from another person. Wesley Madden blew into my life like a hurricane, all roaring winds and crashing waves. Receiving his love was like swimming in the ocean for the first time—you wanted to open your eyes and see everything even when it burned like hell. I used to wonder if Mama sent Wesley to me because she knew I needed saving or if she recognized the good I could bring out in him. Our opposition became the perfect balance, our personalities clashing in ways that could only complement one another. But when you've only known suffering and loss, the glimmer of light shining through the cracks can petrify you. That's a lesson I learned the hardest way possible.

Life comes full circle, huh? Fate must've missed the mark with me.

Full Circle
Ch. 1: Let the Good Times Roll

Celeste

The grass had barely begun to sprout on the ground above my mama's grave, but I ignored the damp soil underneath my bottom. Nana would probably tan my hide when she saw the muddy patches on my jeans. It was worth it to have the quiet moment with Mama.

I had gone to the cemetery to visit her grave every day since we buried her seven weeks ago, shortly before my thirteenth birthday. Talking to her headstone was a crappy replacement for seeing her beautiful smile or feeling her warmth as she held me an extra second longer for a hug, but nothing else brought me any comfort. Missing her felt like a phantom limb; how could I go on in a world without my mama? She had been the center of my world, my very best friend, and my heart ached with the sting of her loss. The future stretched ahead like a barren, arid desert—dusty, painful, and empty—without her bright laugh or delicious cooking.

A car horn honked behind me and I turned abruptly to see Daddy's truck outside the gate. He had the windows rolled down and could have just hollered my name, but we were both stuck in our own downward spirals of grief. Nana figured Daddy didn't know what to say to me to make me feel better, so he stuck to not saying anything at all. Whether that was true or not, even I recognized he would be wasting his breath to try to get my mind off things right now.

Rising slowly, I wiped as much of the debris off my bottom as I could before heading forlornly over to him with my head down. The twinkle had gone from his bright blue eyes and I hated to see yet another reminder of what Mama's death had done to our family. "Good Times Roll" by The Cars echoed faintly from his stereo as I approached, and I stopped next to the driver's side door rather than get in the truck with him.

"Why don't you go hang out somewhere other than the graveyard, sugar bee?" Daddy asked. He always called me sugar bee because he said I was sweeter than honey but buzzed about more than a bumblebee. Normally it gave me all the warm fuzzies on the inside to hear the term of endearment in his gruff voice. Today it merely reminded me of the void I felt.

I shrugged rather than answer him. If we weren't both still reeling, the action would have fired him up because he considered it poor manners not to respond when someone spoke to you. Mama's death meant manners went out the window.

He sighed heavily. "Hop in. I'm gonna take you over to the park." His firm tone warned me that he'd brook no argument.

Neither of us said another word as he followed the gravel path of the cemetery out to the main road. It was late spring here in Georgia, and the sun was bright and high, making the temperature quickly yield to the heat. My tank top was already sticking between my shoulder blades, making me wish I would have worn shorts along with it instead of jeans.

The park was a joint playground and baseball diamond near the town square. Mama and Daddy had always let me play there on days when I didn't have school because it was located across the street from The Comfy Cushion, Mama's restaurant. People came from miles around to eat her recipes, though I always thought she charmed the customers just as much with her flattering words and pretty smiles. Daddy handled the books and all the ordering, a job he took on because he saw how happy it made Mama to cook for everyone. It was the only real restaurant in town, unless you counted the fast food joints right off the highway, but given how my mama's meals always stuck to my ribs, I didn't see how they could hold a candle to her.

On a Saturday afternoon without a cloud in the sky, the park was jampacked with kids. The problem was, I hated being around them now. None of them knew what it felt like to lose someone so special and since everybody in town adored my mother, it rankled me to see their pitying looks. Their eyes followed me as soon as I set foot in the park. Eyes that all held relief that it was my mama and not theirs mixed with uncertainty over what to say to me.

"I'll be in the office for a bit longer," Daddy told me through the car window again. "Just head on over when you're hungry. Marla will whip something up for you." He didn't give me a chance to respond before pulling away to park his truck in his usual spot across the street.

I sighed heavily again. Marla was my mama's best friend who had stepped in to help Daddy with The Comfy Cushion. She seemed to think the only way I could heal was being force fed large casseroles. Even if it was Mama's recipe, it never tasted the same. My stomach wouldn't accept anything Marla made me choke down. The prospect of being made to swallow anything at the moment filled me with dread.

Following the path around the dugout of the baseball diamond where a pickup game was in full swing, I trailed behind the bleachers until I reached the edge of the woods at the back of the park. There was a small dirt trail into the trees that was mostly overgrown with bushes and moss, but I had been down there so many times that the growth didn't bother me. It led down to a small creek where there was a good climbing tree, full of shade with wide branches. I liked to hide up there among the foliage so that the other kids couldn't stare at me, the girl with the dead mama and no friends.

"Hey!" a voice snapped as I hauled myself up to the lowest branch.

It startled me to the point where I misjudged my hand placement and went tumbling face first over the branch and down onto the creek bed below. I was instantly covered in mud and felt a sting above my right eye from where my face landed on a rock. My knees took the brunt of my fall, however, and I cried out in pain on impact.

"Oh my god, are you okay?!" The same voice as before hollered over me. Gentle hands pulled at my shoulders to roll me onto the creek bank and I made eye contact with what must have been an angel. It was a boy around my age with sandy blonde hair and the bluest eyes I had ever seen. A small halo of light shone around his head, making me pinch my leg to check that I wasn't dreaming. People didn't die from falling out of trees, right?

The boy grabbed one of my hands and hauled me to my feet,

helping me to wipe off all the mud on my shins. "I'm so sorry! I didn't mean to scare you!"

My cheeks burned with embarrassment. "It's fine. I'm not hurt."

He brushed the hair away from my face. "Yes, you are. This cut is bleeding."

Having a stranger's hands on my face made my heart race in a way that spooked me. I took a step away from him, backing myself up against the tree. "It's fine. Just a scratch."

The boy smirked at my retreat and stuck his hand out as if to shake mine. "I'm Wesley. Wesley Madden."

Staring blankly at his offered hand, my mind went through a rolodex of Smithson County. I knew every child in our small town of River's Run, Georgia. This boy did not belong here. He had to be a tourist. "Where are you from?"

He smiled, a megawatt smile that made my heart race again. Stuffing his hand back in the pocket of his cargo shorts, he explained, "Originally from Atlanta, but I live here now."

That didn't make sense. Marla was the gossip queen of our county and she hadn't said anything about a new family moving here. Whose house did they buy?

Wesley must have recognized the look of puzzlement on my face because he clarified, "I moved in with my great-aunt Shirley."

I nodded. Miss Shirley Jones was a regular down at The Comfy Cushion, although she had to be pushing 85. "Ain't she a little old to be taking you in?"

He shrugged. "My dad works too much and my mom took off when I was a baby. I hated all of the nannies, so he reached out to my mom's family. Shirley was the only one who offered."

It took everything I had to hold back a snort. What kind of family used a nanny? Was he some rich, spoiled brat?

Rather than responding, I turned and started to climb back up the tree. This boy, no matter how sweet he seemed, wasn't my problem and I was still too depressed to care.

"Wait!" Wesley grabbed onto the leg of my jeans as I paused on the lowest branch. "We need to go get your eye cleaned up. It could get infected."

"How would you know?" I scoffed.

He smirked again. "Let's just say, I've gotten into my fair share of fights."

The retort on the tip of my tongue died with his statement. He looked too scrawny to be much of a fighter to me, but maybe he was just a bully.

"How old are you?" I asked instead.

"Twelve. Thirteen in June, just a couple weeks from now." His blue eyes twinkled as he perused my body, still hoisted onto the lowest branch. "What's your name?"

A warning bell was ringing somewhere in the back of my mind that befriending Wesley Madden would be a bad idea, but there was a gleam in his eye that reminded me of my mama.

Hope.

He looked hopeful, and that was something I didn't have in me to crush.

"Celeste Hendricks," I finally offered.

His megawatt smile returned. "That's a pretty name."

As if sensing my hesitation, Wesley leaned forward with an outstretched hand, waiting for me to accept. Despite myself, I couldn't help but give him a soft smile in return as I enclosed my hand in his. With one tug I was out of the tree and standing next to him, peering up into his crystal blue eyes.

Even though I was a few months older than him, Wesley towered over me. He held my gaze far longer than was necessary and I felt something shift inside me, something I couldn't quite put my finger on. I wondered errantly if it would ever shift back.

For the rest of the afternoon, Wesley and I walked around the park and the playground, telling each other more about our lives. I let him do most of the talking, still too in awe of this angelic boy who paid me this kind of attention. He told me that his dad owned a big corporation and had plans for Wesley to take it over one day, but Wesley kept getting into trouble and fighting at school. I gasped in shock as he described the number of fights he had won, supposedly against much older, bigger kids. It never crossed my mind to question him. Wesley didn't seem too keen on the idea of joining his father's company, but when I asked what else he would want to do with his life, he merely shrugged. "That's a long ways off," he said. "I have plenty of time to figure it out."

We had circled the area more than five times before he threw himself down on the edge of the field beyond the baseball diamond, yanking me down to join him.

"Look at all the clouds! That one kinda looks like a rabbit," he said, pointing upward.

I flopped down so that my head lay right next to him, my body extending in the opposite direction. We were so close that his stray hair tickled my ear. If I turned my head to the left, my face would collide with his.

The shapes he saw in the clouds became increasingly ridiculous, with elaborate back stories that he swore were Native American legends, and I couldn't stop giggling. I never offered my own interpretation of the shapes, content to let him continue talking. After several minutes, his voice faded away and we laid there quietly.

"So how come you aren't with other friends today?" Wesley suddenly asked.

Perhaps it was easier because I couldn't see him, just feel his warm presence, but for once I answered honestly, "I don't really have any. Mama was my best friend."

There was a pregnant pause before he replied softly, "'Was' your best friend...?"

I gulped, tears threatening to spill over. It was the first time I admitted it out loud to someone else. "She died a few months ago. Heart disease."

Wesley leaned up on one elbow to look down at me. "Then I get to be your best friend now." His eyes held no pity, only friendship, for which I was grateful. The assurance in his voice made me feel safe, something I had only ever felt in Daddy's presence. I was reminded of the cosmic shift in my soul from earlier when he shook my hand.

"CELESTE RENEE HENDRICKS, WHERE ARE YOU?!"

Jumping up like my pants were invaded by fire ants, I saw Marla at the park entrance, her hands on her hips. Anger lit up her face. She still had on her work apron, scanning the park for me.

Dang it, I never went back to The Comfy Cushion to eat like Daddy said. Now Marla was gonna scold me til the cows came home.

"I've gotta go," I said to Wesley.

He stood up, too, brushing grass off his tan legs. "Who is that?" he asked, nodding towards Marla.

I sighed. "That's my mama's best friend. She helps Daddy at

the restaurant now." Slowly I walked towards her, not in any hurry for the verbal whiplash I knew was coming my way.

Wesley fell into step beside me. "Does your dad manage a restaurant?"

Nodding, I couldn't keep the pride from my voice as I explained, "We own it. It was my mama's restaurant." I pointed across the street to The Comfy Cushion, the outside lights now on from the timer. It must be a lot later than I thought.

Marla finally took sight of me and although I could tell Wesley's presence by my side surprised her, she continued to frown at me. "Care to explain where you been?!" she snapped. "Had me worried sick! Goodness me, what happened to your eye?!" She gruffly turned my chin upward so that she could examine the cut near my eyebrow.

Before I could respond, Wesley shocked me by saying, "It's my fault, ma'am. I'm new here and I asked her to show me around."

If he had announced he was the fifth member of the Beatles, I don't think Marla could have looked more surprised or confused. Her eyebrows receded towards her hairline as her warm brown eyes darted between the two of us. "Celeste..." she clarified, "...showed you around. Willingly."

Wesley didn't skip a beat. "Sure did. She's the only friend I have in the world right now."

I could tell Marla was fighting the urge to smile because she wanted to stay mad at me, but she couldn't hold back. Long before my mother fell ill, I avoided kids my own age, preferring to cook in the restaurant or learn how to manage the books with Daddy. Friends weren't really a thing on my radar.

"Well, as nice as it is to meet you, Celeste needs to come eat something before she passes out," Marla replied, giving me less of a stink eye than usual. "Why don't you come, too? I've got a slice of pie with your name on it."

My heart leapt, hopeful he would accept.

Wesley smiled at me but shook his head. "I should probably get back. My aunt Shirley didn't know I was leaving."

Marla's jaw clenched, warring over his polite decline and his obvious disrespect to his aunt. "Would that be Miss Shirley Jones over there on Houston Street?"

He nodded. "Yes, ma'am."

It was the "ma'am" that redeemed him, I could tell. She finally dropped her stiff demeanor and nodded. "You give Miss Shirley my best now, young man." Marla gave him another once over before turning back towards The Comfy Cushion. "Say good-bye to your friend and get inside," she called over her shoulder.

I gave him a half-hearted smile as I toed with a small rock at my feet. For the first time ever, I felt a real connection with someone outside of my family, and I didn't want to leave. "Sorry about that," I offered.

"Meet you here after lunch tomorrow?" Wesley asked.

He might as well have handed me a four leaf clover. I tried not to make it too obvious as I beamed at him, nodding and wrapping my arms around my own waist to try and contain my joy. A friend—I had finally made a friend.

Spinning on my heel, I started humming along to the song from Daddy's radio. Maybe, just maybe, I could let the good times roll.